TOUGH LOVE

KERRY KATONA

D0493922

EBURY
PRESS

1 3 5 7 9 10 8 6 4 2

Published in 2007 by Ebury Press, an imprint of Ebury Publishing
A Random House Group Company

Copyright © Kerry Katona 2007

Kerry Katona has asserted her right to be identified as the
author of this Work in accordance with the Copyright, Designs
and Patents Act 1988

The Random House Group Limited Reg. No. 954009
Addresses for companies within the Random House Group
can be found at www.randomhouse.co.uk

A CIP catalogue record for this book is available from
the British Library

The Random House Group Limited makes every effort to ensure
that the papers used in our books are made from trees that have
been legally sourced from well-managed and credibly certified
forests. Our paper procurement policy can be found on
www.rbooks.co.uk/environment

Printed in the UK by CPI Cox & Wyman, Reading, RG1 8EX

ISBN 9780091923198

To buy books by your favourite authors and register for offers visit
www.rbooks.co.uk

chapter one

Leanne opened the paper and looked at the young blue-eyed, blonde-haired vision of tabloid beauty staring back at her, the pert breasts and happy-to-be-there smile. She threw it aside. She wasn't particularly interested in what Mel, 18, of Colchester had to say about the war in Iraq. She knew that the girl's problems extended only as far as whether the spray tan she'd had before the shoot was too orange and if her false eyelashes were alluring or, horror of horrors, made her look like Jackie Stallone. The Knowledge and Knickers speech bubble that the papers insisted on printing above the new breed of page-three girls' heads was always made up in two seconds flat by some hack in Canary Wharf – it had nothing to do with the models. 'That's not Mummy,' Kia, Leanne's seven-year-old daughter, said, climbing on to her mother's knee.

Leanne looked at her and shook her head. 'No, darling, that's a pretty lady.'

'Mummy's pretty too,' Kia said.

Leanne smiled at her daughter, grateful for the compliment. Leanne was pretty. She was five foot five with an hour-glass figure and her blonde hair and green eyes ensured that heads turned when she walked into any room. They had also ensured that until recently her career had been long and lucrative.

She had agonised over telling Kia exactly what she did. She didn't think it appropriate that her young daughter should know that Mummy made her money as a glamour model, but at the same time she was proud of her work, so why should she hide it from her? In the end the choice had been taken out of her hands by her less than thoughtful mother, Tracy: she had given Kia a locket with a picture of a topless Leanne in it. Mother of the Year Tracy wasn't.

In fact, Leanne had recognised Mel. She had been sitting in the waiting room at Figurz Management when Leanne was given what she could only describe as the Right Royal Boot. Jenny, her manager for the past nine years, had summoned her into her spacious office and sat her down. Leanne had known something was wrong as soon as she got the call to go to the office. Jenny didn't usually do the office. She liked to sink a couple of bottles of Pinot Grigio and go over the proofs for whatever men's magazine Leanne had been starring in that week. The office meant bad news.

'I suppose you know why I've asked you here...' Jenny, with her vicious bob and her black-rimmed glasses, had lit a cigarette and leant back in her chair, inhaling hard, then letting a plume of smoke out of her nostrils. Leanne's throat had dried. She had an idea of why she was sitting there, but she wasn't sure she liked it.

'You and me, Lee, we go back a long way.' Leanne hated it when Jenny called her Lee. 'And I've always said I'd be straight up and down with you, haven't I, girl?' Leanne winced. She wanted Jenny to get this over and done with, whatever she was going to say. 'And I've always said, "Tits is tits," haven't I?'

And I've always wondered what the fuck that's supposed to mean, Leanne thought but didn't say. She wouldn't. She was terrified of Jenny, if she was honest.

'Well, tits is tits, but there's younger tits coming through that door, if you know what I'm saying.'

'Look, Jenny,' Leanne's voice wavered, 'I offered to get a boob job and you said no, natural's what everyone wants.' She didn't really want one. Her boobs were big enough as it was. She didn't need ginormous plastic orbs bobbing around so she couldn't see her feet.

'That's true, sweetheart. Natural is what everyone wants, but so's young. And you might be young to some bloke in his fifties, but twenty-five's over the hill to an eighteen-year-old brickie who wants a quick lump in his trousers while he's eating his corned-beef sandwiches. You get where I'm coming from?'

Leanne got where Jenny was coming from – loud and clear. She was telling her that her lucrative career as a glamour model was coming to an end. Leanne would have liked to think that in this situation she would stand up and tell Jenny exactly where she could shove her Eric Morecambe glasses, but she didn't. When it came down to it, she avoided conflict at all costs. With a mother like hers you didn't need to look for a fight – they came to you.

'What about my fan base?' Leanne had asked meekly.

'They're a fickle bunch. They move on quickly, and that's what I'm here to spot.' Jenny looked at Leanne, who was fighting back tears now. She could have kicked herself: she didn't want to break down in front of the hard-faced witch. 'I'm not saying you won't work again, sweetheart, just that you might have to do it with your top on.'

Leanne had stumbled out on to the street near Battersea Bridge. She got well away from the office before she fell in a heap and started crying. She'd had such a nice life for the last six years – parties, premières, free holidays if she put her name to the travel company – and now Jenny, the number-one glamour agent in the country, was telling her it was over. What was she going to do?

She stood up, tears streaming down her face, and looked around for a taxi. Typical! There wasn't one in sight. Leanne walked on with her thumb out like a hitch-hiker, until a cab pulled up beside her, splashing mud up her leg. Brilliant! Could today get any worse? she wondered aloud.

As she climbed in, the driver stared at her. 'You're that Jodie Marsh, ain'tcha?' he asked.

Yes, she decided. It could.

*

'Get out here and fucking talk to me!' a man's voice screamed.

Tracy turned up the volume on *Jeremy Kyle*. She'd rather listen to someone else's problems than confront her own. Suddenly there was a loud banging on the back door, something she was well used to.

'I said, "Fucking talk to me!"'

Tracy raised an eyebrow and stuck a spoon into the tub of Dairylea she had grabbed from the fridge for breakfast; she had nothing else in and she was damned if she was going outside the house to get an ear-twisting from her ex-husband. Just as she was about to find out the result of the paternity test on TV an almighty whack put paid to her morning of loafing around. She turned to see a foot sticking through her boarded-up back door.

'For the love of God, Paul!' she shouted, jumping up from the settee and heading over to the door. The foot was waggling around. Its owner was obviously trying to free it.

'Let me in, and we'll have this out once and for all.'

'I'm calling the police. You're not allowed anywhere near here,' Tracy reminded him.

'This is my fucking house!'

'It's the council's fucking house. Get your facts right, dickhead.' Tracy stood back and kicked the foot as hard as she could.

'Ow!' the disembodied voice wailed. 'You bitch!' The foot disappeared.

'Now, fuck off, or I'm calling the police and you'll end up back in the nick!' Tracy returned to the settee. This wasn't the scene of domestic violence she liked to paint but it was how she and Paul were with each other since they had split so acrimoniously. She was used to the frequent ructions and bored with them.

Paul and Tracy had been together since they were teenagers. He had always fancied himself as a bit of a hard man around the estate, but his hard-man credentials didn't stretch much further than thumping people when he'd laid into the Stella Artois a bit harder than he should have. When they'd first met, Tracy had believed the hype. He'd been the tough lad at school, the one everyone fancied, but a few years with him had soon put paid to any romantic notions she'd had about him. He was a lazy waster who prided himself on not having had to get out of bed before ten o'clock since he'd left school. Something of a feat in itself, Tracy had often thought, seeing as they had five kids together.

Tracy loved her kids, she really did, but she often thought they didn't understand what she'd gone through, what she'd given up, to raise them. She'd been a looker when she was younger, could have been a model like Leanne, but instead she'd ended up sitting out her life in Bolingbroke Estate, Bradington's number-one problem area, so they were always being informed. Leanne didn't know she was born, Tracy thought. Granted, she'd had to go out and work when she was fourteen, but there was nothing wrong with that, Tracy told herself. Bit of grafting to pay some board had done none of her kids any harm.

The rot had set in between her and Paul years ago. He'd thought that having children meant giving up. He'd soon stopped looking at Tracy as anything other than the mother to his kids, and she'd wanted more. She'd wanted some romance in her life, but there was a slim chance of that when she had five kids in tow and the only place for a night out was the Beacon, a dump of a pub where the men were men and the women looked like men.

Three years ago, on Tracy's forty-fifth birthday, Paul had produced the straw that finally broke the camel's back. He'd been promising to take Tracy out all year. They'd go into town and have a proper knees-up – they'd even go to a club. Tracy had bought a new outfit, courtesy of some cash that Leanne had put her way, and then Paul hadn't come home. She'd waited all night for him and in the end had gone into town on her own and got blind drunk. She couldn't remember what had happened, but her youngest daughter, Jodie, had informed her that when she and her mates found Tracy she was draped round some thirty-year-old and had been sick down her top. Eventually Paul came home all apologies but Tracy had known things had to change.

Along with *Jeremy Kyle*, one of Tracy's pleasures in life was *The Late Nite Love-In* on Bradington Community

Radio. The voice of the DJ, Kent Graham, was enough to make her go weak at the knees. After Paul's no-show and the subsequent arguments, in which he had defended going on a three-day bender, Tracy had decided to do something for herself for once. Never mind sorting her rabble out. She was going to look after number one. She had picked up the phone and rung the radio station, then asked to be put through to Kent, saying she was an old school friend. When she finally had him on the phone, she put on her best, most seductive voice and asked him out. And Kent, to her utter amazement, said yes.

What followed was a whirlwind romance. At first, Tracy thought he might only be interested in her because she was Leanne's mum. Her daughter was the local celebrity and everyone, as far as Tracy could see, wanted a piece of her, and if that meant going through her mother, then so be it. But it soon became apparent to Tracy that Kent wanted her for herself.

A month later, Paul had found out. Tracy soon tired of hiding her new love and became more and more brazen in her choice of venue when meeting him. She wanted Paul to see that someone else was more interested in her than he was in the bottom of a pint glass. She was finally spotted by one of the locals from the Beacon, being pushed on the swings in Bolingbroke Park by Kent. She had thought Paul would realise that this spelled the end of their marriage. The kids were all grown-up now: Jodie still lived at home but was working at the Beacon; Karina had moved in with

Gaz; Scott and his girlfriend Charly had a flat on the other side of the estate; and Markie was in prison but was due out any time now. Leanne, of course, little Princess Tippy Toes, as Tracy liked to call her, if not to her face, was off setting the world alight. They didn't need a mum and dad – she and Paul had done their bit, Tracy thought rather grandly. She didn't understand that her 'bit' couldn't be considered first-class parenting.

Paul didn't take it well. He broke every window in the house and posted a lit rag through the door. The whole thing got dragged through the papers because someone on the street saw a quick buck to be made. It was good reading: the page-three girl, the psycho dad and the DJ. Tracy had played the injured wife, but the truth was that she enjoyed winding her ex-husband up. She'd even got the police to install a panic button in case of violent attack. Paul had laughed at this, thinking it was a joke, when he had come round to have his monthly Shout-at-Tracy-from-the-Garden. She had pressed it, and he'd found out the hard way that it was anything but a joke. He had spent the night in Bradington Bridewell with his belt and shoelaces confiscated.

As for Kent, he'd stuck with Tracy through thick and thin. He felt he'd met his soulmate. He'd say, 'I feel like I can tell you anything.'

Tracy would reply, 'Me too.' But there were a few things she thought it was best not to let him in on, such as that when they'd all ended up in the tabloids she had grasped there was money to be made. Ever since, she had been anonymously drip-feeding the papers stories about Leanne to make herself a nice bit of coin on the side. Now if she could only get Leanne to spill the beans on who Kia's dad was, which she had been tight-lipped about from day one, Tracy'd have two weeks in La Manga and a plasma-screen telly sorted. She had an idea who it was, though. And if it was who she thought, then it was tabloid dynamite.

Tracy liked to think that what stopped her finding out more was that she was concerned about Kia: she didn't want her dragged through the papers like the rest of her family had been. But she knew she could rationalise it, if push came to shove and a large cheque from the *News of the Screws* was winging its way in her direction. Her other, bigger, concern was that she didn't think Kent would be very understanding about her on-the-side income. He could be a right uptight sod sometimes, she thought. She'd sit schtum on that one for the time being.

With Paul still shouting outside, Tracy wandered over to the panic button and pressed it. A few minutes later the police were at her door. She prepared herself for another Oscar-winning performance.

'Thank God you came so quickly, officers,' she said, fighting back crocodile tears – they came so easily to her. 'I thought he was going to kill me.' If there was one thing Tracy loved more than *Jeremy Kyle*, it was a good drama.

*

Lisa Leighton looked out over the beautiful blue crystal waters of Lake Garda and snapped the magazine shut. Ever since her husband Jay had moved to Milano Atletico she had had the weekly gossip magazines shipped out from the UK just to see how many column inches she and her beloved had notched up that week. It had been Lisa's idea to move to Italy three years ago. Jay's reputation had been getting slightly out of hand back home but she knew that if she could get him away from the hangers-on they might be able to get on with their lives in the way she wanted. For the most part her plan had worked. The move had seen the Leightons go from being the UK's golden couple to a European phenomenon.

Lisa based herself in Italy and London. She quite liked Italy, but found the language barrier tough. Also, everyone went on about Milan being the fashion capital of the world but the place was an overgrown industrial estate and the clothes were like something her mother would have worn out for a night on the tiles in Essex, all gold lamé and appliqué clowns.

It was strange to be so famous, but Lisa felt she had the hang of it now. She had grown used to being photographed everywhere she went, and so had Jay. But that was more to do with the fact that she let the paparazzi know where she was going to be than their popularity.

Since the move her own career had rocketed. When

they had lived in the UK she had been a TV presenter. She'd started off on a music channel but had soon been noticed for her good looks and bright on-screen personality. The main channels had snapped her up. Now she had her own column in a weekly glossy, her own fashion show on UK Lifetime TV and her own perfume, Suggestive, by Lisa Leighton. It actually smelt of turps, but she wasn't wearing it: her loyal public was and that suited her fine.

Even now, ten years after she and Jay had first got together, she knew she could expect to see herself and him on the front cover of at least one of the weekly magazines with a couple of mentions from Rav Singh or the 3 AM. girls thrown in. But this week there was nothing. All anyone was interested in was Leanne bloody Crompton. There were pictures of the glamour model getting into her car with her face screwed up – she was obviously asking for privacy – and the rest were old reruns that Lisa had seen a thousand times.

Did people really fall for this? she wondered, not for the first time. If the press didn't have a picture, or a story for that matter, they would delve into their archives and use an old one. Lisa should know: they'd dined out for months on Jay's alleged affair with a Manchester Rovers female physiotherapist, using the picture of her massaging cramp out of his leg at the FA Cup final over and over again. Lisa knew that she'd massaged more than his leg, but she wasn't about to let the mask of her perfect marriage slip any time soon.

She knew she and Jay were worth far more together than they were apart, and so did he.

Just when Lisa had thought that Leanne Crompton might drift into obscurity she'd reared her not-so-ugly head again. Even when she was papped with a scrunched-up face she looked all right, Lisa thought grudgingly. She herself daren't go out of the house without having every one of her long auburn tresses in place, her green contact lenses in and her Fake Bake professionally applied. She knew that if the paps caught her first thing in the morning they'd jump out of their pasty skins, shortly before snapping their shutter lenses and making themselves at least ten grand for the picture. She was naturally pretty, Lisa, but not naturally stunning. That bit took work. But years of eating only protein and constant high-end professional grooming had made her the svelte size eight über-redhead she was today.

Lisa didn't mind reading about Leanne when it was bad news. In fact she enjoyed it. Leanne, it appeared, had finally been dumped by her agency. The magazines were talking about it being the end of her. But Lisa knew that if Leanne was smart it could be the making of her. She could turn her hard-luck story into a lucrative rags-to-riches, riches-to-rags story. But Lisa didn't have Leanne down as smart. She had her down as Bradington scum. And people like her, Lisa knew, didn't think to look at the bigger picture and plan a career. They spent money when they had it and panicked when they didn't. And if Leanne started panicking, God only knew what would come out of her mouth. Well, Lisa wasn't about to take any risks.

She picked up the phone and dialled Jay's number. It went to answer-machine before she remembered he was having one of his tattoos lasered off. He'd had it for three months and thought it read *'my country, my life, my heart, my wife'* in Sanskrit. But it had turned out that the tattooist had been a Manchester City fan and apparently it read *'I flick turds for a living.'* She wouldn't mind but he hadn't played for Manchester Rovers for years.

Lisa rose from her sun-lounger and walked across the balcony of the villa they were renting from George Clooney. They'd never met him but that didn't matter – she knew they would now be associated for ever with him in the public's consciousness. For a moment, she wondered what to do, then picked up her phone and called Mike Atkinson, their head of security.

'I think we might have a little problem that needs attending to,' she said, splaying her free hand and checking that her perfectly manicured nails didn't need a touch-up.

*

Leanne walked along the Thames by the imposing Tate Modern with Kia, looking at the sky-line. St Paul's Cathedral rose up on the other side of the river and the buildings in the Square Mile vied to be noticed too. Leanne loved and hated London. She had worked in the capital since she was sixteen, moving in a year later, but she had always felt like an outsider. She envied the Sloaney young women in the coffee shops around Regent Street who could order a double mocha choco skinny latte and not feel they had to apologise for their pain-in-the-arse order. She still felt grand when she asked for a cappuccino.

She had come for a walk to clear her head. She lived in a house in Greenwich. The rent was astronomical but until last week Leanne hadn't cared. She'd always had money coming in and spent it accordingly. But this morning she had sat down and opened the credit-card statements she usually tossed to one side to discover that she was in trouble.

She glanced down at Kia, who was wearing her favourite Dolce and Gabbana trainers with her Matthew Williamson for Kids jumper, and her heart sank. Her poor little girl had grown used to having the best of everything, and Leanne had grown used to assuming that she could give her the best of everything.

She took out her mobile phone and rang Directory Inquiries. 'Can I have the number for Pink Models, please?' Pink Models were Figurz Management's biggest rivals.

The operator put her through. 'Hello, can I speak to Meagan Richards, please?' Meagan had been Jenny's arch enemy.

'May I ask who's calling?' the receptionist asked, in a nasal voice.

'It's Leanne Crompton.' She felt nervous to be ringing up and asking for work, which she hadn't had to do since she'd first done the rounds in Bradington, looking for a cash-in-hand Saturday job.

'One moment, please.'

The receptionist must have pushed the wrong button. Instead of Meagan's polite business voice, Leanne heard, 'Leanne Crompton? Ha! She gets dropped by Hag Features and thinks she can come crawling to me? Let her sweat. Tell her to call back tomorrow. She's old news, anyway.'

Leanne clicked the phone off, feeling sick. She had a strong suspicion that she and Kia were in for a rocky year.

*

Karina was off her head. Gaz, her boyfriend, had been dealing coke for a year or two but had suddenly landed a massive stash, and while he was off working as a bouncer at Bradington's current number-one night spot, Cloud Nine, she had been charged with dealing it up and hiding it. Never one to pass up the opportunity to test Gaz's wares, Karina had tucked into the coke like a kid in a sweet shop. She was now on day two of a paranoid bender, which had started with her being Queen of the World and was ending with her scrabbling around on the floor, taking the coke out of the settee cushions and sewing it into her two-year-old daughter Izzy's teddy bears. Which was a good idea, as it turned out, because when she heard a loud knocking at the door, it wasn't just her paranoia at play, it really was the police.

'We've a warrant to search the premises, Miss Crompton,' the police officer said, and barged past her.

Karina reverted to the cocky madam she'd been at school and started telling the police what she thought of them.

'Nothing better to do? Haven't you got some tom you should be shaking down for free blow-jobs or something?' she asked sarcastically.

'Good afternoon to you too,' the police officer said.

Karina was trying her best to act normal, but she had no way of knowing whether she was pulling it off. She flattened herself against the wall and looked on as the police tore the flat apart.

'What you looking for, then?' she asked, aware that her eyes were like saucers.

'I think you know, don't you?' The police officer stared at her, raising an eyebrow, as his colleague upturned cushions and rifled through drawers. 'Mind if we look in the bedrooms?'

'No, go ahead. You'll do what the fuck you please anyway,' Karina said, trying to pretend that she wasn't completely bricking it.

'No need for the bad language. What did your mother teach you? Oh, that's right, nothing – your mum's a scumbag.' The two coppers fell about laughing as Karina scowled at them.

'Don't bring my mum into it.'

The copper looked at her. She knew that he knew she was as high as a kite.

She began to scratch. She wasn't itchy, just felt that she needed to get out of her skin. Her mind raced. They were going to find the stuff and all Gaz's hard work would be down the drain. She'd be put in prison and Izzy would be taken into care and it would be all her fault. Karina was trying to keep calm, but her already racing heart was thumping in her chest.

The coppers swaggered back into the living room where Karina was standing, sure that this was the moment when she would be arrested. 'Well, looks like it's your lucky day,' the copper said. 'We can't find anything.'

Relief flooded through her. 'I told you,' she said defiantly.

'Anyway, say hello to that lovely sister of yours, won't you, from all the lads? Can't have her posters up any more – the political-correctness mob's gone mad. But she's up here.' The copper tapped his temple.

'You make me sick,' Karina said, as the coppers let themselves out, smiling. But it wasn't just them who made her sick. Her sister, bloody Leanne – Leannecrompton, everyone said it as if it was one word, like Madonna – made her nauseous too. With her fancy clothes and her smart life and her bleating all the time about being down-to-earth. She could afford to be, Karina thought. I'd be down-to-earth if I had a Mini Cooper S and four holidays a year. *Bloody*

Leanne. She felt the stab of envy she often experienced when she thought about her sister. Not that she'd tell her. Leanne was too good a meal ticket for Karina to start falling out with her now.

*

Jodie leant over the bar and made sure that her low-cut top gave Dave, one of the regulars, a good look at her ample cleavage. 'And your own, love,' he said, as he always did. Jodie got the best tips at the Beacon. There was a fight every night and there were more boards than windows on the outside of the building. She didn't particularly like the place, but it was a good stopgap for the time being – and she got the attention from the male regulars that she craved.

She had worked there for a year but knew she wouldn't have to stay much longer, not if Brian Spencer had anything to do with it. He had walked into the pub a week ago and asked the manager, Val, where the lovely younger sister of Leanne Crompton could be found. Jodie had shimmied across to him, swung her long blonde hair over her shoulder and announced, 'You're looking at her.'

He had managed two seconds of eye contact before his gaze came to rest on her chest. Jodie didn't mind. She knew, as her sister had found, that they were going to be her fortune. Brian had slid his business card across the bar. 'Call me. I think I could represent you,' he had said, then ordered a Campari and soda.

Val had taken the ancient bottle down and sniffed it slyly. Nobody had ordered Campari at the Beacon for at least three years.

Jodie had looked at the card with delight: Brian Spencer Management. She had tried and failed before to get someone to take her seriously as a glamour model. When she was younger she had thought things would be as easy for her as they had been for Leanne, who'd been an overnight success. But when Jodie had sent her amateur pictures to Leanne's horrible manager she had been told, 'Yeah, love, I see where you're coming from but you're not the full package like your sister. You're a bit of a barrel and your features are too clustered. Don't get me wrong, sweets, you're a pretty little thing, you just ain't Leanne.'

She had shelved her ideas of fame and fortune and instead had gone on an extreme diet, slimming down to a size six. Her mum had noticed that she was often sick in the middle of the night, but Jodie had passed it off as a bad stomach, and as her mum didn't think about much other than herself for any length of time, she carried on being sick. Every time someone told her how good she was looking, Jodie thought it was all worth it. She could see in the mirror now that her once-chubby face had been transformed. Her eyes were huge and blue and her cheekbones were sharp. Her hair had been brown when Jodie had sent her pictures to Jenny, but now it was blonde, well coloured and styled – she had made a deal with JoJo at the hairdresser's: JoJo did her highlights for free and in return Jodie shoved her as many Bacardi Breezers as she could get down her face on Friday and Saturday nights at the Beacon.

Until Brian had walked through the door, Jodie had been annoyed with Leanne. She thought her sister could have helped her more. OK, she'd taken Jodie to celebrity parties where she'd met Calum Best and Duncan out of Blue, but so what? She was still living at her mum's and pulling pints at the Beacon. Leanne should have made Jenny take her on, or at least give her a chance.

Anyway, she was going to show that Jenny. She was going to go all the way with Brian Spencer managing her. She didn't know whether Brian could manage a piss-up in a brewery but that didn't matter to her. She wanted the kudos of having a manager. And that was what Brian was.

'Val says you've got yourself a manager,' Dave said, still staring at her boobs.

'Yeah, that's right. He's got an office in town. I'm calling him soon to get some pictures taken.'

'Want me to take some pictures for you?' Dave leered.

'Why don't you pop off to the toilet and have a wank, Dave? Get it out of your system.'

Val looked on and smiled approvingly. She didn't want to lose Jodie as a member of staff. She might not be the sharpest knife in the drawer but her tongue was like a razor.

chapter two

Leanne pulled out her credit card and handed it to the girl behind the counter, willing it to work. The girl looked at the name and then at Leanne, obviously recognising her but not letting on. Leanne was used to that. Sometimes she preferred the people who charged across the street to say, 'You're that Leanne Crompton, aren't you?' to the ones who smugly ignored her.

'I'm sorry. Your card seems to have been declined.' The girl gave her a disingenuous smile.

Leanne felt her cheeks redden. 'Well,' she said, 'I can't think why.'

The girl looked at her with *faux* compassion. 'Maybe one of your others will go through,' she said, sticking the knife in.

Leanne bundled her purse into her bag. 'No, it's fine. I'll ring the bank and find out what's going on.' She grabbed Kia's hand and fled the shop. She felt completely foolish.

'You OK, Mummy?' Kia asked.

'Yes, darling, I'm fine. Come on, let's get a cab.' Leanne had twenty pounds in her purse and she knew

Jenny owed her some money but she wasn't sure how much or when she'd get it. 'Actually, just for fun, shall we get the Tube?'

'What's the Tube?' Kia asked.

Leanne looked at her daughter worriedly. Unless she could sort out something quickly, Kia's bubble would burst. And Leanne didn't want that.

*

Scott heaved the box of knock-off clothes out of the boot of his C reg BMW and struggled to his mum's front door. He glanced round and saw his girlfriend, Charly, getting out of the car as if she was expecting a team of paparazzi to be there. She had on a denim mini-skirt, her spray tan was perfectly applied and her vest top showed just enough cleavage. She was clutching an oversized handbag that would have cost nine hundred quid if Scott hadn't got his mate, Johnny, a security guard at a local warehouse, to nick it and sell it on to him for two hundred. That was a lot of money for a bag, Scott had thought, but he didn't care if it kept Charly sweet. She was his darling and he'd spend whatever he earned to keep her happy.

She slid her Chanel sunglasses on to her face and gazed at Scott's mum's house half in disgust, half in despair. 'Five minutes, Scott, I mean it,' she said as her dog, Mitzi, a yappy little Shih Tzu, jumped out of the car. 'Mummy won't keep you in this shit-hole with the nasty woman for long, baby,' she said to the dog.

'Fuck off, Char. Anyone'd think you grew up in fucking Cheshire, not Canterbury Avenue.' It was the toughest street in Bolingbroke. And Charly's family was the hardest on it.

'Don't tell me to fuck off,' Charly said, all precious.

Scott bit back the retort that flew to his lips. He didn't want an argument, he never wanted an argument, but he got one every day with Charly. There was no love lost between his mum, Tracy, and Charly, but Scott loved his mum and it was the only thing he asked of his girlfriend that, once a week, she would go round to Tracy's with him for a cup of tea and to hand over the week's contraband. Tracy thought Charly had ideas above her station and was bleeding her son dry, and Charly thought Tracy was a scumbag who'd sell her own kids. Scott hopped about hopelessly between the two main women in his life, trying unsuccessfully to keep the peace.

Now he hammered on the boarded-up door. He'd have to get it fixed, he thought.

Tracy opened it. ''Ello, son,' she said, standing back to let Scott in. Charly shimmied up to the door. Tracy gave her a withering look, but the girl walked straight past her. 'Morning, Princess,' Tracy said.

She shut the door and walked into the living room. 'Come on, then, let the dog see the rabbit.' She began to rummage through Scott's box.

'Fuck me, Mum! Give me chance to get through the door.' He bustled past her.

'Kettle's on, what more d'you want?' Tracy pulled

28

out a Louis Vuitton clutch bag, a Sergio Tacchini tracksuit and a number of watches that had Rolex stamped on them but had never been anywhere near a Rolex factory. 'Fucking minter,' she said gleefully. 'I've got ten orders for these trackies down at the Beacon and no fucker can get their hands on them 'cept my Scotty.' She pinched her son's cheek.

'Gerroff,' Scott said, pulling back. Now he looked at his mum properly for the first time since he'd come in. She had a big purple bruise above her cheek and her eye was swollen. 'Fuck's done that?' he asked. Charly raised an eyebrow, unseen behind her huge shades.

'Don't start, Scotty,' Tracy said. 'It'll just make things worse.'

'Mum, tell me!' he demanded.

'Your dad was round the other day.'

'I'll fucking murder him.'

'I never said he did it …' Tracy said, her eyes filling with tears.

'I'll knock his fucking teeth down his throat.'

'Don't, son.'

'Where is he?'

Tracy shrugged. She didn't know.

'And what's Kent done about it? Fuck all, I bet.'

'You know Kent. He's not a fighter.'

'No? He's a fucker, in't he? Giving it all that when it suits –' Scott put up a hand in the shape of a crab claw to indicate a lot of yapping '– but when the shit hits the fan, where is he? Behind the fucking couch, that's where.'

29

'Don't, Scotty,' Tracy said mournfully. 'He's a good man, Kent is. I don't want to bother him with all my shit.'

'No? Well, I do, he's a pussy. He should be standing up for you.'

Tracy dabbed her eyes and Charly sighed. Tracy threw her a dirty look.

'Well, if he won't, I will.' Scott grabbed his mobile phone.

'Who you calling?' Tracy asked, sounding worried.

'Our Markie. He should be out by now. He'll find out where Dad's gone. Then I'll go and see the old bastard and warn him off.'

Tracy hugged her son. 'You're a good lad to me, aren't you? What would I do without you?' Her chin rested on his shoulder as Scott hugged her back. She was looking straight at Charly, unknown to Scott, who was busy trying to get through to his brother.

Charly slipped her glasses down and eyeballed Tracy coldly. Tracy eyeballed her back and mouthed, 'Twat.' Tracy Crompton was not a woman to be messed with. But then again, neither was Charly.

*

Markie walked out of Strangeways, Manchester's notorious city-centre prison, and down the road to the busy street he had watched from his cell as he counted down the days until he'd be a free man, able to stand down there, eat, sleep and piss when he liked. About ten minutes later he came to a car he thought would do the job. Old enough not to have an immobiliser, new enough not to break down three minutes after he'd started it. He looked around to see if anyone was watching, and it seemed no one was. He pulled a coat-hanger out of his bag and slipped it deftly down the inside of the door. The button popped up on the inside and then he was sitting inside the T reg Astra, ready to hotwire it within a minute of laying eyes on it.

He fired the vehicle into life and put it in gear. Sluggish, he thought, not like the Subaru Impreza or the Range Rover he was used to, but it'd do for the time being. And, anyway, he just wanted to get from A to B. He didn't need his collar feeling today. He had an important day ahead of him soon and he needed to keep his head down between now and then.

His phone began to ring. 'Scott' came up on the screen. Markie ignored it. He loved his brother, but he was as daft as a brush. If Markie'd let him, he'd ring him to ask him how to get out of bed in the morning. Markie had had two years of relative peace, with no access to his mobile in prison, but as soon as he was out Scott was calling. His brother must be psychic. He did feel sorry for him, though, pussy-whipped by that bird of his. Markie didn't like her and the ice-queen routine didn't wash with him. She was a Canterbarbarian, as they called them on Bolingbroke. A scrubber from Canterbury Avenue. No amount of Chanel gear was going to cover up *that* fact. He'd talk to Scott when he was ready. First things first, Markie thought as he pulled up outside Pandora's massage parlour.

He parked the car round the back, pretty sure that the police in Manchester had better things to do than look for a stolen shit-heap. That was what he liked about Manchester: it was anonymous. No one getting up his nose and knowing his business, unlike Bradington where everyone wanted to know his inside-leg measurement and talk about the latest wank they'd had over his sister, Leanne. Not that many people dared talk about Leanne to Markie. He'd always been protective of her. But since she'd moved to London they'd grown apart. It wasn't anyone's fault. London was a long way away and Markie hadn't been able to visit for a while since he'd been staying in Manchester at Her Majesty's pleasure doing his two-year stint.

He walked into the reception area. The flock wallpaper was peeling off the walls and the gold desk was shabby. Behind it sat a young woman, about twenty, wearing a see-through baby-doll négligée, flicking through a copy of *Heat* magazine. When she saw Markie she jumped to attention. 'Markie.' She flushed and pulled at the négligée self-consciously. This pleased Markie. He knew he was good-looking, but not in that pretty-boy Brad Pitt way. Women always fancied him, but he hadn't been sure he still had the touch, having been out of circulation for all this time.

'Hello, darl.' He walked round the back of the desk,

pressed 'No Sale' on the till and looked at the notes in the drawer. He counted out two hundred pounds and pocketed the money. Then he took the car keys out of one of the change compartments. He looked at the girl, who was gazing at him, mesmerised, and read her name badge. 'Not got a kiss for Daddy, Cleo?' She smiled at him gratefully, and dropped to her knees. Markie guided her head to exactly where he wanted it. There was nothing better than a good blow-job after a long stretch, he thought, as he watched the eager Cleo bobbing up and down.

Fifteen minutes later, he walked out of Pandora's and over to the Range Rover Vogue that was parked next to the Astra he'd just dumped. It was exactly where his mate Swing had said he'd leave it. Good lad, thought Markie. He jumped inside and turned on the heated leather seats, then fired up his beast of a car. He loved this one. He pulled out from the kerb and pointed it in the direction of the motorway. He had to be home soon, or he'd be wearing his bollocks as earrings. He scrolled through his phone until he came to 'Mandy' and pressed dial.

The phone was answered almost immediately.

'Markie!' a voice shrieked. 'Need me to pick you up?'

'Nah, babe, I'm sorted. Just some business to attend to first.'

'Aw! I've missed you so bad.'

'I've missed you an' all. All set for the big day, sweetheart?'

'I'm dead nervous. But the dress fits perfectly. Two weeks to go. I can't believe it!'

'Why you nervous?'

'Just our families. I don't want a big kick-off when they all get pissed. And I swear to God, if your Leanne turns up wearing white and tries to upstage me ...'

'Keep your knickers on. Our Lee wouldn't do that.' Although our Jodie might've. Good job she's a bridesmaid and has to wear what she's told, Markie thought.

'Are you nervous?' Mandy asked. She had been planning their big day since Markie had been sent down.

'You know what?' Markie thought about the servicing he'd just received. 'I couldn't be calmer.'

*

It had been two weeks since Leanne had parted company with Jenny and she'd lined up a meeting with another glamour agency, Coco Management. It wasn't as well regarded as Pink, but she hadn't had the nerve to ring Meagan back after what she'd heard. Kia was at school and Leanne was getting ready to go out.

The last few weeks had been a struggle. She had never been under the illusion that she was surrounded by friends in London. But she'd thought she might be able to call on a few old acquaintances to help her until she was back on her feet again. She had fifteen thousand pounds outstanding on credit cards, her rent was fifteen hundred a month and then she had to live.

When Jenny had given her the boot, Leanne had had two thousand pounds in the bank. This had dwindled to nothing. *What have I spent it on?* Leanne fretted.

The hard fact was she had spent it on a lifestyle she'd been told she deserved but couldn't afford. When she was growing up she'd go to the pub, have a few vodka-and-oranges and get in free to any club in Bradington, thanks to Markie. But in London she had quickly become accustomed to the champagne lifestyle she had encountered at Atlantic and China Whites – the places to be when she had first arrived. Often the drinks were free but when they weren't Leanne might find herself spending more than a thousand pounds on a night out with her friends.

When any of her family visited Leanne would put them up at the Dorchester or Claridges; she wanted to show them how well she was doing and the only way she knew to do this was to splash the cash she'd never had before. She'd stopped thinking about the value of a pound and bought whatever she'd liked the look of. The same went for Kia. All of the little girl's clothes were designer, all of her bedroom furniture was from Selfridges. Nothing was too good for Leanne's child. Leanne had an accountant but he told her when her tax was due, not what she could and couldn't buy.

When she had called a couple of the girls she had modelled with over the past few years, girls she had helped when they'd started out, she had been gutted to discover how quickly people could turn their backs on her. She just needed a couple of grand to tide her over but no one wanted to help. She should ask Markie, she knew, but something was stopping her. They used to be so close, but she'd only seen him twice since he'd been inside – she couldn't just turn up on his doorstep now and ask for two grand. Anyway, you never knew with Markie: he was flush one week and on his uppers the next. Leanne knew she had to get herself out of this situation, but she didn't know how.

She sat at the solid oak table in the beautiful marble kitchen, neither of which she owned, and began to flick through her portfolio. Looking back on her nine years of modelling, she felt a mix of nostalgia, pride and sadness. She had been so young when she'd started out. So fresh-faced. There was the picture of her in the Maldives, wearing a bikini bottom made of shells. She looked so happy. She had been so happy. Then there was the one of her at the carwash – it had become a massive-selling poster all over the world. If Jenny had been a better manager, Leanne would have got residuals on that, but as she was young and starting out, Jenny had agreed a one-off fee.

Leanne shook her head as she turned another page. Her heart thumped when she saw the picture she hadn't looked at for seven years. There she was, painted in the colours of the famous football club, surrounded by the first team. And there he was. She flipped the page. She needed to be in the right frame of mind for her meeting, and daydreaming over pictures that stirred old memories wouldn't help.

With everything ready, Leanne checked her reflection in the mirror one last time, grabbed her bags and coat, then went to switch on the alarm. The intercom buzzed – she'd had it fitted when she was being pestered on a daily basis by the papers. She wasn't expecting anyone, but answered it anyway. 'Hello?'

'Delivery for Ms Crompton.'

'Won't be a minute.'

As she opened the door a stocky man in a balaclava burst in, grabbed her by the throat and hit her. Leanne screamed and reeled back against the wall. He pressed his mouth to Leanne's ear and spoke in a low, menacing voice: 'Rumours are circulating about that bastard kiddie of yours and who its daddy is.'

'I don't know what you're talking about,' Leanne said. Her voice shook with terror.

'I think you do. You're on your arse and you need some cash. Well, be a good girl and just keep getting your tits out to pay the bills, yeah? Don't want you resorting to any funny business.'

Hot, panicky tears stung her eyes. She fought them back.

'If our friend – and you do know who I'm talking about, sweetheart, don't muck me around – is in any way implicated, you're dead meat, understand? He's got a wife and a reputation to protect, and we don't want the good British public thinking he's a naughty boy, now, do we?'

Leanne shook her head. The man loosened his grip round her neck.

'Good girl.' He walked out, unrolling the balaclava – Leanne glimpsed the back of his bald head – and closing the door behind him. She crumpled to the floor, sobbing.

chapter three

Leanne was standing outside a modern apartment block at the back of Spitalfields Market, pressing the door buzzer. This once run-down area of London was now *the* place for trendy young things to live, and Jenna James was the country's current favourite. She had been plucked from obscurity in the North East by the pop mogul Ian Welsh to front his new band, Girls on Top. Leanne and she had been introduced on a night out and at first Jenna had been star-struck, telling Leanne how amazing she was. Leanne had taken the flattery lightly, knowing that the then eighteen-year-old was nervous.

As the night wore on, the pair became separated from the group they were with, and Jenna had broken down, crying, telling Leanne she was homesick and felt out of place in London. Leanne empathised with her. She knew exactly what Jenna meant when she said she felt stupid opening her mouth. It didn't matter how successful Leanne became, she was still intimidated by the people around her in the capital. Everyone seemed cleverer, wittier and sharper than she was. Hearing Jenna say that she felt the same had been a blessed relief. She was so used to young starlets who were utterly confident in their own skin.

But that conversation with Jenna had been five years ago and she was now engaged to one of Britain's most bankable actors, her solo album had just been released to rave reviews and she had her own clothing range in Topshop.

At last Jenna's breathless voice said, 'Hello?'

'It's me,' Leanne said.

'Who's me?' Jenna asked, sounding rushed.

'Leanne,' she said, a little irked but trying not to show it. Jenna buzzed her in and she waited for the lift, hoping that her friend would help her make sense of everything that was happening to her. She needed someone else who was public property to tell her not to worry, her profile was high enough for her to get other work. Leanne knew that if she was on her own she could stay in London and slog it out. Something would turn up. But she had Kia to think about: she needed to know where the next pay cheque was coming from.

As the lift door opened, Jenna was hopping into a leopard-print stiletto. 'Aright, darlin'?' she said, in her Newcastle brogue.

'Hiya,' Leanne said. 'How are you?' Jenna was obviously great, she thought, looking at her friend's long tanned legs and perfect honey-highlighted hair.

'I'm all right, but I've got to be in Soho in an hour,' Jenna said.

Leanne's heart sank. When she had texted Jenna to meet up, she had asked if she could take her out to lunch for a heart-to-heart.

'Leonardo DiCaprio's manager wants to meet me. I got my agent to tell him if he thinks I can act then he's barking up the wrong tree.'

Leanne smiled weakly. Leonardo's *people* were talking to Jenna's *people*. Great, she thought. She'd forgotten what it was like to have 'people'. 'Cool,' she said. 'You're doing so well, aren't you?'

'Well, I'm OK, I suppose.' Jenna shrugged. Understatement of the century, Leanne thought. 'What's up with you? You sounded like your knickers were in a bit of a twist in your text. Coffee?' She went into the kitchen. It was huge, bigger than Leanne's entire house and far more upmarket. The appliances were stainless-steel Miele and the utensils were Philippe Starck design classics. Leanne was lucky if she could find a spoon that didn't look as if Uri Geller had been at it.

She weighed Jenna up for a moment. Five years ago she'd have been able to say to her, 'I'm on my arse, Jen, and I've no idea what I'm going to do.' That had been when Jenna thought Leanne held the keys to the celebrity kingdom and knew exactly what she was doing. But today Leanne felt she was a mild inconvenience to her friend. 'I've had a run of bad luck, and I just wanted to see a friendly face,' she said.

Jenna was filling the coffee machine. 'Aw, babes.' She stopped what she was doing, tottered to where

Leanne was standing and gave her a limp hug. Leanne patted Jenna's back – she didn't know how to respond. What she needed now was a big bear-hug and someone to say, 'Don't let the bastards get you down.' She was beginning to think she'd come to the wrong place. 'Come on, tell us what's wrong.'

Leanne looked at Jenna, with her great career and her fabulous life, and realised there and then that Jenna wasn't interested in her, and who could blame her? It wasn't that Jenna was a nasty person, far from it. She was a sweet-natured girl, but she didn't want to hear about Leanne's problems. They weren't true friends. In the public's mind they were bosom buddies because they had been photographed together many times, but they rarely saw one another. 'I'm just a bit down. But I'll be all right,' Leanne said, forcing a smile.

Jenna looked relieved. 'Course you will, chicken,' she said brightly, clearly glad that Leanne hadn't turned up to burst her celebrity bubble.

Half an hour later, Leanne was walking towards Liverpool Street station with a heavy heart. She had to be at Coco Management for three o'clock but until then she was free. Jenna had left her with a smile and a promise that they'd go out for drinks soon, but Leanne had a sneaky suspicion that that would never happen.

She grabbed her phone as she walked along and scrolled through the address book. Then she stopped and leaned against a wall. A shocking thought had occurred to her. At her lowest ebb, there wasn't one person she could call on in London. All of the people she had ever hung around with in the city she had met through work and she knew that, like Jenna, they would only be interested in her if things were going well. The people who *would* listen to her and actually care were more than a hundred miles away in Bradington. She scrolled to 'Mum' and pressed call.

'Bloody hell, stranger, we thought you'd fallen off the face of the earth,' Tracy said. Leanne tried to reply but the lump in her throat turned her voice to a squeak. 'What's up wi' you?' Tracy asked, in her usual brash way. But, brash as she was, she was still Leanne's mum and the person she needed to talk to now.

She swallowed the lump. 'I just wanted to say hello.' Then the tears were flowing.

'You crying, Lee? Bloody hell, Kent, our Lee's sobbing,' Tracy squawked. 'Someone been at you?' She always went into defensive mode when she thought someone had harmed her kids. *She* could be as rotten as she wanted but if anyone outside the family laid a finger on them they'd have her to answer to.

'No.' Leanne tried to pull herself together. 'I'm all right, just a bit homesick.'

'That lot in the *Mirror* was making out you were on your arse the other day. You're not, are you?'

'No, I'm fine, Mum. Just a rocky patch. I'm changing agents.'

'Well, you can always come back here.'

Leanne could hear her lighting a cigarette.

'Thanks,' she said. She knew her mother didn't think it would come to that, but Leanne wasn't so sure. If she didn't sort something out soon, she wouldn't stay in London where there was nothing for her and Kia.

''S all right, love, any time. Kent, pass us the remote, will you?'

Leanne half smiled. 'See you, then.'

'Ta-ra.'

Leanne pocketed her phone and headed on up the street.

''Ere, that's Leanne Crompton, phwoar! Show us your tits, love,' a passing man exclaimed.

A large part of Leanne wanted to slap him across the face and say, 'Don't be so rude!' But a little bit was secretly pleased that she was still recognised. She pulled her cap down over her face, silently chastising herself for being grateful to some oaf, and marched off in the direction of the station.

*

'Miss Crompton.' Eddie Ball walked into the reception area of Coco Management and thrust out his hand, casting a lascivious eye over Leanne. Eddie was everything she had expected of men in the glamour-modelling world but had rarely experienced. Desperate times call for desperate measures, she thought. She took a deep breath and plastered on a smile.

'Come through, come through.' He let his eyes

settle on Leanne's chest. She pulled her cardigan tighter.

'So, then, what took you so long to come to see Uncle Eddie?'

Bit forward, Leanne thought. She'd only met the guy twice before. 'I've been having a break,' she said.

'Rumour has it you've been touting yourself around and having doors closed in your face.' Eddie smiled as if that might cancel out the meanness of what he'd just said.

Leanne shuffled in her seat. 'Who told you that?' She tried to keep the smile on her face.

'Oh, it's a small industry.'

'Isn't it just?' she said breezily.

'I like you, Leanne. But I think you know as well as I do that your career as a glamour model is over. You need to diversify.'

'In what way?' she asked, trying to keep the shock and hurt out of her voice.

'Well, I've got a business on the side where I know for certain you could earn big bucks.' He looked Leanne in the eye.

'Really?' She was all ears now. Maybe it was presenting, she thought optimistically.

'Yes, really,' Eddie said, grabbing a portfolio from behind him. 'Have a look at this little lot.'

Leanne opened the folder and began to leaf through it. She recognised a few girls from years back. Women who would now be in their thirties.

'They work all over the world. See Leonie?' Eddie

said, pointing at the woman on the page Leanne was looking at. 'Earned two hundred grand last year tax free while she was living it up in Dubai.' Leanne wasn't sure about moving abroad, but for that kind of money ... 'A girl like you, Leanne, I think we're talking closer to a million.'

Suddenly the penny dropped from a great height. 'Are these women hookers?' she asked plainly, too horrified to be outraged yet.

'Good God, no! Hookers stand on street corners, Leanne. These are high-class ladies offering a bespoke service to our bank of high-net-worth male clients.' Evidently Eddie believed his own hype.

'High-class hookers, then,' Leanne said, an edge to her voice now that she knew what Eddie was suggesting.

Eddie sat back in his chair. 'Call it what you want, my love, but it's more money than you'll ever see again – *and* you'll get to live the life and call the shots. If you want to be sniffy about it then good luck. But don't come crying to me when you're scanning beans in Kwik Save.'

Leanne stood up. 'Thanks for the vote of confidence, Eddie. I'll see myself out.' She left his office, slamming the door behind her. But once she was out in the street her confidence left her and fresh tears welled ...

At home with Kia that evening she couldn't get Eddie Ball out of her mind. Maybe this was the end of the line for her. Maybe her choices really were *that* limited. She had thought she'd be able to make some money, maybe get a contract with *Reveal* magazine or something, but the truth was that if any of the magazines wanted to publish a story about her, they didn't need to pay her. They would get a picture of her from a paparazzo and write what they wanted. Well, she thought angrily, as she jabbed at the remote control, I'd rather scan beans for a living than do anything Eddie bloody Ball suggests. Although at that moment she couldn't even see how she'd swing herself a job in Kwik Save. The truth was, she wasn't qualified for anything. As she tormented herself with her morose thoughts Kia, who had been sitting cross-legged in front of the TV, got up, came to her and gave her a big hug.

'I love you, Mummy,' she said.

Leanne looked at her beautiful daughter and thought her heart might burst. 'I love you too, sweet-heart.' She held Kia tightly to her. No matter what happened, she thought, at least they had each other.

chapter four

Leanne looked around the little terrace house that had been her home for nearly four years. It had been a heartbreaking decision to leave London because she knew that she was saying goodbye to her career. But the simple fact was, she could no longer afford to live in the city.

The furniture was still there but the house had been stripped bare of her belongings, which were now packed into a removal truck. Her heart plummeted when she placed the last of her possessions – a few coat-hangers and a couple of Kia's teddy bears – in the back of the van. Jenny had told her several times when she was earning well to see a financial adviser but Leanne had always put it off. She didn't really like talking about money and had thought things would be all right. Well, so much for that, she had thought yesterday, when her bank had refused her an extension to her overdraft.

Leanne loved Greenwich and the thought of having to leave was too much for her. Everyone else wanted to live in Notting Hill or Camden Town and be seen falling out of a pub with Jude Law, but Leanne had wanted somewhere safe and quiet for Kia, whose dad had first brought Leanne to Greenwich. They had hidden themselves in the Rose and Crown and he had declared undying love to her. He had only been able to stay with her for an hour but that was how it had always been: snatched moments and promises that were never kept. After that encounter, Leanne had gone from the park to Greenwich High Street as if she was walking on air. While she was strolling along the row of tiny houses, which looked as if someone had uprooted a picture-postcard English village and deposited it in the middle of London, she had decided that when she had enough money she would move there. After her first major shoot, when she'd appeared in *Packed*, the top men's magazine, she had spotted that this house was available for rent. She and little Kia had moved in the following day.

'You all set, love?' the van driver asked.

Leanne nodded.

'I don't want to go!' Kia exploded.

Leanne knelt in front of her and pulled her close. 'We don't have a choice, darling. I'm really sorry.'

'Jemima Forster says it's because we're tramps that we have to move,' Kia shouted, then dissolved into floods of tears.

'That's not true,' said Leanne, firmly, 'and if I see Jemima Forster again, I'll tell her exactly what I think of her for saying that.' She stroked her daughter's hair. She had a feeling that Kia wasn't going to see her school friends again. Unless Leanne could find some decent money. And that didn't look like it was going to happen any time soon.

*

Leanne drove along the M60 following the removal van. When she saw the familiar exit for Bradington, her stomach performed flip-flops. *This is it*, she thought. I'm back where I started.

She drove past the old sports centre where Markie had taken her and the others swimming when they were kids. He used to like to see who could hold their breath under water longest. Jodie would always win, popping up with a beetroot face well after everyone else had given up. She drove up to the roundabout at the top of Manchester Road. One way led to Bilsey, a small, quaint village, and the other to Bolingbroke, the sprawling estate where Leanne had grown up. She took the Bolingbroke turning. She had been in touch with Jodie, who seemed to be looking forward to having her back. Leanne had always enjoyed her sister's visits to her in London. Jodie was good fun, and since Leanne had moved away, she had been the one sibling who had kept in close touch with her.

Karina had been distant, but Leanne put that down to the fact that she was getting on with her life. However, recent reports from Jodie had suggested that Karina was into coke and Leanne didn't think she'd meant the fizzy drink. Coke seemed to be a bit of a problem in her family. Leanne didn't understand the attraction. She hated the thought of snorting something and she certainly didn't like the effect it had on people. A lot of celebrities she knew took it and it made them go on about themselves incessantly, and the celebrities Leanne knew liked nothing more than talking about themselves.

Canterbury Avenue – the gateway to Bolingbroke – snaked away from the well-to-do houses of Bilsey and into a maze of 1960s concrete housing. Over the years the council had tried a number of initiatives to improve the area – sleeping policemen, speed cameras, even shoving hanging baskets everywhere. Leanne had admired them on one of her visits back home but her mother had dismissed them, with the immortal words, 'You can't polish a turd.'

Kia, who had been asleep for most of the journey, stirred. 'Are we at Nana Tracy's, Mummy?' she asked. 'It smells funny at her house, doesn't it?' She said it as matter-of-factly as if she'd been talking about the weather.

Leanne sighed. 'It smells of smoke sometimes.'

'Hmm.'

'Once I've got us sorted, Kia, we'll get our own place, I promise. It'll be like an adventure,' she told her.

'Like when we went to the Maldives with Simon and Greg?' Kia asked excitedly. Simon and Greg were a couple who worked together. Simon was the photographer, Greg his manager. They had taken a real shine to Kia on a photo shoot in the Indian Ocean. Kia had loved every minute of it, playing in the sea and being fussed over.

Leanne smiled sadly. 'Yeah, a bit like that,' she said.

*

Jodie had called her mum the day before to find out if they were going to do something to mark Leanne's homecoming. 'What? Like get a life-size poster of her from *Loaded* magazine and roll it down the side of the house? Really rub it in? She'll be wanting to skulk back in like she never left, won't she?' Tracy had retorted.

'Tell you what, Mum,' Jodie said, 'remind me not to come to you when I'm feeling a bit sorry for myself, eh?'

Tracy had waved her hand and said, 'I tell it like it is. People don't like it? They can lump it.' Jodie had put the phone down and decided to organise something herself.

She had called Markie, Karina and Scott and told them to be at Tracy's at two the following day. Markie had said he'd meet them for food later but the others agreed. Jodie visited one of the many town-centre pound shops – Bradington might not have much but it had pound shops by the dozen – and bought a Welcome Home banner with some balloons. She had taken a couple of bottles from the Beacon that were intended for the optics but she would replace them.

She wanted Leanne to feel as good as possible when she got home. Jodie had experienced Leanne's life in London and it had been glamorous, whatever her sister had said when she came to Bradington and tried to play it down.

Jodie waltzed into Tracy's with her box of goodies. Charly was sitting on one of the kitchen stools, looking as unimpressed with life as ever. 'Here –' Jodie threw a balloon at her '– you're good at blowing things.' Charly gave her a sarcastic smile, but did as she was told.

'Our Lee's in the *Sun* again,' Scott said, flattening the paper on the breakfast bar. Everyone took a cursory glance; it wasn't news. '"Leanne Crompton Heads Home. The glamour model has been plagued with financial difficulties since she was dropped by her manager. Now the blonde bombshell will have to fend for herself back up north."' Underneath the printed article there was a mock-up of Leanne as a cleaner, Leanne as a lollipop lady, Leanne as a milkwoman and Leanne as a police officer: the tabloid's helpful suggestions for her next step up the career ladder.

'She'll never make a copper.' Tracy blew up a balloon.

'Think she's dreading coming back?' Scott asked.

'I would be, wouldn't you?' Charly said, as if Scott was thick to imagine otherwise.

'Out of here like a shot you'd be, wouldn't you?' Tracy snapped her fingers and raised an accusatory eyebrow at Charly.

'Oh, and given half a chance you'd stick around for the high life in Bolingbroke?' Charly said, with a withering stare.

'Knock it on the head, you two, for one afternoon.' Jodie shimmied over to the fireplace and attached the banner above it. She stood back. 'Well, it looks shit but it'll have to do.'

A car pulled up outside. 'She's here!' Jodie shouted.

They all gathered in the kitchen. Tracy poured herself a tumbler of vodka and added the tiniest dash of Coke to the top. Jodie couldn't believe it: her mum would be on her backside before tea-time. She gave her a disapproving look.

'If I can't celebrate my girl coming home, what can I celebrate?' Tracy said, and had a swig.

The door opened and Leanne came in. 'Hello,' she said, in a tiny voice.

'Welcome home!' they chorused. Jodie ran over to hug her sister, Tracy put 'Welcome Home' by Peters and Lee on her stereo, Charly stood up, tugged at her skirt and slid over to give Leanne a peck on the cheek, and Scott hugged Kia. Leanne smiled at them and burst into tears.

*

Leanne was still in shock. She was sitting in the Kathmandu restaurant, Bradington's best curry house, as her family talked over her. Karina and Tracy were as drunk as lords and Tracy was speaking to the waiter as if he had just stepped off a plane from Nepal. Scott was fiddling with Charly's jacket, trying to take it off for her while she made a half-hearted attempt to talk to Kia. Then the door opened and Markie walked in. Leanne's heart leapt. She jumped to her feet and ran to her brother. 'Markie!' She flung herself into his arms.

Markie hugged her. 'Welcome back, darl.' He kissed the top of her head. 'You don't want to be in London, you want to be up here where the action is,' he said, with his tongue in his cheek.

'That's why I came. It got a bit quiet in London. Not enough parties, you know how it is.'

'You're over the hill, but we don't care, do we?' Tracy shouted from the other end of the table. Kent looked mortified and whispered something in her ear. 'Oh, "sssh" yerself, yer great big girl,' she slurred.

'Hello, Uncle Markie,' Kia said, as Markie walked over to kiss her. He chatted to her for a minute or two, then went to sit in the spare seat next to Leanne.

As everyone else resumed their conversation, Leanne turned to Markie and said, 'How was … er … the last two years?'

'Prison was shit.'

'Markie, I wanted to visit more than I did …'

'If I had a penny for everyone who's said that to me …'

He wasn't trying to lay a guilt trip on her, she knew that, he was genuinely perplexed as to why she hadn't been more often. Leanne didn't really have an answer. 'I just don't like prisons,' she said lamely.

'Well, that makes two of us. Difference is, I didn't have a choice about visiting.' Markie waved the waiter over and ordered a beer.

Leanne hung her head. 'I'm really sorry.'

Mark half smiled. 'Don't worry about it, darling. You've not been having the best time, have you?'

Leanne was about to explain the last couple of weeks to him when all hell broke loose at the other end of the table. Kent was holding Tracy in something very similar to a half-nelson and one of the waiters was saying, 'You must all leave now!'

'What did I say? I didn't say nowt!' Tracy was shouting.

Scott was yelling to another waiter, 'Come on then, mate, start on a woman, think you're hard? Have a go at a real man.'

The waiter took Scott at his word and lifted him off the ground by the scruff of the neck. Markie stepped in. 'Put him down.' The waiter dropped him like a hot stone. 'We're leaving,' Markie said. Tracy was now out on the street trying to get past Kent to come back inside. 'Whatever she or he said, I'm sorry.' He threw a bunch of tenners on to the table. 'Have a nice night.'

Leanne had grabbed Kia's hand, expecting her to cry but she seemed mesmerised. She led her out of the restaurant. She couldn't believe that their first night back had ended in a brawl. 'What did you say?' she asked her mother.

'I didn't bloody say anything! He was giving me the eye!' Tracy shouted. Leanne doubted that that was the case. Tracy gave the restaurant a one-fingered salute, then stomped up the street. Everyone trudged after her.

'Nothing changes, eh?' Markie said to Leanne.

Leanne smiled wryly at her brother. But something *had* changed. A few years ago Markie would have piled in with Scott but not now: he was far calmer, more measured. She wondered how long it would last.

chapter five

Lisa was sitting in her first-class seat on the flight back to the UK from Thailand, enjoying a foot massage. She and Jay had been away for a week and now they were returning permanently to the UK. Lisa wanted to reclaim her crown as the country's number one celebrity. She had found it hard to maintain that status in Italy even though she had constantly fed pictures to the press. Anyway, it was all part of her plan. They were renting a mansion in Alderley Edge and Jay would return for his swan song at Manchester Rovers before bowing out to national applause.

The trip to Thailand had been billed in the press as a romantic gift from a besotted husband to his wife for their tenth wedding anniversary, which was great PR even though they had been there mainly on business. Lisa looked through the photos in her lap. She couldn't quite decide: a little girl to take shopping, dress up and be friends with when she was older, or a little boy who'd love his mum uncondi-tionally. Boys were less complicated than girls, Lisa thought.

'What d'you think?' she asked, holding up a picture of a pretty little girl to the woman massaging her feet.

'She's beautiful.' Lisa nodded. She was. She put the picture to one side and picked up that month's edition of *Vogue*, which had a picture of her and Jay on the cover. He was standing upright and she was draped around him. The only thing saving their modesty was a strategically placed Union Jack. She liked it. Mario had done an amazing job. It was part of the campaign for Jay's return to the UK. He was thirty now, and in football that was virtually geriatric. Lisa had her eye on their future career. She had invested in her own swimwear and underwear line, which was only being stocked in upmarket stores, and Jay had signed a five-year deal with a large men's clothing firm. He was also awaiting confirmation of a number of lucrative sponsorship deals for everything from aftershave to hats.

Lisa was fairly sure that her efforts to place Jay in the national consciousness as the man whom other men wanted to be and women wanted to be with had worked. Now the brand needed managing. And she was the woman to do it.

Just then Jay came out of the toilet. He flattened his shirt with his palm and stared at the floor. Lisa's eyes bored into him as he came back to his seat. In the background one of the male cabin crew was staring at him. Lisa turned on him the glare she'd had fixed on her husband. The young man pretended that another passenger somewhere behind Lisa and

Jay had caught his eye. When he bustled past, Lisa said, 'Nice arse.'

The woman who was massaging her feet glanced up, obviously trying to figure out why there was such a frosty atmosphere between the golden couple.

'Do you have to?' Jay said curtly, grabbing a copy of the in-flight magazine and pretending to leaf through it.

'No. I don't *have* to. And neither do you, but you do.'

'Leave it.' Jay jerked his head at the masseuse, indicating that he didn't want to have such a conversation in front of her.

'Fine,' Lisa snapped. 'Here.' She thrust the pictures of the Thai kids at him. 'Choose one of those.'

Jay began to shuffle through them. Lisa gazed out of the window at the foothills of the Himalayas below. Five years ago this sort of argument would have upset her and she would have been running to the toilets to have a good cry, but not any more. She couldn't work out if she'd become used to her relationship with Jay or tired of it. Either way, there was no chance she was going to demand a divorce as she had in the early days: she was too long in the tooth for all that drama. She knew how the fame game worked and played it to her advantage, rather than being its victim. She peered at the lush green landscape and wondered about the life going on 30,000 feet below her. How many people have heard of me down there, she thought, then settled back in her seat and fell asleep.

*

Hanley Farm Estate on the outskirts of Bradington wasn't the sort of estate that the Cromptons were used to. It was the closest thing that Bradington had to a stately home, and for the past eighteen months Mandy had been in her element organising the wedding of the decade. The small fact that her husband-to-be, Markie, had been banged up for the last two years hadn't bothered her too much: if he'd been around he'd only have got in the way. He had been restricted to telling her where to get the money from when she needed another injection of cash for two hundred metres of pink taffeta or a fairytale-castle cake.

Jodie had watched all of this with bemusement. As chief bridesmaid to nine others, she had to help Mandy with the arrangements. Mandy and Markie had been together for years. They had first met when she was at school, but now, at the age of twenty-five, Mandy was champing at the bit to become Mrs Crompton. Jodie knew that Mandy and Markie had a fiery relationship: she was all mouth and he was all temper. A bit of Jodie wasn't even sure why they were getting married, other than for the day out, but she was as guilty as anyone of wanting to play along with it.

She had been taken aback when Mandy had asked her to be chief bridesmaid, but she suspected it was because Mandy's sister, Chanese, was such a troglodyte that she'd make the pictures look bad and Mandy wanted them in the *Bradington Gazette*. Chanese had been relegated to ordinary bridesmaid status, which wasn't much of an honour considering there were so many others.

It was 7 a.m. and Jodie and Mandy were at Hanley Farm putting the finishing touches to the wedding tables. Mandy was wandering around the place settings in a pink tracksuit with her hair in curlers, her face black with the San Tropez spray tan she had yet to wash off, checking that everything was in order.

'Who put Tamsin next to Billy?' she shrieked. 'She'll go off her fucking head!'

Jodie bit her bottom lip. That *was* a cock-up. Billy, Jodie's cousin, had slipped Tamsin, Mandy's cousin, some acid a few years ago and she'd finished up sectioned with drug-induced psychosis. His defence had been 'I thought it'd be a laugh.' Tamsin wasn't laughing when the police found her up a tree naked, stroking a grapefruit. Mandy picked up Tamsin's place card and swapped it with her other cousin Dale's from another table.

Jodie watched what she was doing and thought carefully about the consequences. 'Won't it kick off with Dale and Billy if you put them together?'

Mandy rolled her eyes and slammed down Dale's place card. 'Well, if it does, they'll have me to fucking answer to.'

Jodie decided to remain silent. She didn't fancy rocking the boat with Mandy on her big day. She was volatile at the best of times, but today Jodie knew she'd go off like a rocket if riled. Mandy stood back and huffed in satisfaction. 'It looks mint, doesn't it?'

Jodie nodded. 'Yeah, top.' And indeed it did, Jodie thought. *Over the* top. But she wasn't about to say that to Mandy. The best thing she could do was keep her head down and nod when spoken to. Which would be a bit hard for Jodie, who was used to telling everyone exactly what she thought. Tomorrow she could tell Mandy what a colossal pain in the arse she'd been, but today Jodie was keeping it buttoned. And when the speeches and pretend crying were out of the way she could get as pissed as a newt and finally relax.

Mandy folded her arms and smiled. She pointed to her head. 'Hair extensions – a grand. Chocolate fountain – four hundred quid. Ceramic swans – six hundred quid. Marrying Markie Crompton – priceless.'

Jodie forced a smile. She wasn't sure she'd make it through the day without vomiting. Not because of the tack, she wasn't afraid of a bit of tack – she worked at the Beacon, for God's sake – but at Mandy thinking she and Markie were so perfect. Give me a break, Jodie thought. She knew her brother was the furthest thing from husband material in the north of England. But Jodie wasn't the one to spill the beans: she was sticking to her role of nodding dog for the day. If Mandy was ever to find out about Markie, it wasn't going to be from her.

chapter six

Markie peeled his head off the pillow and looked at his alarm clock: 11.15. 'Shit!' he said, jumping out of bed. 'Swing?' he shouted. There was no reply. *Where the bloody hell is that numbskull?* Markie was meant to be at Hanley Farm at twelve but here he was, stinking like a brewery.

Last night he and a few of the lads had gone out in Manchester for his big send-off. They had ended up back at Pandora's and Mac 'The Knife' Derbyshire, Markie's sometime business partner, had ensured that four girls had been waiting for Markie when he arrived. As a result he was shattered. He looked at his reflection and wondered if maybe he was getting too old for all this. He was thirty-two now; probably for the best that he was getting married. Not that he was about to throw in the towel, but four birds in one go was a bit much, even by his standards.

Markie hopped into the shower and washed quickly. He knew he'd have to shave his stubble. Mandy wanted him to look like Brad Pitt today and he'd have to pull something out of the bag sharpish if he was going to look that good.

forward and hoovered up a line like the old pro she was. Leanne dropped her voice: 'I thought you'd knocked that shit on the head.'

Tracy threw back her head and sniffed hard. 'Special occasions. And what's a more special occasion than my baby boy getting married?'

'Put it away. I don't want Kia to see you doing that.' Leanne glared at her.

'Bloody hell. Anyone'd think you were pure as the driven snow.'

Leanne could hardly believe it – but Tracy never failed to surpass herself. 'The only reason I ever took that stuff was because you gave it me!'

Tracy flicked a hand dismissively. 'Oh, boo-hoo! Loads of kids would love a mum who was cool about doing drugs.'

'Cool?' Leanne could feel herself losing it. 'You call coming in from school and having to take heroin cool?'

'Oh, come on, I wasn't into the scag for long.'

'Long enough to make me take it with you when I was only fifteen.'

'No one forced you.'

Leanne had had enough. 'No? I come in. You're off your head. You tell me you need someone to talk to and the only way you'll feel right about talking is if I'm on your "wavelength". So I chase the dragon to have a conversation with my own mother. What bit of that is you not forcing me?'

Tracy raised an eyebrow and Leanne turned. Kia was standing by the door holding her handbag.

'Why are you shouting?' the little girl asked.

Leanne smiled and replied, through gritted teeth, 'We're not shouting, sweetheart, Mummy and Nana always talk like this. It's just a game.'

Tracy put her baking tray back into the oven with a knowing snigger.

Leanne straightened Kia's dress. What a start to the day, she thought. She felt physically sick. Her mum had always dipped in and out of drug-taking and Leanne knew the signs that showed a bender was in the offing. Tracy would use a special occasion as an excuse to tuck into the coke. Leanne had seen her in some real messes and couldn't face another, not at Markie's wedding with everyone there.

'Now then?' Kent stuck his Elvis-inspired head round the door. Leanne felt relieved. She hoped he could pull her mother into line. 'How's my darlin'?' He went over to Tracy, who put her arms round him and kissed him on the lips. Leanne cringed but not as much as she did a moment later when their tongues got involved. Tracy snaked her hand down to Kent's belt and Kent tried to pull back, although he was obviously enjoying it.

'Eurgh!' Kia said, clapping her hands over her eyes.

'Eurgh's right!' Leanne said, and grabbed her daughter's hand. 'I know it's your house, Mum, but can you do that in private?'

Outside, Leanne started her car, wondering what on earth she'd done to deserve her mother.

*

Jodie, Chanese, Karina and the other seven brides-maids were trying to get Mandy and her Lady Di-influenced wedding dress into the carriage she had booked. It was proving easier said than done.

'Couldn't you have got a longer train?' Jodie said, her vow of silence forgotten.

'I don't need you getting all lippy today, Jode. Just help me into this fucking thing,' Mandy snapped.

Mandy's poor father, Keith, who was neither use nor ornament, was sitting in the orb-like carriage clutching at his daughter's back as if that might help. 'Dad, will you give it a rest? You're doing my head in!' Keith sat back, chastised, and Jodie gave him a small smile. Poor bugger, she thought.

Once Mandy was in, the carriage set off for Hanley Farm. Jodie and Karina breathed a sigh of relief. 'D'you think she'll chill out once we get to the recep-tion?' Karina asked.

'God knows.' Jodie watched the horse-drawn vehicle pull round the corner.

'Here.' Karina rummaged in the little pink flower bag that each bridesmaid had. 'Take this.' She passed Jodie a wrap of coke.

Jodie took it so as not to arouse suspicion and hid it in her own bag. 'You know I don't take drugs,' she said.

Karina giggled. 'By the end of today you'll be jacking up heroin if she keeps on like that.'

Jodie smiled reluctantly. What the hell have we got ourselves into? she wondered.

chapter seven

Leanne was sitting in a row with Kia, Scott and Charly. She didn't mind Charly. Tracy always said of her, 'I know her type.' Well, Leanne knew her type too: she'd met a thousand of them in London, hard-faced girls who wanted a way out of their humdrum lives, but that didn't make them bad. Charly just needed a foot up in life, and Leanne hoped that Scott was enough for her. Somehow she couldn't be sure that he was. She'd done all right, Charly, as far as Leanne could see. And she could have been a lot worse: she was a Metcalfe, and the Metcalfes made the Cromptons look like the Waltons.

The grand entrance hall of Hanley Farm had been turned into a chapel for the afternoon, with twenty rows of benches on either side, pink roses adorning the ends. It was beginning to fill up. Leanne didn't recognise many people but they all seemed to know who she was. A few of the men had done the not-so-sly double-take she was used to. She sometimes felt like wearing a badge that read, *Yes, I am who you think I am*. It seemed that Mandy had invited all of

Bradington. Leanne really hoped that everything went to plan. Mandy had been so on edge about everything that she knew the tiniest wrinkle would ruin her day. But her future sister-in-law's nerves weren't just pre-wedding jitters. Mandy had lost a lot of weight lately. She had always been slim, but now she was a size six and shrinking. Before Leanne had moved back to Bradington, she had confided one night when she was drunk and in confessional mode that she had been taking slimming powder, lots of it.

'Speed?' Leanne had asked, appalled.

'God, Leanne, you're such a bloody goody-goody sometimes.'

'I'm not – I just don't want you to wreck your insides.'

'I'd sell my insides on frigging eBay if it meant I'd get into Vicky Beckham's size zeros,' Mandy had admitted. Well, she wasn't that far off a size zero now, Leanne had thought when she saw Mandy yesterday. She didn't have the heart to tell her she looked ill and, besides, Mandy was so jumpy with the amount of amphetamine she was shoving down her neck that Leanne couldn't be sure she wouldn't swing for her.

She glanced round and saw Markie come in at the back of the hall. He caught her eye and winked. She beamed at him. She'd never thought she'd see the day when Mandy finally got Markie down the aisle. At that moment, Mandy's mum, Rita, turned round and breathed an obvious sigh of relief that the bride-groom had shown up. She adjusted her rather too large duck-egg-blue hat and returned her eyes to the front of the hall.

Behind Markie came Paul and Scott. Leanne needed to talk to her dad. He hadn't spoken to her in months. She'd argued with him earlier this year, telling him he was making a rod for his own back by constantly pursuing Tracy, but he hadn't listened. In fact, he'd put the phone down on her, then refused to take her calls. She wished he'd get on with his life.

Tracy was sitting at the front with Kent. When she saw her ex-husband she made a big show of dusting some non-existence speck off Kent's shoulder, then kissed his cheek. As Paul took his seat, Leanne felt the atmosphere chill. Tracy cleared her throat and looked straight ahead. Everyone knew that Paul wasn't allowed near her but for their son's sake they were putting aside their differences for the day. Leanne knew this was a generous gesture on both their parts, considering their history. She wondered how well they'd fare when her mum's coke really kicked in and her dad had a few Stellas inside him. For now, though, they were doing their best impressions of civilised human beings.

Four men filed to the front of the hall to take their places alongside Markie. Leanne felt herself flush. She smiled down at Kia to distract herself, then looked up again and caught the eye of the person responsible for the change in her colour – Tony O'Brien. Tony and Markie had been friends since they were children but, more importantly, Tony had been Leanne's first love.

Tony gave her a half-smile, and Leanne sent him a little wave before returning her gaze to her feet, annoyed that she felt embarrassed.

Tony was seven years older than her, and when he had first taken the fifteen-year-old Leanne out, he had sworn her to secrecy. They both knew that if Markie found out he'd go mad. 'He'll have my bollocks,' Tony told Leanne, and she'd laughed until she realised he was serious. Leanne and Tony had been an item for two years before she moved to London, and no one had ever known. Plenty of people half-suspected but she and Tony had kept it hidden. By the time she was old enough to tell anyone she felt they had left it too long. She was sure that her relationship with him had taught her how to keep a secret.

The benches filled up quickly and Markie was standing at the front now, staring ahead. He looked nervous, Leanne thought. Sandra Davidson, an old neighbour, was taking her seat on the bench in front of Leanne and turned to hug her. 'Awright, sweet'eart,' she said, in her sixty-a-day voice. 'You're lookin' beautiful as ever.'

'Thanks, Sandra,' Leanne murmured.

'You still down south?'

'No.' Leanne shook her head, ashamed. 'I'm back here.'

'Oh, good.' Sandra smiled and squeezed her hand. She was about the tenth person since Leanne had arrived back in Bradington to react positively. What Leanne saw as monumental failure, others saw as her return to where she belonged. It was as if her family and friends had known she'd be back and thought little of it. She just wished someone could have told her sooner and saved her all the heartache of trying to set up home in London.

A hush fell over the congregation and the harpist began to pluck at her instrument. Then Celine Dion started to sing 'My Heart Will Go On'. Of course, Leanne thought. Everyone turned round to see Mandy, followed by her twenty-foot train and ten bridesmaids, enter the hall. As much as this sort of over-the-topness wasn't really Leanne's bag, she thought Mandy looked stunning. She wished Markie would turn to look at his bride – that was what Mandy wanted – but he was staring at the registrar as if he was petrified. When Mandy and Keith, her dad, reached the front, Markie gave her an awkward smile. Mandy was crying, and her mum, Rita, was flapping her hands in front of her face as if she was trying to stave off tears.

The registrar began the ceremony and everyone settled in. Leanne was watching her father like a hawk. He kept staring at Tracy but whenever Tracy caught his eye he quickly faced forward.

The vows came and went without a hitch, and no one had stood up when the registrar asked, 'Does anyone know of any reason why these two should not be joined in matrimony?' which was a blessed relief. Leanne had had money on one of Markie's joker mates jumping to his feet.

As the ceremony came to a close, the registrar took a step back and looked at the newly weds. 'You may now kiss the bride,' he said.

Markie moved forward to Mandy, who took her new husband's face in her hands and kissed him passionately. When her tongue went into action Leanne had to look away. 'Eurgh!' Kia said, for the second time that day.

Leanne put a finger to her lips to shush her but, really, she agreed with her wholeheartedly. Apparently Markie's mates shared their opinion, doing the silent shoulder shake that indicated they were laughing. Markie pulled back, mortified, and looked at Mandy as if to ask, What was that about? Mandy grinned manically. She was wired. Leanne winced. This had the makings of a very long day.

*

Tracy came out of the toilet cubicle. She had just been to powder her nose again. The door opened and Karina walked in, her puffball dress barely fitting through the door.

'The bloody Sugar Plum Fairy! What do you look like?' Tracy cackled.

'"You look nice, Karina." Thanks, Mum,' Karina said sarcastically, bustling into a cubicle.

'Glad all that bollocks is out of the way,' Tracy said, as she fixed her pearlised lipstick. 'Now we can get wrecked.'

'Yeah, well, try not to cause any trouble,' Karina shouted from inside the cubicle.

'Me? Trouble?' Tracy sniffed with true indignation.

'God, I know. What am I on about? Sorry. You wouldn't know trouble if it came up and sat on you, would you, Mum?'

Tracy looked at herself in the mirror and a scheming smile spread across her face. 'That's right, darlin',' she said. 'Course I wouldn't.'

She walked out of the ladies' and into the main hall, which had been transformed for the wedding dinner. The tables were bedecked with pink balloons and there was a pink chocolate fountain in the corner that was drawing quite a crowd, but nowhere near as much of one as the bar, and the pink *pièce de résistance*: the fairytale-castle cake. On top of it Tracy noted that the two heads poking out of a turret that were meant to be Mandy and Markie looked more like characters from *Fraggle Rock*.

Kent was waiting for her, Tracy noticed. He was always waiting for her. When they'd first got together she'd loved how attentive he was. Compared to that idiot ex-husband of hers, Kent was a godsend. But after three years together the flowers he gave her and the songs he played for her on his graveyard-shift radio show had less and less impact, and the other things – like his insistence on wearing a thong with Homer Simpson's head on it and the way he called the Who and the Rolling Stones 'the boys' like he knew them – were getting on her nerves. He was a nice bloke, Kent, but she ran rings round him and knew it. He was a good shag, though, and there was a lot to be said for that, Tracy thought.

'Awright, darling?' He grabbed her round the waist.

'Gerroff!' Tracy said. Then she saw Paul eyeballing her from the other side of the room, and took the opportunity to stick her tongue down Kent's throat. That'll show him, she thought.

'Starting early, aren't we?' Mandy's mother said disdainfully as she swept past. Tracy pulled back and looked at her. There was no love lost between the two women.

'Your price-tag's sticking out, Rita.' Mandy's mum felt the back of her mother-of-the-bride jacket. 'Oh, sorry. You'll be leaving it in, won't you? Sending it back to the catalogue tomorrow?' Tracy asked.

Rita gave her an evil glare. 'It's from bloody Next. Where'd you get your rig-out? Poundstretcher?'

Tracy had enjoyed the exchange. She liked winding Rita up. She waved the other woman away. 'Now, now, mother-of-the-bride, no need to see your arse.'

Rita turned on her heel and walked off. Tracy smiled.

'Bloody hell, love, can't you wind your neck in just for one day?' Kent asked nervously, patting down the back of his DA hairstyle.

'You don't know how to enjoy yourself, you miserable sod, that's your problem.'

Paul was over by the bar with the lads. He'd been watching Rita and Tracy's little chat and was laughing as Rita stomped past him. He raised his pint to Tracy. She stared blankly at him, but a bit of her was quite pleased that someone had noticed and appreciated what she'd been up to.

chapter eight

Leanne and Kia were sitting at the top table with Karina and Jodie. Jodie looked great, Leanne thought. When she was little, Jodie had always been the chubby ugly duckling of the family but now she was blossoming. Most of the guests had taken their seats, and even Paul and Tracy had managed to sit down without one pouring a pint over the other's head. Mandy had decided that they would have the speeches before the meal. She said it was so that those speaking could enjoy their food afterwards and not have it spoilt with nerves, but Leanne knew the real reason was so they didn't get blind drunk and say something they shouldn't.

First up was Mandy's dad. Poor Keith, Leanne thought, he was absolutely terrified. He said all the usual stuff: how beautiful his daughter looked, how stunning the bridesmaids were, how much he was looking forward to welcoming Markie into the family. At this particular declaration Rita shifted uneasily in her chair and repositioned her hat for the umpteenth time. When he sat down, everyone clapped and cheered – they'd known how nervous he'd be.

Then Markie stood up. Leanne gulped some wine. She really wanted her brother to say the nice things that a groom should say at his wedding.

'Well, she finally got me up the aisle' was his opening gambit. Leanne slid down in her chair, but to her surprise this remark went down well, and everyone whooped. He continued, 'Me and Mand have been together now, for, ooh, how long, Mand?'

'Long enough,' Mandy replied, and everyone laughed.

'And I thought it was about time I made an honest woman of her. Well, as honest as she's ever going to get.' The rest of Markie's speech was short and sweet, and exactly what Leanne had expected. Nothing mushy, just to the point and funny. Everyone clapped and he took his seat, glancing briefly at Mandy and smiling tightly. Leanne was beginning to feel uneasy about how he was behaving with his new wife. The wedding seemed too much for him. Maybe it was, she thought. He's only just come out of prison.

Swing got unsteadily to his feet and Jodie whispered in Leanne's ear, 'He's pissed!'

Leanne cringed. Now that he was standing up, she could see he was on the ropes. He looked down at the crib cards he had prepared for his speech. 'Markie, mate, from one jail sentence to another, eh?' There was a ripple of polite laughter. 'Fuck it!' he said, and tossed the cards to one side. 'Right. I've known Markie since I was ten, and he's always been a cunt.'

There was a round of 'Hear, hear,' from the men in

the room, and quite a few shocked gasps from the women.

'No, seriously, though,' Swing went on. 'He is. And Mandy.' Swing turned his drunken gaze on her. 'Mandy, Mandy, Mandy. What is there to say about Mandy that we don't know already?' There was an awkward pause as he lurched sideways. Mandy shuffled uneasily in her chair. ''Cept that I shagged her at a pool party in Ibiza last year.' The room fell silent. Before anyone had chance to react, Markie had grabbed his best man by the throat.

'That's not true!' Mandy jumped to her feet. 'It's not true!'

Everyone leapt up – they didn't want to miss whatever happened next. 'It was only a fucking warm-up joke,' Swing said, staggering backwards.

'Get 'im the fuck out of here,' Markie ordered.

Mandy collapsed in floods of tears and was comforted by her multitude of bridesmaids. Markie got back on the microphone.

'Right, sorry, everyone. Swing's a dick, as we all know, and I should have had our Scotty as best man, but I gave Swing the gig 'cause he's me oldest mate – won't make that mistake again.' The 'again' made everyone laugh and broke the tension. 'Scotty, can you come up here and say a few words?' Markie asked.

Scott stood up and Markie went to comfort Mandy. 'It's all right, sweetheart,' he said, and kissed her forehead. 'Come on, don't spoil your big day.'

As Scott cleared his throat Leanne finally relaxed.

At last Markie had shown his bride some real emotion – even if he had had to knock the best man out cold first. And as Mandy smiled gratefully at her groom Leanne realised that, for all the pink and the wedding bluster, the only thing she had really wanted was that kiss.

*

It was eight o'clock in the evening, the DJ was playing 'Come On Eileen' and everyone was happily drunk, as far as Tracy could tell. Swing had been put to bed and told not to reappear. He'd never been the brightest star in the sky, even as a kid, she remembered. The lads used to bet him that he wouldn't do something just to see if he would; he never disappointed them. He once ended up in hospital for a week after they'd got him to go down the metal twenty-foot 'death-slide' in the park head first with a bin bag over his entire body. Unbeknown to Swing, Markie had put two litres of cooking oil down the slide before he got to the top to attempt his daring feat. That was where he'd got his nickname. He'd come off the end at nearly a hundred miles an hour and broken both legs. If he hadn't, he'd probably have gone up again for another go.

A hush fell over the room and an usher announced that the bride and groom would have their first dance. Markie took Mandy in his arms as the opening chords to 'All Day And All Of The Night' played. That had been Markie's choice. Tracy knew that he'd compromised with Mandy, saying, 'You can have that Celine Dion shit as long as we have the Kinks for the first dance.'

Tracy knew that Paul would be looking at her. Markie liked the Kinks because Paul and Tracy used to listen to them when they were young. Kent was holding Tracy's hand and joggling it about in time to the song. Tracy caught Paul's eye and yanked it free. As Markie and Mandy danced and others began to join them on the floor, she saw Paul walking towards her.

He stopped in front of her. 'I know I'm not meant to be within a hundred yards of you, but could I have the honour of this dance?' he asked. Tracy looked at Kent, who was about to defend her honour.

'For our Markie, then. Go on.' Paul took Tracy's hand and led her on to the dance floor. She knew she was getting funny looks from her kids and from the other guests, but she didn't care. She was drunk, she was as high as a kite and she loved this song. As Paul spun her round the floor he whispered, 'I've come into some decent cash.'

Tracy's eyes widened and she pulled back. 'You what?'

'You heard. I've got moolah and lots of it.'

'Where from?' Tracy asked disbelievingly.

'Like I said, I came into it.'

'You've never had a pot to piss in and neither's anyone else you know. How've you come into it?'

Paul tapped his nose and spun Tracy round. 'Fifty grand,' he said, as the song ended.

Tracy was transfixed, gaping at him.

'Now, off you go, back to lover-boy,' Paul said. He waved at Kent, then turned on his heel and headed over to his son and daughter-in-law to congratulate them on their choice of song.

Tracy walked back to Kent, who looked like a puppy that'd just been kicked. Suddenly she had the overwhelming feeling she'd backed the wrong horse.

'Everything all right?' Kent asked nervously.

'Yeah, why wouldn't it be?' Tracy snapped.

Kent wrapped his mouth around the straw in his drink and sucked hard.

Tracy rolled her eyes. Now what was she going to do?

*

Leanne had taken Kia to bed just before the first dance. The child had been complaining for an hour that she was tired. They were staying in one of the rooms at Hanley Farm and Leanne was happy to go up with her daughter. She didn't want the embarrassment of being partnerless for the evening and there was a good chance that she would be. She had tried to get Tony's attention a number of times but he was preoccupied with his female guest, so she decided to leave well alone.

'When are we going back to London?' Kia asked, as Leanne tucked her into bed.

'Darling,' Leanne said, stroking Kia's hair, 'we're

not going to be able to go back to London for a while. Things have changed and we've come up here because this is where our family is.'

Kia looked at her with big wide eyes. 'But me and you are family, Mum. We don't need anyone else.'

It almost broke Leanne's heart to hear her daughter say that. 'I know, but I need to be here because I can't work in London any more.'

'Why not?' Kia asked.

'There isn't work for me.'

'Why don't you get a job in a shop?' Kia asked.

Leanne wasn't about to get into a discussion about the economic realities of living in London. 'I've never worked in one before. Anyway, we're here now and you'll have new friends soon. And you can play out on the streets, not like in London.'

'I don't like it here. It's scruffy,' Kia said, pulling the bedclothes over herself sulkily.

Leanne stood up. Kia was just going to have to get used to living in Bradington – they couldn't afford to go anywhere else.

She kissed the little girl good night and left the room, quietly closing the door.

'Boo!' a male voice said.

Leanne nearly jumped out of her skin. Her hand flew to her heart, which was pounding, and she whirled round. Tony was standing behind her. 'You scared me!'

'Sorry.' Tony smiled at her with twinkly-eyed warmth. He put his arms round her and Leanne hugged him back. It was so good to see him. 'How've you been?' he asked.

'Better,' Leanne admitted.

'Come on, tell Uncle Tony.'

Leanne didn't want to have to go over everything again, especially not with Tony. The girl who had gone off to the bright lights and big city comes crawling back. That was a story she'd leave the press to write. 'Who's your girlfriend?' she asked, trying to sound casual. 'She's very pretty.'

'Yes, she is. But she's not my girlfriend.'

Leanne felt her heart skip. Tony was single? That couldn't be possible. 'She's my wife.' Her heart dropped into her stilettos.

'Oh. Wow,' she faltered. 'Congratulations.'

'Thanks. But you don't have to congratulate me.' Leanne could feel Tony looking at her as he always had when they were younger. 'We married for a visa. She's Russian. She's one of the dancers at the new club, Poles Apart.'

'Good job she's not Polish, eh?' Leanne joked lamely. Tony laughed heartily. He'd always laughed at her jokes. One of the few people who had, she thought.

'She's got to live with me. Have toothbrushes in the same pot, all the usual bollocks. But I don't mind. Not like I was seeing anyone.' He let the words hang in the air.

'No. Right,' Leanne said, cutting her gaze away from him. Even though she and Tony had been an item for a long time he still unnerved her. Not that he was frightening, far from it. He just made her feel different from the way she felt with other men. 'Best get back downstairs, then.'

'Yeah. At least Swing's flat on his back.' Tony gestured to a door on the landing. Evidently it led into the room that now contained the useless best man.

'What on earth did he have to say that for?' Leanne mused.

'Because he doesn't know when to shut his trap.' Tony sounded tense.

Leanne looked at him. She'd thought Swing had been joking but ... 'Is there some truth in it?' She was shocked that there might be.

'Listen.' Tony lowered his voice. 'Swing's a very sorry man who's been living in your brother's shadow since the year dot.'

Leanne's mind was whirring. Mandy had been in Ibiza last year, but had Swing? And surely she wouldn't have gone anywhere near him, would she?

'So did he?' Tony shook his head and began to walk away. 'All right,' Leanne said, 'I'll put it another way. Where did Swing go on holiday last year?'

Tony stopped to look at her. 'Ibiza. But I swear to God, Leanne, if your Markie finds out he was anywhere near an easyJet flight last year then he's a dead man. OK?'

Leanne followed Tony downstairs.

*

87

Markie was ready to kill someone. He had come up to the bridal suite to freshen up and was about to go back downstairs when he'd heard his sister and Tony talking. He stood, his hands against the door, breathing hard, trying to get himself together and decide what to do. He knew that something must have gone on while he'd been inside, he wasn't a complete idiot – two years was a long time to wait – but she could have had the decency to do it with someone he didn't know. But Swing? That fucking imbecile? Well, she must have been desperate, Markie thought. The thing that bugged him most was that, if she'd stoop low enough to shag one of his mates, there must've been others.

He left the room, walked down the corridor and hammered on Swing's door. There was no answer. He spotted a porter along the corridor and, composing himself, approached the young man.

''Scuse me, mate. It's my wedding day and my best man's flat out in there and I just want to check he's all right.'

'The one you got by the scruff of the neck?' the lad asked.

Cheeky sod, Markie thought. 'One and the same. It's all blown over. He just told a joke I didn't find very funny, that's all.'

The lad looked at Markie, obviously decided that he was telling the truth and swiped his skeleton key along the electronic code reader. The door opened.

'Ta, mate,' Markie said, and handed the delighted

boy a twenty-pound note. It was a small price to pay to see that dickhead Swing get what he deserved.

Five minutes later, Markie came out of the room, nursing a bruised fist, and headed down to the hall. He stopped at the bottom of the staircase when he saw Gemma, Mandy's nineteen-year-old cousin, one of the bridesmaids. Gemma didn't make any secret of the fact that she fancied Markie and had done throughout her teenage years. But because Markie wasn't about to try it on with someone so close to Mandy, she knew her flirting wouldn't get her into hot water. Until now.

'Hiya, Bridegroom. Don't you look handsome?' a tipsy Gemma said.

'Hi, Gemma. I don't know if it's because I'm officially off limits now, but I want to tell you that you're beautiful.'

'Really?' Stunned, Gemma, batted her false eyelashes.

'Yeah, really.' Markie let his gaze fall on her chest. 'It's weird because now that I'm married I want what I can't have …' Gemma flushed. 'Do you know what I mean?'

Gemma nodded.

'Come here.' She moved closer. Markie leant forward and whispered, 'Ever done something you shouldn't?'

'All the time,' Gemma said, clearly trying to sound confident.

Markie took a key out of his pocket. 'Meet me in my room in five minutes.'

'But I can't. It's the bridal suite.'

'Well, that'll make it all the naughtier, won't it?' Markie winked and left Gemma staring at the key he had pushed into her hand.

He went back into the reception and straight to his bride. He wanted to hurt her, but he knew he had to keep calm. No scene. Not yet. He whispered something into Mandy's ear, and a wide smile spread across her face. As he turned round she slapped his backside. Markie bit his tongue. That's the last time you'll do that, he thought.

He was waiting behind the bridal-suite door as Gemma opened it. She was trembling as she closed it behind her. Markie began to kiss her, running his hands roughly all over her. She quickly grabbed his hand, guided it to the top of her thigh and gasped as he pushed his fingers inside her. She was trying to unbuckle his belt but he turned her round and pushed himself into her. Markie was pounding into Mandy's bridesmaid when the door opened and his wife was staring at them.

'Remind you of Ibiza, Mand? You fucking slag!' Markie spat.

Gemma jumped away from him and began to cry with shame.

'You bastard!' Mandy shouted, flying at Markie, who was tucking himself in.

He grabbed her arm and threw her against the wall. 'I know about you and Swing.'

'Nothing fucking happened, you piece of shit.'

'Save it. He admitted it. Shortly before I kicked fuck out of him.' He looked at his wife in disgust. 'Get your stuff out of our flat tomorrow and then get the fuck out of my life.' Markie walked to the door, leaving the two cousins sobbing. Before he left the room, he turned back. 'You might want to call an ambulance for lover-boy by the way. Room 230.'

Markie could hear Mandy screaming at Gemma as he walked along the corridor. He went downstairs and straight out of the place where only eight hours before he had been married. He didn't want to go back to the wedding party: if he did, he wouldn't be responsible for his own actions.

chapter nine

Tracy noticed a commotion in the corner and thought they'd done quite well to get so late into the evening without a fight. She was far too wired to go and investigate. She hadn't had a knees-up like this in a long time. She'd had enough coke to kill a small cow but was on the lookout for more. Since Paul's financial bombshell earlier, she had been trying to get back to him to find out more but Kent was stuck to her like a limpet, stroking her hair and constantly asking when she was going to take him to bed.

'I'm tired, babe,' he said now, pushing his bottom lip out like a sulky five-year-old.

Tracy felt embarrassed. If any of her lot saw him acting like this she'd never live it down. 'Go to bed, then,' she snapped.

Kent looked genuinely put out. He stood up in a huff. 'All right, then, I will.' He grabbed his double-breasted suit jacket and flounced out. Tracy watched him go. Now for some real fun, she thought. She caught Karina's eye and put her finger to her nose. Karina walked across to her and handed her another wrap of coke.

'Your dad say anything to you about having some good luck lately?' Tracy asked. She wouldn't say too much: she didn't want everyone getting wind of him having money.

'Dad? You're kidding, aren't you? The man who could land in a bed of roses and still come out smelling of shit.' Karina wandered off to find Gaz, and Tracy scanned the room for Paul. She didn't have to look far: he was propping up the bar, watching her.

Tracy sashayed over to him. 'So then, hot shot. If you're so rolling in it, you can get me a drink in.'

Paul smiled. 'Two brandy and Babychams, love, and make them doubles,' he said to the girl behind the bar. He turned to his ex-wife and winked at the extravagance of his order. Tracy was impressed.

'Well, then?' she said, picking up her glass, which the girl had placed before her.

'Well then what?'

'You know what. Where's the money come from?'

'I won it.'

Tracy choked on her drink. 'You!' she exclaimed. Paul had to be the unluckiest man she ever knew. The only time he'd ever backed a Grand National winner was the year the result was declared void after a false start.

'Me.' He nodded. 'I did a place pot at the bookie's. Rovers for the treble, Sunderland to come back up, and the winner of the first two horses past the post at the Derby.'

'Well, bugger me,' Tracy said.

Paul grinned, pleased with himself. 'So how're you and Geoff getting on?'

'Kent,' Tracy said pointedly.

'He wasn't christened bloody Kent.' Paul sniggered.

'We have our ups and downs …' Tracy said, holding her ex-husband's gaze. 'We don't have the same connection me and you had.'

'That connection hasn't owt to do with my fifty grand, has it?'

'I don't want your bloody money,' Tracy said angrily. She hated it when people saw through her. She was usually cleverer than that. Anyway, it wasn't just the money. Kent was getting on her nerves and she wanted her old life back. 'You start thinking when you get a bit older. About your family,' she added, with drunken sentimentality. 'But I couldn't have it how it was before, you getting all violent.'

'Contrary to popular belief I've never laid a finger on you! You're the only woman I know who says, "I walked into a door," and means it.' He glared at her. 'Making me out to look like a wife-beater.'

'I meant coming round and putting your foot through the door.'

'You're the one who's always sending me texts and then when I try to talk to you you act like you haven't. What d'you expect me to do?'

Not put your foot through the door, Tracy thought, but she wasn't about to argue the toss. At this point Scott came running over from the other side of the room and pushed his dad backwards. 'Everything all right, Mum?'

'Course it is, soft arse,' Paul said.

'I wasn't asking you,' Scott told him sharply.

'Me and your dad are getting on great, as it happens.' Tracy raised her glass and clinked it against Paul's.

Scott stared at them, nonplussed, as if they'd dropped out of the sky. Then he said, 'You're getting on great but Mandy and Markie are kicking off with each other. What's going on?'

'Why the hell are they kicking off already?' Paul asked, looking concerned.

Tracy took a swig of her drink. 'Because they're married,' she said, worldly wise. Paul sighed and nodded – she was right. Scott rolled his eyes to the heavens and stalked off.

'He's a nowty get, isn't he?' Tracy said.

'Gets it from you,' Paul said.

Tracy rattled her ice cubes. 'Shut it, you, and fill her up.' Tonight was shaping up quite well, she thought.

chapter ten

Leanne was watching TV in Tracy's living room. It was the day after the wedding and everyone had checked out of Hanley Farm at eleven and made their way home. The events of the previous evening were still playing on her mind. Tracy and Kent had had an argument at the desk this morning, which culminated with Tracy shouting, 'Can't a mum enjoy her son's bleeding wedding in peace?' The fact that her son had decided his marriage was over long before she'd had her last line of celebratory coke was, it seemed, a minor detail.

Leanne had no idea what had happened to Markie. Mandy, in floods of tears, had told her he'd walked out because he'd overheard what she and Tony had been saying to each other about her and Swing. All morning Tony had been trying to contact him, but without success.

Leanne sighed, then stood up to make some tea. At that moment, to her complete astonishment, Markie came through the door, looking like he'd been dragged through several hedges backwards. 'Bloody hell!' she exclaimed. 'Where've you been? We've been worried sick!'

'Not worried sick enough to tell me my new wife's a slag.' The colour drained from Leanne's face. 'I heard you and Tony having a nice little chinwag about Mandy's trip to Ibiza.'

'Mandy told me – and I didn't have time to say anything to you. By the time I came to look for you you'd disappeared.'

'You wouldn't have told me anyway.'

'No. Because this is how you react to things. Swing's in hospital, you know. You've shattered his jaw.'

'Is that all?'

'Is that *all*?' Leanne echoed, her voice rising. 'You could have killed him!'

Suddenly the door flew open. Tracy was standing there, hair all over the place, yesterday's makeup smudged under her eyes, stained dressing-gown wrapped round her. 'Will you fucking well pack it in? My head's splitting as it is.'

'Fucking hell. *What Ever Happened to Baby Jane?*,' Markie said sarcastically.

Tracy glared at him. 'And what the bleeding hell happened to you? Mandy crying, that fat cousin of hers bawling, Swing in hospital with a broken jaw and no one's saying anything!'

'It's over with me and Mandy,' Markie said flatly.

'Over? It's not even bleeding begun!' Tracy said. 'Well, I'll tell you something, if it is over, I want that Breville back I bought you.'

'Have the fucking thing.'

'I will.' Tracy slammed the door and headed back upstairs to bed.

'I can't understand it, can you? I mean, she only had fourteen vodkas, ten Breezers, sixty B & H and two grams of coke that I know of.' Markie grabbed the television's remote control. Leanne knew better than to try to get him to talk. He flicked on to Sky News and caught the banner at the bottom of the screen – 'Leighton Adoption Media Scrum'. He paled and looked as if he might switch over.

'Leave it on,' Leanne said. 'They're bloody every-where, those two.'

Markie sat down, but she could see that he was uncomfortable about what was now on the screen. They were watching Lisa and Jay Leighton holding a baby and being bustled through the large wrought-iron gates of a country house. A spokesperson was saying, 'Lisa and Jay have today officially adopted a Thai baby, Mae-Khao. The couple have asked that they be allowed some privacy in order to bond with the new arrival. The couple have said in their state-ment that the child will be renamed Blest Leighton, because they feel truly blessed by the gift they have been given.' Leanne stared at the screen in disbelief.

A Sky reporter took up the story: 'Rumours have surrounded the celebrity couple for years with regard to their childless marriage, but their spokesperson insists that they will have their own children when they are ready. For the moment they are happy to give a better life to a child born into poverty.' He went on to talk generally about the Leightons but everyone in the country already knew everything he was telling them unless they'd been living in a cave for the past decade.

Leanne tucked her knees under her chin and stared at the TV: the wedding in a hillside mansion in the Scottish Highlands; the A list party they threw every year in the grounds of their Italian mansion; Lisa having dinner with Victoria Beckham and Katie Holmes; Jay showing Tom Cruise a good night out in Mayfair; and the one that stung her most, the staged picture of Jay giving Lisa a happy-go-lucky shoulder ride on the beach in Cancún the week after news broke about his affair with an unnamed celebrity.

Leanne could feel Markie watching her. A single tear plopped down her cheek and she rubbed her nose with the back of her hand.

'You all right, mate?' Markie asked, softening.

Leanne shook her head. She knew that if she said anything she'd collapse into floods of tears.

'Come here.' Markie held out his arms.

She got up and went across to where he was sitting, fell into them and began to sob. Markie stroked her hair, allowing her to cry, not asking what was wrong.

After a minute or so, she pulled back, her face swollen with tears, and looked at her brother. 'I'm sorry, Markie.' She sniffed and took the tissue he was offering her. 'You've got your own shit to deal with. It's just all this –' She waved her arm around to indicate Tracy's house '– it's too much to get my head round, if you know what I mean.'

'That makes two of us, darl.' He pushed the hair away from her eyes.

'What am I doing, Markie? I had everything I wanted and I've blown it, haven't I?'

'You've not "blown it", you're just having a bad patch, same as me.'

'It's not the same! I'm not a bad person!' Leanne cried. Immediately she knew she'd gone too far.

'And I am?' he asked.

'I didn't mean it like that. I'm just feeling sorry myself, that's all.'

Markie got up and went into the kitchen. Leanne picked up the remote control and switched off Sky News. Then she followed her brother. In the kitchen she said, 'Markie, I didn't mean it.'

He was slapping bacon on to a baking tray.

'There's coke on that,' she pointed out.

Markie's shoulders dropped. 'Fucking brilliant,' he said, took off the bacon, dusted it and the tray, then replaced it and stuck it in the oven. He looked at his sister. 'Am I that hard to talk to?'

'You're not hard to talk to at all. It's just what you do when you find stuff out, that's the worrying thing.'

'Look, Lee, I've been in Strangeways for two years. And let me tell you, it fucks with your head. And then I come out to this.'

Did Markie mean he'd been abused while he was in prison? She'd read it happened quite a lot but she'd thought he knew how to handle himself. 'What did they do?' she asked, panic-stricken.

'Jesus, Leanne, I didn't get bummed in the showers! I was just in a room like the fucking box room upstairs for all that time listening to some half-wit junkie from Eccles peck me head night and day.' He smiled for the first time, amused by his sister's assumption. He pointed at his backside. 'Only person getting up there is the undertaker to pull me giblets out.'

'Markie!' Leanne threw a tea towel at him.

'Yesterday should never have happened,' he said.

'Try telling Mandy that.'

'Fuck Mandy. I've been a mug to that girl since I met her and what happens? She shags Swing, while I'm bankrolling her and her shitty ideas – that bloody nail bar, for instance, what happened to that?'

Leanne knew only too well what had happened to it: it had gone bust, as had the tanning salon. The last thing Bradington had needed was another of those. It had already had one on every corner.

'I propose to her before I go inside,' he went on, 'big grand gesture, keep her quiet.' Leanne raised an eyebrow. 'Don't look at me like that, Lee, you know what she's like as well as anyone. If Teddy Sheringham walked in here now, she'd be off like a shot. All she's bothered about is money in her pocket and having the biggest and best in town. She didn't love me. I knew that. We were just used to each other, you know how it is.'

Leanne didn't, really. 'Why go through with it, then?'

'I didn't know she'd shagged one of my best mates, did I?' Markie said bitterly.

'Come on. You know what I mean. Why let her go to all that trouble if you just thought she'd up and leave?'

Markie opened the fridge and sniffed the milk bottle, then swigged from it. He thought for a moment. 'I didn't have time not to go through with it, did I? I'm in the nick blissfully unaware that she's planning a wedding to rival Liz Hurley's when I come out. What am I meant to say? "Tell you what, sweets, cancel the plumed horses, I don't think we'll be needing 'em."' Markie sighed.

'Well, I wouldn't like to have to say no to Mandy,' Leanne said, looking up just in time to see a Transit van screech to a halt outside the house and a livid Mandy jump out of the passenger seat. Her brother, Neil, got out of the driver's side and stomped to the back of the vehicle. He pulled up the shutter noisily as Mandy hammered on the front door.

'I know you're in there, you fucking wanker!' she yelled.

Markie jumped to his feet. Leanne went up to Kia; she knew her daughter would be scared if she heard this commotion.

At the top of the stairs she found the little girl coming out of the bedroom they were sharing. 'What's wrong, Mummy?' Kia asked.

Leanne took her hand. 'Nothing, darling. Auntie Mandy and Uncle Markie are a bit cross with each other ...'

'Get out here now, you piece of shit!' Mandy screamed.

Leanne winced. From the landing window, she could see Neil throwing Markie's belongings on to the ground: chairs, a mattress and bags of clothes.

'You can fuck off, you deranged bitch!' Markie shouted through the glass door.

'I will not fuck off. You've ruined everything!' Mandy shrieked. Then she smashed her fist into the glass-panelled front door, shattering the pane, which sliced into her hand.

'Fuckin' hell!' Markie bellowed.

The door to Tracy's bedroom flew open. 'What the bleedin' hell is she up to?' Tracy stormed down the stairs.

Now, to Leanne's horror, Neil was dousing all of Markie's things with petrol. Mandy was moaning, blood dripping all over the pavement from her hand.

'Now listen here, you,' Tracy shouted, through the hole in her front door. 'If I hear another fucking dicky bird out of you it'll be more than a chopped-up hand you've got, you hear me?'

Leanne pulled Kia close to her, trying to shield her from the violence that she found all too familiar. She could feel her daughter shaking.

'And you can get fucked, you mad bitch!' Mandy howled.

'Mad? That's rich coming from you!' Tracy roared back.

Markie, who had been in the front room weighing

up his options, suddenly burst past his mum. 'Leave her to me.' He threw open the front door and Leanne saw him shove Mandy to one side as a ball of flame knocked him backwards off his feet. Tracy followed Markie outside to shout at her daughter-in-law.

'You're dead' was all Leanne heard her brother say to Neil, and then a bone-shattering thump. Mandy began screaming again but this time she was pleading with Markie to leave her brother alone. Markie was asking Neil why he was getting involved, helping his slag of a sister, and all hell seemed to be breaking loose. Leanne took Kia, who had begun to sob, into their bedroom and shut the door. She grabbed her iPod and put on one of Kia's favourite songs from *The Little Mermaid*.

'I don't like it here, Mummy,' Kia sobbed.

Neither do I, Leanne thought, as she listened to Mandy and her mother screaming at the top of their lungs and Markie dealing out the pasting of a lifetime to Neil while his worldly belongings blazed to cinders.

chapter eleven

Scott was sitting in front of the TV watching *Extreme Makeover* and rubbing Charly's shoulders as she painted her nails. 'Can't we watch something else?' he complained.

'Like what? *Police, Camera, Action*?' Charly said sarcastically.

'Well. Yeah.' Scott loved that programme. He knew a few people who'd been on it. Felons, not coppers, of course.

Scott was happy staying in with Charly for the time being. Yesterday he'd had enough excitement to last him a lifetime and, anyway, whenever he went out, someone wanted to ask him about what had really gone on at the wedding, why Swing was in hospital, why Markie was holed up at his mum's. Scott was playing daft but he didn't have to play anything: he hadn't a clue what had gone on. All he knew was that they'd all been having a blinding time, then Mandy's crying and the party's over.

'I want to see what she looks like,' Charly said, of the woman with the bandaged face on the screen.

'She looks like shit,' Scotty said, kneading her shoulder.

'When it's done, you div.' Charly wriggled to get Scott to work his hand a bit further down her back.

'Well, switch it back on when it's nearly finished. No point watching all the gory bits.'

Charly turned round and eyeballed him as if he was the thickest person she had ever met.

'Scott, if I'm going to get my tits done to 34FF, don't you think I might want to know what I'll have to go through? This is research.'

'Who's paying for that, then?' Scott asked. It was news to him.

'I am. I'll get a credit card.' Charly swung her head back to the TV.

'No one'll give you one.'

'Well, I'll just have to get the money another way, won't I?'

Scott thought for a moment. 'What d'you mean by that?'

'I don't mean anything. I'll just have to get a job.'

'But you're not qualified to do anything.'

'There's something I'm good at.'

Scott didn't like where this was going. 'Such as?'

'You know! I could work at Poles Apart.' Scott dug his fingers into her shoulder. 'Ow!' she squealed.

'You are not working in a pole-dancing club!' Scott spat.

'I just want to be independent and you keep holding me back.'

Scott looked at his beautiful girlfriend. He couldn't think of anything worse than a load of leering men paying money to watch her dance. 'How much do new boobs cost?'

'About five grand.'

'Right.' He wondered where on earth he'd ever get that kind of money. He'd have to shift one hell of a lot of knock-off gear. 'I'll see what I can do.'

Charly jumped up and hugged him. 'I love you, Scott Crompton.' She kissed him on the lips.

He smiled. 'I love you too.' And he did. With all his heart.

*

It was Kia's first day at school and she was nervous. But not as nervous as Leanne. Leanne had enrolled her at Bolingbroke Primary last week, the school that she herself had attended twenty years previously. There had been little involved in the process. Not like the hoop-jumping exercise she had gone through to get Kia into that private prep school in London.

She walked Kia to her classroom door and the teacher came out to greet them. 'Hi, Kia, I'm Ms O'Donnell,' she said. Leanne warmed to her immediately. 'Now, we're going to have a lot of fun today, aren't we?' Kia nodded shyly. Ms O'Donnell looked at Leanne and smiled. 'I'm sure she'll be fine. My name's Helen.' Leanne shook her outstretched hand. No teacher at the school in London had ever introduced themselves by their first name.

She kissed her daughter and the teacher took Kia's hand. As the little girl gazed round her new classroom, Helen said to Leanne, 'I'll come out to see you when school's finished and tell you how she's done.'

'Thanks. I'd really appreciate that. Oh, I'm Leanne by the way. Sorry, how rude.'

'No need to apologise.' Helen smiled. 'I know who you are. My boyfriend's a massive fan.'

Leanne blushed. No one had mentioned her public persona for several days and she had been getting used to the anonymity. But she had spent the last five years in and out of the tabloids so she could hardly expect no one to recognise her.

At 3.30, she was waiting for Kia outside her classroom. Her stomach was in knots. She hoped that Kia had had a nice day but she feared the worst. The door opened and the children piled out. Kia ran to her mother, and Helen followed her, beaming.

'It's been really good today, Mum, and I've got some new friends, Jada and Beth, and I've been doing reading and it was bigger books than we did back at home but I was good at it, I think, and we did a painting and I painted Tower Bridge!' Kia gabbled, and held up a picture that was thick with wet paint. A few blobs trickled off and hit the floor. 'And no one else had been to London, so Miss showed them some pictures in a book and everyone was really excited that I used to live there.'

Leanne rummaged in her bag, produced a tissue and mopped up the paint.

'I think it's fair to say that Kia's enjoyed herself today, haven't you, Kia?' the teacher asked, and Kia nodded vigorously.

'I can't tell you how made up I am,' Leanne said. 'I wasn't sure how she was going to settle in.'

'They think I talk funny, Mummy,' Kia said, giggling. 'I don't, do I?'

'She's brought the house down today. All the kids wanted to be her friend. I don't think there'll be any problem with her fitting in,' Helen said.

Leanne smiled with utter relief. 'That is such good news.'

'So, we'll see you again tomorrow, won't we, Kia?'

Kia looked proudly at her picture. 'Can I put this on the fridge at Nana Tracy's?'

In the car, Leanne was still smiling when her phone rang. Kia dived into her handbag and grabbed it, as she always did when Leanne was driving. 'Withheld number, Mum. Shall I answer it?'

'If you want,' Leanne said, only half paying attention as she steered the car through the Bolingbroke Estate.

'Hello, my mum's phone,' Kia said. She looked blankly at the handset. 'They've put the phone down.'

Leanne shrugged. 'Probably a wrong number,' she said, as she pulled up outside the house. 'Go and show Nana Tracy what you've done.' She hoped her mother had managed to get out of her dressing-gown. She didn't want Kia to get the impression that swigging whisky till two in the morning and not getting dressed the next day was normal. Although at Tracy's house it always had been, and she wasn't about to change that because Leanne and Kia were lodging there.

chapter twelve

Lisa watched the nanny as she changed the baby's nappy and thought she might leave that task entirely to her staff. She wasn't sure she'd be any good at it – and, anyway, what was the point of keeping a dog and barking yourself?

It had been nearly a week since she had drop-called Leanne Crompton, but she knew she needed to speak to her today. Last week she had merely been hedging her bets, she had wanted to frighten Leanne a little, but after today's revelation, courtesy of her press officer, she had to speak to her – and fast. But first, she needed a word with her wayward husband.

She picked up her Vertu phone and scrolled to Jay's number. She liked to pretend to herself that she was past caring about his indiscretions but that wasn't true. The only way she knew how to cope with his behaviour was not to think about it. Some days, and this was one of them, she wondered why she stayed. There must be someone out there for her, someone better than Jay, but if she ever left him, someone else would jump in and take the spoils that came with being Mrs

Leighton – and there was no way Lisa was about to let that happen. But it meant she had to take the downside when it came, as well as the up. And there were plenty of downsides with Jay.

'Yello,' Jay said.

Lisa hated it when he said that. 'No, that wasn't the colour I was thinking of,' she said. 'I was thinking more about brown.'

'You what?' Jay asked, in his Yorkshire brogue.

'The colour of shit? The stuff you're up to your neck in? Again?'

'What?' Jay asked, sounding panicked. 'What've done?'

Lisa looked at the notepad in front of her. 'Some little slag by the name of Catherine York, who appar ently is a beauty therapist at Tan Tilisers in Wilmslow is claiming she gave you more than a back, sack and crack when you went to see her last week.' She waited for him to pretend it hadn't happened, like he usually did. And she always wanted to believe him even though she knew he was *always* on the lookout for sex.

'She went down on me,' Jay said piteously.

'You are pathetic!' Lisa shouted. 'Can't you have wank like everyone else?'

'I didn't mean it to happen,' he whined.

'You never do, do you? Well, I'll tell you something you'd better sort it out sharpish, because not even Ma Clifford could dig you out of this shit.'

'Why? Has she gone to the papers?' Jay asked, th fear evident in his voice.

'Gone to them? She's conducting a bidding war! And I know what that means. It means they'll all be sniffing round Leanne Crompton again, asking her if that kid is yours.'

'She's got a name. It's Kia.'

'Oh, he cares now!' Lisa said, throwing an arm into the air.

'Why would Leanne want to say something? She's not interested in trying to ruin us.'

Lisa's jaw set. 'Really? Well, that's where you're wrong. Leanne is now on her arse, back at home with her skanky family and, so I hear, broke. What better way to make a quick buck than to come after us? It's not like she's going to get her head down and do a real day's work, is it? She gets her tits out for a living, for God's sake. If that avenue of money has dried up, then I fear, my dear, that we are fucked.'

'No, we're not. Let me talk to her.'

'No bloody way.' Lisa shook her head, adamant. 'I do the talking. You just lie low for a while and keep your pants zipped.'

'Lisa?' Jay said.

'What?'

'I love you,' he said pathetically.

Lisa snapped the phone off. The thing that hurt most was that she knew a bit of Jay did love her. When they had first started dating, she had only just begun presenting a late-night TV show called *Think You're It?* and Jay had worked his way up to the first team at Manchester Rovers. He had been so shy when

113

he asked her out; he couldn't even look her in the eye. He wasn't the smouldering, confident man he was today, the man who stared out from billboards the world over. He was just a lad from Leeds. They soon got engaged and Lisa quickly became the girl to envy as Jay grew from boy to man. She had also been responsible for prising him out of his uniform of tracksuit and trainers and making him the style icon he had become.

Over the years, though, the lifestyle and adulation had simply gone to Jay's head. He knew that generally he could have any woman he wanted and this in itself seemed to act as an aphrodisiac. It had sent Lisa the other way: knowing that everyone fancied her husband, and that he knew it, actually put her off him. She couldn't remember the last time they'd had anything other than mechanical sex. She sometimes wanted to try to get back to how they had been with one another when they'd first got together, making love and meaning it. But she had long ago resigned herself to the fact that that was in the past, and that after ten years together they couldn't expect to be swinging from the chandeliers.

She threw back her head and covered her eyes. *I am not going to cry!*

'Are you OK, Mrs Leighton?' The nanny, Jeanine, asked.

'I'm fine. Just fine.'

'Would you like a cup of tea?'

Jeanine was about her mum's age, Lisa thought,

which was great because it meant that hopefully she wouldn't try to leap on Jay, and she had come with brilliant references. There was something about her that just seemed kind. It was a long time since Lisa had been around a person who wanted genuinely to help and not just to be connected with her for the kudos it brought.

'Tell you what,' she said, 'you sit down and I'll make it. Give me something to do while I'm making this phone call.'

'Don't be silly!' Jeanine looked shocked.

'I said sit down!' Lisa said, pretending to be annoyed. Jeanine smiled and did as she was told.

Lisa wandered into her vast kitchen and put the kettle on. She looked at the number she had for Leanne, then steeled herself and pressed dial.

Leanne picked up.

'Leanne. It's Lisa Leighton.' She did her best not to let on that her heart was trying to thump its way out of her chest.

'What do you want?' Leanne said, sounding alarmed.

'I want to meet. Me and you. Iron out a few things.'

'I don't have anything to say to you.' She sounded choked now.

'Well, I've got a few things I'd like to say to you.'

'What – like you did when you sent that thug to my house?'

Lisa bit her lip. She didn't know whether to deny that she had had any involvement in Leanne's being warned not to talk to anyone about Kia's father. Then

115

she decided she was better off telling the truth. 'That [
one of the things I was going to talk to you about.' Sh[
swallowed hard. 'I wanted to apologise.'

'Right,' Leanne said.

She wasn't giving much away, Lisa noticed.

'I want to see you face to face and make things righ[
between us.' Leanne didn't reply so Lisa ploughed on[
'I'll come to you. You name the place and the da[
Somewhere we won't get papped.'

'We won't get papped unless you ring them [
Leanne said.

Lisa bit back a stinging response. 'I'll be on my ow[
in an unmarked car. Don't worry.'

'But I am worried, Lisa. You don't do anything tha[
doesn't benefit you directly,' Leanne said coldly.

'Well, take it from me that this will benefit both [
us, right?' Lisa wasn't about to beg the little tramp.

'OK, meet me at the playing-fields near St Blais[
School in Bradington at twelve tomorrow. You'll fin[
it on sat nav. I'll be on the bench near the gates. W[
can go for a walk.'

'Fine. I'll be there.' Lisa hung up.

She turned to find Jeanine standing in the doorwa[
'I haven't really time for a brew, Mrs Leighton.' Sh[
smiled. 'I really should be getting home now.'

'Are you sure?' Lisa asked; she'd almost made i[
Jeanine nodded. 'What time does Carmella get here[
Until they could find a full-time live-in nanny, Lis[
was making do with a day shift and an evening shi[
from the nearby agency.

'She's just pulled up outside.' Jeanine was putting her coat on.

'Well, thanks for your help today. I'm sure I'll get the hang of having a kid one day!' Lisa said, laughing.

'People don't realise how much work it is having a baby. See you tomorrow.' Jeanine smiled and left her.

'See you tomorrow,' Lisa echoed.

She walked into the dining-room with her mug of tea and saw the notepad on which she had scribbled Jay's latest misdemeanours. A burst of adrenalin shot through her. The pad had been moved. She automatically looked over her shoulder and watched Jeanine's car pull away. *God, Lisa, chill out!* She had to stop being so paranoid. Just because lots of women wanted to make a quick buck off her husband's unwillingness to keep his pants up didn't mean that everyone did. Lisa shook her head at her silliness. Sometimes she was her own worst enemy.

chapter thirteen

Leanne put the phone down, her hand shaking.

'What's up wi' you? Look like you've seen a ghost,' Tracy said.

'Nothing. I'm just off out.'

'Where you going?' Tracy asked.

Leanne could see it was killing her mum to know what her conversation had been about. Tracy knew her so well that she must have worked out it had tipped her over the edge.

'Markie's.' She grabbed her coat.

Her brother had moved into an apartment in town. As soon as the wedding furore had died down, he had left Tracy's, as Leanne had known he would. He needed his own space. Going from Strangeways to Tracy's was like jumping into the fire because the frying pan was becoming tiresome.

Markie was battling with Mandy about their old place, which was his but she was saying he'd have to burn it down before she'd move out. He didn't want to get heavy with her but if she didn't clear out soon he knew he'd have to do something about it. He had told

Leanne that he had an associate sitting outside the apartment, waiting for Mandy to step outside. The man was going to let himself in, throw her stuff out and change the locks. Leanne knew that Markie was trying to keep his head with Mandy, but there was only so far she could push him before he exploded.

She hopped into her car and started the engine. It was only one o'clock, so she had plenty of time to seek Markie's advice before she had to pick up Kia. She'd been thinking about her car. It was her prized possession and she knew that at the end of the month she'd have to give it back and rely on Bradington's finest bus service to get her from A to B. Leanne had been feeling increasingly that her time in the limelight had been a dream – until she'd had the call from Lisa Leighton, asking for a clandestine meeting. At that point, she'd known for sure that she wasn't dreaming.

She drove out of Bolingbroke and along the tree-lined streets leading to the city centre. She had never really looked at Bradington before. She knew the streets like the back of her hand, and had she been asked to describe Bradington she would probably have said, 'It's full of roundabouts.' But it wasn't as bad as she remembered it. A lot of the grotty shop-fronts had been replaced and the old Victorian houses along the main road had had a face lift so the place was almost presentable.

Markie had given Leanne the address of his flat in Little Venice. She had laughed. 'Give me a break!

Venice in Bradington?' But as she pulled the car up alongside the old mill at the side of the canal, she understood why the place had acquired its name. It looked almost Italian. Markie was standing on his balcony. 'Park anywhere,' he shouted, waving at a couple of empty spaces.

A few minutes later she was stepping out of the lift to find her brother waiting for her. 'Shit here, innit?' he said, giving his sister a hug.

'Yeah, rubbish.' She giggled.

Markie led her through to the duplex apartment. There was hardly a stick of furniture. 'You can have the chair.' He pointed to the only one in the room.

'Mandy really has cleared you out.'

'She can have it, the deranged bint, clinging on to some shit bits of furniture like that's going to make me go back to her.' Markie shrugged, clearly not interested in talking about his ex.

'Is she still doing a sit-in at your old place?'

'Course she is. She'll get sick of it, though. I know her. She'll lose her rag, and when she moves out, the lads'll go in.'

Leanne rolled her eyes. 'Nothing's ever simple, is it?'

'Not if your surname's Crompton. So, what's up with you?'

Leanne took a deep breath. 'I've got to meet someone tomorrow and I want your advice.'

'Go on.' Markie said.

'It's Lisa Leighton.' Leanne bit her lip.

Markie whistled. 'Bloody hell! And do I need to know what you're meeting her about?'

'I think you can guess, can't you?' Leanne said.

'So Kia's Jay Leighton's, then? Fuck me.' Markie shook his head.

Leanne knew what he was thinking. His little niece, whom he loved to pieces, her dad just happened to be the best footballer to come out of Britain in the last twenty years and one half of the country's most famous couple. 'I bet you're thinking I was a right star-struck silly cow, aren't you?'

'Did you see that goal against Barcelona in the Cup Final in 1999? I'd have shagged him!' Markie chortled.

Leanne's stomach knotted. 'Thanks.'

'Lee, I'm sorry, I was only joking.' He went over to her and gave her a hug.

Leanne burst into tears. 'You're the first person I've ever told and then you make a joke of it. I just wanted your advice and you're doing what I bet everyone else will do when they find out – laugh at me!'

'Aw, come on, I didn't mean it,' Markie said, stroking her hair.

Leanne pulled back. 'Kia and I don't need Jay. We never have. But I didn't go with him just because he was famous.' She leant back in the chair and began the story. Markie listened, intrigued.

When Leanne was eighteen she had been in a club in London with other models signed to Figurz Management when a guy she took to be a doorman had approached her. He asked if she would come upstairs to one of the private rooms. Immediately assuming she had done something wrong, she had followed him up three flights of stairs.

When she arrived at a door he had let her in and shut it behind her. Leanne had wondered what was going on until she heard a voice from the corner of the darkened room. 'Hi.'

'Hi,' she had replied nervously.

Suddenly a light had been flicked on and, to Leanne's surprise, Jay Leighton was standing in front of her. She knew all about Jay. Bradington wasn't far from Manchester and he was, at the time, Manchester Rovers' number-one player – her brother Scott idolised him. He was also very good-looking which was why Leanne and legions of other women knew who he was.

'I'm sorry to bring you up here like this, but, well, I wanted to get you on your own.' He had smiled shyly. Had someone suggested to Leanne that this unlikely situation might ever arise, she would have told them that she'd ask him where his wife was. But she didn't. She was captivated.

Jay poured Leanne a glass of champagne and she had stayed, talking to him, until the early hours. He told her she shouldn't believe all she read in the papers but he didn't mention Lisa. At the end of the night he had kissed her lips and asked his driver to drop her home. He had promised to call and he had. They always met in secret, private rooms in private members' bars, hotels where he booked in as Mr A. Bennett.

He had told her several times that it was only a matter of time before he and Lisa split up, but there was always another lucrative *Hello!* spread to do or another charity football gig that he and Lisa had agreed to. Leanne believed him when he said he loved her, when he said his marriage was stale, that he wanted to be with her, and only her.

The affair lasted less than four months, but that was long enough for Leanne to fall for him. It was intense, heady and she was swept along by it. When she found out she was pregnant she had panicked. But then, she reasoned, Jay would be OK about it. He was leaving Lisa soon – and they were living separate lives anyway. Lisa was always off filming, and he split his time between Manchester and London.

Jay had hit the roof and demanded that she have an abortion. It was the first time Leanne had seen this side of him and it scared her. He told her Lisa would kill him, that it would ruin everything for him. Leanne couldn't believe what she was hearing. She told him she wanted nothing more to do with him. And from that day until the rumours started to circulate that Jay might not be the devoted husband he appeared, she hadn't.

'So you've not seen him since?'

'Once. At a film première. He does this really intense stare, like he's trying to psych you out. I just stared back.'

'Glad to hear it.'

'And everything was all right – well, not great, but

123

me and Kia ticked along, working out what to do, and then the other week …' Leanne began to sob again.

'Go on.'

She told him about the man pretending to deliver something, then threatening her.

'*What*?' His eyes sparked with fury.

'I don't know if he sent him …'

'I'll have that fucker killed.'

Leanne laughed at the absurdity of the notion. 'Jay Leighton? Bloody hell, Markie, that's never going to happen.'

Markie stared at her. 'If anything happens to you, we'll see how serious I am,' he said.

'I've agreed to meet Lisa,' she said, hanging her head.

'Why?' Markie was incredulous. 'You don't owe that bitch anything.'

'Maybe not. But I want to hear what she's got to say. After years of silence it might be about Jay and Kia.'

'Yeah, and she might want to stick the fucking knife in.'

Leanne grabbed his hand. 'Markie, will you come with me? Not to meet her, just stay in the car, see that nothing happens.'

Markie nodded. 'OK, if you want me to. But if she lays a finger on you I'll be back inside – but this time for murder.'

*

Tracy gazed at Kent with contempt. He was feeding his parrots, Elvis and Presley, and singing 'Love Me Tender' to them. Tracy had taught one to say 'piss off', but at a time when it should have been most forthcoming, it was mute. It even seemed to be enjoying Kent's strangled rendition. He turned, dusting bird food off his hands, then pointed both index fingers at Tracy and sang, 'For my darling, I love you, and …'

'Kent.' Tracy arched an eyebrow. He went on singing. 'Kent!' she shouted.

He looked at her blankly. 'I thought you liked my Elvis.'

'Me and you need to have a word,' she said, sparking up a cigarette. 'Sit down.' She waved at the armchair opposite where she was standing.

Kent sat. 'What's wrong, babe?' he asked.

His hang-dog expression made her want to slap his face. 'Me and you. That's what's wrong.' Tracy exhaled a long plume of smoke.

'But we're perfect, aren't we, doll?'

'No, "doll", we're not. You've been swanning around here like you own the place, and I've been fetching and carrying for you for too long.' Even Tracy couldn't quite believe she had said this. She didn't fetch and carry anything.

'What you on about? I do all the housework!' Kent exclaimed.

'There you go, shouting the odds,' Tracy said, with a sigh, as if this was just part and parcel of what she had to put up with.

'Course I'm shouting. You're acting up, saying there's something wrong with me and you, when me and you are all I've got,' Kent said, as if he hadn't a clue what she was talking about.

Tracy was sick of feeling sorry for him. The hearts-and-flowers days had long gone and she wanted a real man – a man who could provide for her, not just play soppy songs on a community radio station, then sign on the sick for his weekly crust. '"Me and you are all I've got"?' she echoed. 'Me and you are all you've been arsed to get, you mean. You never see any of your old mates. I'm beginning to think you haven't got any. And you're stuck in this house day in, day out …'

'You've always said you liked having me around,' Kent expostulated.

Tracy's jaw set. What Kent had said was true, but she wanted to swing things round to the way she saw them, and she could swear black was white if it meant getting her own way. '"Around" as in being near me, not under my feet.'

'But I love you, Trace. I thought being under your feet was where you liked me,' he whined.

Tracy was losing her rag. Give me strength, she thought. What did she have to do to get a blazing row out of the man? Set fire to him?

'Well, I don't love you, Kent, not any more,' she said, and meant it. He got on her nerves. He'd been good for a time, but now he had to go.

Kent steadied himself on the armchair. He was

visibly crumbling. 'You can't do this to me, not after all we've been through.'

'What have we been through, Kent? Two trips to Magaluf and a tattoo apiece. It isn't exactly *Romeo and Juliet*.' He was making her scoff at him now, but Tracy couldn't help herself.

'You said those tattoos meant we'd be together for ever,' Kent said desperately, grabbing at his trouser belt, wanting to reveal the one on his bum cheek that read 'T&K'.

'Yeah, well, me, Blackpool and being pissed is not a good combination.' Tracy shuddered as he dropped his trousers. 'Pull your pants up, I've seen it.' She sighed. She decided to take a different tack. 'Look, the thing is, I don't want to hurt you, Kent, I just want you to understand that it's finished. I don't know any other way to do this other than be honest with you.'

'We've got a home together, a life together.' He fell into a chair and began to cry.

'I want you out of here. Tonight. It's the only way.'

'And what if I say I'm not going?' The tears had gone. Now he was sulking, like a scolded child.

Tracy thought for a moment. 'I'd say I'm calling our Markie.'

*

Much later that evening, Tracy was tucking into her wine box, feeling mournful about her and Kent. He had gathered some of his belongings and said he was

going to stay with his brother on the other side of
Bradington. He'd told Tracy she'd change her mind,
and when she did it might be too late, but Tracy didn't
think so. She put on the song he always played for her,
'Ma Chérie Amour' by Stevie Wonder and cried into
her drink. When the song had finished she poured
some more, hit play and cried all over again. After
about an hour she felt she'd got something, she wasn't
sure what, out of her system. She grabbed her phone,
scrolled to Paul's number and pressed call.

'Hello.'

'Just wondering if you were doing anything
tonight,' she said innocently.

'I thought you might call this week.'

Tracy knew that that was a veiled dig, but she
brushed it aside. She had a thick skin.

*

What is this place? Lisa thought, as she drove through
Bradington to where she was meant to meet Leanne.
No one was following her, she was sure. It wasn't as
hard to lose the paparazzi as she often made out it was.
All she did was ask her bodyguard to leave his wife's
car at a service station on the outskirts of Manchester.
There, she had pulled up in her Bentley GT, gone
inside, changed in the toilets, walked out and jumped
into the Avensis that was waiting for her. Bob's your
uncle. Bodyguard's wife gets the GT for the afternoon,
Lisa gets a car that won't be followed.

Lisa looked at the sat nav. It indicated that she was less than a mile away from the school where she had agreed to meet Leanne.

She was nervous, which was unusual now. In the early days stage fright had been a problem before she did a live performance. She had once presented *A Song for Europe* and fluffed her lines. Her heart had been pounding but she'd managed to pull things round. Yet now she was driving anonymously through a small northern town and feeling more anxious than she ever had in any of the major cities of the world she had visited in the public eye.

Lisa pulled the car over to the kerb. 'St Blaise High School', the sign read. She fixed her makeup in the rear-view mirror and then, pulling her bag to her chest, she stepped out of the car. In the distance she could see a small figure with blonde hair sitting on a bench. 'Leanne Crompton,' she said to herself, as she began to walk down the hill to the school playing-fields.

Contrary to popular belief, Lisa had been in the same room as Leanne just once. The press conjured up an image of the celebrity world, in which everyone knows everyone else and they all go to the same places like one big happy family, but the truth was, Lisa knew what Leanne looked like from the pictures she had seen of her in the papers. The one time they had nearly met had been excruciating for all concerned.

It had been at a film première, a big American blockbuster starring Tom Cruise. He had done his usual three-hour autograph-signing outside the Odeon in London's Leicester Square and the attendant guests had had to wait inside, drinking warm wine and eating second-rate nibbles.

Lisa and Jay had arrived later than most people, because they were nearly as big a draw as Mr Cruise. Nobody had warned them that Leanne would be there.

The couple had walked in to a warm round of applause, started by the general public and taken up half-heartedly by the celebrities, and Lisa had caught her eye. Leanne Crompton was with the little girl whom Leanne knew, Lisa and Jay knew, and most of the British public suspected, was Jay's.

Jay had assured Lisa that he had looked through Leanne. Lisa had snapped that he might have thought to 'look through' her when he'd first met her. After that, it had been painful to sit through a two-hour film and attend the drinks party afterwards. Thankfully Leanne had had the good grace to go home before the party.

Lisa neared the bench where Leanne was sitting. She looked smaller than Lisa remembered. She was wearing a simple white shirt, blue jeans and a pair of shades, with her hair tied back in a pony-tail.

'Leanne,' Lisa said flatly. Leanne stood up to greet her. The women didn't shake hands, just looked at one another.

'Lisa,' Leanne said, matching Lisa's tone.

'Thank you for coming.'

'I don't think we need to start off with pleasantries, do we? What do you want?' Leanne asked, sounding tired.

Lisa looked around furtively. 'Are you wearing a wire?' she asked.

'Am I what?' Leanne burst out laughing.

'A wire. You know what I mean.'

'You've got a high opinion of yourself. It's not *The bloody Sopranos*, you know.'

'I can't be too sure.'

'Oh, shut up, Lisa,' Leanne said, and pulled up her top. 'Look, no wire, you paranoid idiot.' She sat down again. 'Come on, spit it out.'

'I know that that little girl of yours –'

'Kia,' Leanne snapped. 'She's got a name, and you know what it is.'

'Kia. I know she's is closely related to my husband.' Lisa sat down next to Leanne on the bench but stared straight ahead.

'Look,' Leanne said, 'just so you know, I never meant for any of this to happen. I'm not stupid, but Jay fed me line after line and I fell for it. That's all I'm saying.'

'Why did you keep her?' Lisa asked.

Leanne leapt to her feet. 'If it's a personal heart-to-heart you're after, you've come to the wrong place. You sent some bloke round to frighten me the other week and then you want me to meet you and, like a mug, I do. Then you ask me this! You've got a bloody nerve.'

'I'm sorry,' Lisa said, and she was. She didn't want to rile Leanne. 'I just wanted to agree a severance settlement with you.'

'A what?' Leanne asked.

Lisa took some documents out of her bag. 'A severance settlement. I've got some papers here, non-disclosure agreements, that I'd like you to sign, and a cheque for eight hundred thousand pounds. I know that things must be difficult for you at the moment and I want to help. Then we'll let sleeping dogs lie.'

'*What?*' Leanne shrieked.

'I thought you might like it.'

'*Like* it? You're more demented that I thought you were. This is my daughter we're talking about, not some "sleeping dog". As for your money, you can shove it, because I don't need it and I certainly don't want it.'

Lisa stood up. 'But if you go to the papers, it won't be just our lives you'll ruin. It'll be yours.' She paused for effect. There was no way she was leaving without these documents having been signed. 'And Kia's.'

'Well, for your information, I've never been to the papers. I don't use them like you do, Lisa. And I don't care if I have to go and work in a chippy rather than sell my story to the highest bidder. Because that's what I'll do.'

Lisa put the papers back into her bag. She couldn't believe Leanne's stupid brought-up-the-hard-way attitude. The money could set her up for life. If she didn't take it she was a fool.

Suddenly she noticed that a tall, handsome man was heading in their direction. It was the last thing she needed – some guy recognising them and wanting a picture or an autograph.

As he got closer it became clear that he knew Leanne. 'Everything all right, Lee?'

'Fine. Lisa Leighton and her eight-hundred-grand cheque were just leaving.'

The man didn't pause to consider the sum in question. 'Bribery. That'd look interesting in court – and in the papers for that matter,' he said, his eyes narrowing.

'I came here to speak to Leanne.'

'Well, I'm her brother Markie. You talk to her, you talk to me,' Markie said, stepping closer to Lisa. 'Now, why don't you fuck off back to your mansion and tell that mincing shit husband of yours that if he ever wants to see his kid, fine, we'll sort something, but not to get his missus to do his dirty work.'

Lisa was shocked. How could she have put herself in such a compromising position?

'And if Leanne gets any more visitors of the sort you sent her in London I'll be coming to see you and you won't like me when I'm angry.'

As he spoke, Lisa saw a lunatic glint in his eye. She turned and walked away, not looking back, feeling like a complete fool, focusing on the car at the top of the hill.

The last thing she heard as she negotiated her way in her Louboutin heels was Leanne's brother saying, 'She's not much to look at in real life.' These words hit her harder than Leanne's refusal to guarantee her silence.

chapter fourteen

When Tracy woke, her head was thumping. She needed water and a fag, but first she had to piece together the events of the previous evening. She prised open her eyes and confirmed that, yes, the man whose life she had made a misery for the past few years was back in her bed, and Kent had gone. Paul was lying on his back with his mouth open, catching flies. Tracy tried not to get angry about his mere existence. She'd have to give him a bit of time to bed in so they could get used to one another again.

She was fairly sure they'd had sex, but she couldn't be one hundred per cent certain. On the floor beside the bed she saw an overflowing ashtray and a couple of empty cans draped with her bra. She pushed back the duvet and got up.

'Morning,' Paul said, smacking his lips as if he'd just eaten something he'd enjoyed.

'Morning, yerself. What you making for breakfast?' Tracy asked, pulling on her knickers and running her fingers through her greasy hair.

'I'm not making breakfast, my sweet,' Paul said, sitting up.

'Get fucked. You are,' Tracy said, in her usual charming manner.

'Let me finish. I'm taking you out for a slap-up two-for-one at the Beacon and an all-dayer. What do you say to that?'

This was the man who had rarely bought her a pint in the past and now he was offering to take her all-day drinking. This was a turn-up for the books. 'You're on,' she said. Now that Paul had come into some cash it looked like he was finally pulling his finger out.

The Beacon was as it always was on a Monday afternoon – packed with hardened drinkers making the most of the pint-for-a-pound-before-three offer. Tracy and Paul ordered fish and chips and a pint of strong lager from Val, who was eyeing them suspiciously. 'You look like you want to say something, Val,' Tracy said pointedly.

Val smirked. 'I'm saying nothing.' She placed the pints in front of Tracy and Paul.

'What the …?'

Tracy turned, to find Jodie standing behind her, gaping. 'What? Can't me and your dad come for a bit of lunch without everyone gawping?'

'Er, yeah, you could, if you hadn't spent the last three years ringing the police on 'im and calling him all the names under the sun,' Jodie said, wagging her head from side to side like a *Jerry Springer* guest. Tracy flipped her daughter the bird. 'Nice,' Jodie said. She turned to her dad. 'And what about you, you mug?'

'Why am I a mug?' he asked, wounded.

'D'you want a list?' Jodie said. 'What a pair.'

'Who puts a roof over your head?' Tracy snarled.

Jodie pretended to think for a minute. 'Er, the council.'

'Me, that's who. If I hadn't filled out the forms for the house, you wouldn't be living in it,' Tracy said, and meant it.

Jodie looked at Val. 'Heard this? Mother of the Decade?'

Val laughed.

Tracy wasn't about to stand around with all the nosy regulars eavesdropping on her business.

'I'm not listening to this. Me and your dad are going to sit over there, mind our own business, eat our dinner –'

'And get pissed out of your heads,' Jodie finished.

'So what if we do? It's none of your frigging business, is it, you nosy cow?' Tracy walked over to a table in the corner, Paul following. 'Mouth on her,' Tracy said.

'Don't know where she got it from,' Paul said, without a hint of irony.

Tracy shook her head. 'Neither do I.'

A few hours later, Tracy and Paul were deep in conversation. 'You can fuck off with that. It was "Chirpy Chirpy Cheep Cheep".' Tracy slammed her half-full pint glass on the table.

'That song came out in 1971. We didn't know each other then,' Paul said.

'We did. Our Markie was born in seventy-five. We were at school together, you mong. Course we knew each other.' Tracy sat back in her chair, swigging her lager triumphantly.

'Our song was "Live And Let Die".' Paul was adamant.

'No, we liked it, but it wasn't our bloody song. Jesus, you'd forget your head if it were loose,' Tracy said. The two were so lost in their argument that they didn't hear the door behind them fly open and a drunken Kent fall through it. But Jodie did.

'Val!' she exclaimed.

Val grabbed the baseball bat that was mounted behind the bar. 'Is he going to cause trouble?' she asked.

'God knows.' They watched Kent lurch towards where Tracy and Paul were sitting.

'I fucking knew it!' he shouted.

Tracy swivelled round in her chair. 'Don't show me up in here!'

'You're showing yourself up, going back with him after everything we had.' Kent burst into tears. 'I love you. I fucking love you.'

Paul stood up and went over to Kent to steady him. 'Gerroff me!' Kent said, swinging at Paul, missing him, spinning round and falling in a heap on the floor.

Val had been watching all of this unfurl and put down the baseball bat because it was clear she wouldn't need it. She walked over to Kent. 'Come on, you, out!' she said, hauling him to his feet.

He began to sing "I (who have nothing)" through the tears.

'That's right, love,' Val said, as she deposited him outside the pub.

'I can't believe he's just done that,' Tracy said, more to herself than anyone else.

Jodie, who had lived in the same house as Kent for the past three years, wasn't quite as shocked as her mother that he had turned up drunk and desperate. 'What can't you believe? Until yesterday he thought he was spending the rest of his life with you.' She threw her mother a withering look.

'Well, you know what thought did,' Paul said, draining his pint.

'Is this you two back together, then?' Jodie asked wearily.

Paul looked at Tracy and she looked at him as he dragged another wad of twenty-pound notes out of his pocket. 'I think it is,' Tracy said. She gave her daughter a smile that told Jodie this was the last she wanted to hear about it.

chapter fifteen

Leanne had left Kia playing with Jodie, who had
offered to put her to bed. As there was no sign of
Tracy, she had been glad of the offer. Jodie had filled
her in on the spectacle Kent had made of himself in
the pub. Leanne wasn't his biggest fan – she thought
he was a pushover who did everything Tracy said – but
he hadn't deserved the way Tracy had treated him,
reinstating Paul in the house and expecting Kent to
weather it. But Leanne knew that that was how Tracy
operated. She must have grown tired of Kent, but
she'd never have got rid of him without a back-up
plan. Leanne couldn't work out yet why her dad was
that plan. Tracy had done nothing but badmouth him
since they'd split up. She was sure, though, that her
mother's reasons would become clear at some stage.
Until then, Leanne had other things to worry about.

She walked into the dusty, old-man's pub tucked
away in a part of Bradington she didn't know. The
barmaid stared at her as if she was trying to work out
whether or not it was her. Leanne stuck her head
down and walked to the side of the bar. In the corner,

a man, wearing a baseball cap pulled down to obscure his face, was hunched over a pint. She went over to him. 'Tony?'

His face was badly swollen, the left side purple with bruising and the eye shut. 'Thanks for coming.'

'Oh, my God!' Leanne sank into a chair. 'Who did this to you?'

Tony laughed bitterly. 'Come on, Leanne, who do you think?'

She knew straight away. 'Markie?'

'Well, he doesn't have to get his hands dirty, does he? He just gets someone else to do it. I should know. I've dished it out for him enough times.' Tony picked up his pint and winced as he sipped.

'Why, though?' Leanne asked, reaching across the table to touch his arm.

'Swing.'

'But you didn't do anything. We just had a conversation.'

'Well, you might see it like that but your brother doesn't and I can't say I blame him. I knew about Mandy and Swing and I never said anything. I'd be fucked off too, wouldn't you?'

'Maybe, but I wouldn't go around doling out beatings.' Leanne got to her feet. 'I'm going to his place now to tell him exactly what I think.'

'No, Leanne, you're not. Sit down.' Leanne did as she was told. 'I wanted to talk to you because even though he's your brother there's no one else I trust.'

Leanne felt an overwhelming rush of love for him.

If things had been different, if he hadn't always been so bound by what Markie thought, maybe they could have made a go of it.

'I feel like such a dick,' he went on. 'I've got fuck-all now – and what for? Just because I knew what a slag Mandy was.'

'You shouldn't be so hard on yourself,' Leanne murmured.

Tony's face contorted. 'Easier said than done, Lee. I've got no job and no fucker else'll take me on because they know your Markie'll have something to say. I lost you because I never stood up to him.'

Leanne flushed. She'd never heard him admit this before.

'And,' Tony went on, 'to put the tin hat on it, I've got some Russian bint cluttering up my flat, pretending she's my missus.'

Despite herself, Leanne burst out laughing.

Tony stared at her, until a reluctant smile broke across his battered features. 'Good, innit?'

'Well, me and Kia are going to get a place when I've got a bit of money together. You're welcome to kip in the spare room.'

'If I moved into a place with you, Leanne, it wouldn't be to kip in the spare room.' He gazed at her, and she shifted uncomfortably on her rear. 'D'you ever think about me and you before you went off to set the world alight?'

This comment irked Leanne. 'I didn't go off to set the world alight, did I? I went to London to earn some money and someone made a promise that they'd come with me but they never did.'

'That was because I knew you wanted to be left alone. You didn't want some bonehead from Bradington following you around when you were hanging out with all those famous people.'

'Bloody hell, Tony! That was exactly what I wanted, and you knew it.'

'I thought you were breaking it to me gently.'

'Really? Well, you're a bigger div than I gave you credit for, aren't you?'

Tony took Leanne's hand, but she pulled it away. 'I didn't know,' he said.

'I bloody well loved you, but you just went cold. I thought it was because you didn't want Markie to find out.'

Tony sat back in his chair. 'Well, this is a fuck-up, isn't it? And I was going to see if you fancied going out for the night when I don't look like the Elephant Man any more, but I suppose that's not going to happen now, is it?'

Leanne sighed. Seeing Tony again had made her realise how much she had missed him. 'Well, it could, I suppose … The only thing is, you've got a wife.'

'She doesn't understand me,' Tony quipped.

I've heard that before, Leanne thought. 'In that case, yeah, why not? Let's go out.'

'Great,' Tony said, winking at her with his functioning eye. 'Whatever happens though, Lee, I don't want you to say anything to Markie about us.'

'Not all this again, Tony. I'm twenty-five, I can't do it. If we go out on a date, who cares what my brother thinks?'

'Look at the state of my face. Do you think he wants me going out with you?'

'I don't care what he wants,' Leanne said.

'You do.'

'For now, Tony – but only for now. I'm not hiding any more.'

Tony nodded. 'You shouldn't have to,' he said seriously.

'*We* shouldn't have to,' Leanne said, and she meant it this time.

*

It was past ten o'clock when Leanne got back to the house and Jodie was sitting on the settee watching the TV and plaiting Kia's hair. 'What you doing still up?'

Kia looked at Leanne, who saw straight away that the little girl was shattered. 'Jodie said I could.'

'She was wide awake,' Jodie said, 'so we decided to watch some telly.'

'Come on,' Leanne said, putting out her hand for Kia to hold. 'Let's have you.'

Kia got up and walked past her mum into the hall. Leanne leant back into the room and whispered, 'Little secret for you. She says she's wide awake even when she's completely knackered.' Jodie shrugged.

Leanne wasn't bothered. At least Jodie had agreed

to look after Kia, and she played with her too. Tracy just gave her some ancient felt-tips and told her to colour in that day's paper.

As Kia trudged up the stairs, she asked, 'Where's Nana?'

'Oh, she'll be back soon.'

'Poor Kent,' Kia said next.

Leanne's heart sank. Her little daughter was just like she had been at that age, feeling sorry for anyone on the receiving end of Tracy's whims. 'Kent's fine,' she lied. 'He just had to go and live somewhere else.'

'He said that Nana was a bitch and that she'd used him. How can you use a person, Mummy?'

Oh God, Leanne thought. 'How do you know he said that, Kia?' She tried to sound nonchalant.

'He came round. He smelt funny. Jodie said that it was because Granddad's your daddy and that mummies and daddies are meant to be together.'

'Did she?' Leanne said, passing Kia her nightdress.

'Yes.'

'Let's go and brush your teeth.'

'Why don't I have a daddy?'

Leanne felt as if someone had just kicked her in the stomach. Her daughter was gazing up at her trustingly. 'Not everyone has a daddy, darling.'

'I'd like one, though. How do you get one?' Kia's eyes were nearly shut with exhaustion.

Leanne was on the verge of tears but hid it. 'It's not that easy, Kia. You've got a mummy and it's just you and me for now, OK?'

'OK,' said Kia. 'Where's my toothbrush?'

Leanne passed it to her. She hoped Kia would go to sleep and wake up the following day having forgotten the conversation they'd just had.

chapter sixteen

Tracy bent her head down to the hob and lit a cigarette. It was early but she was up because yet again she was dying of thirst. Tracy's hangovers were hellish. As she lifted her head, sucking in the first nicotine of the day, she saw Scott outside pointing at a newspaper he was pressing to the window. She tried to make sense of what he was trying to say, but he ran to the door and burst in.

'Page five of the *Sun*,' he said, flicking to the relevant page.

'What's she done this time?'

'Not Leanne. You!' Scott said.

'Me? Fuck off!' Tracy said excitedly.

Scott spread out the page for her to see. 'Super (strength) Gran', the headline read. There was a picture of Tracy in the park, with Kia on the swings. Tracy was smoking a fag and drinking from a can of super-strength lager. She read aloud, '"Leanne Crompton's mum was a sight for sore heads as she pushed her granddaughter Kia in the park in their home town of Bradington. Leanne, who was nowhere to be seen, has recently moved back to Bradington after her career hit the rocks. Kia, seven, whose paternity is a hot topic of gossip, but has never been confirmed, seemed happy enough to play with her fag-ash granny ..." Fucking cheek! I wouldn't mind but that was the only drink I had all day,' she said, as if the world had gone mad.

'Leanne's going to kick off when she sees it.'

'I don't bloody think so,' Tracy said. 'I've been minding that little 'un for her anytime she wants.'

The door from the hall opened and Leanne walked in. Tracy folded the paper and shoved it under the table. 'What's up?' Leanne asked.

'Nowt,' Tracy said. 'You in court?' she asked, trying to change the subject. Leanne was wearing a suit, something her mum had thought she'd never see.

'Primark. Twenty quid for the lot. What d'you think?' She gave them a twirl.

'Very nice. I've always said you can carry anything off.' Tracy nodded approvingly.

Leanne looked at her suspiciously – Uh-oh, overdid it. Rumbled, thought Tracy – then grabbed the paper from under the table. 'What page?' she asked Scott.

'It's not you –'

'Page!'

'Five,' Scott said sheepishly.

Tracy threw him a look. Hopeless, she thought.

Leanne took in the picture of her mum and Kia. Tracy pre-empted the attack. 'All I try to do is help and look what happens. I get put in the papers because you're famous. I never asked no one to take my picture. I was just minding my own business, doing a bit of *free* child-minding.'

'Swigging at a can of super-strength while you were looking after your granddaughter,' Leanne interjected.

'That's right. Twist everything,' Tracy said.

'I'll get a child-minder,' Leanne said. Tracy threw her a murderous look. 'To save you the embarrassment of being followed by the paps.'

'No, no. I don't mind looking after Kia. I'll just have to keep an eye out,' Tracy said.

'No need, Mum. I start work today. I'll get a child-minder for after school, and I'm sure Markie will be flexible.' Leanne folded the paper and threw it aside.

'Markie?' Tracy said.

'I'm his new PA.'

'Well, I'm sure that'll be interesting,' Tracy sneered.

'I'm sure it will,' Leanne agreed.

Kia peeped round the door in her school uniform. 'Ready, Mummy,' she said.

'Right,' Leanne said. 'We've had our breakfast, haven't we, mate?' Kia nodded. 'So we're off. See you later.'

Tracy waited until the front door had closed before she said, in all seriousness, 'I give my life to my children on a plate and what do I get? Grief, that's what.'

Scott threw her a look.

'What's the face for?' she asked. 'Bloody hell, I can't do right for doing wrong. I'm off back to bed.' She pulled her towelling dressing-gown round her and stomped up the stairs.

*

Leanne walked into Markie's office. She wasn't sure how Markie had managed to keep his finger in so many seemingly legitimate pies during his time inside, but the fact that he and Mac Derbyshire had an office in the smarter part of town and Markie was still co-owner of two of Bradington's nightclubs, a takeaway and two hair salons (these were the businesses Leanne knew about) testified to her brother's influence and Mac's belief in him as a partner.

'A'right, sis, get the kettle on,' Markie said, winking at her. He was sitting behind a desk, struggling with a pile of papers.

Leanne wanted to launch into him about Tony but bit her tongue. 'So, this is my office then?' she asked.

'Pretty much. You've got the run of it. There's the other two admin girls Mac has downstairs but I want you to do all my stuff and get involved in promotions. If you want to. I think your name's still got a lot of clout round here. It'll pull the punters in. But settle in and see what you think.'

'I don't know the first thing about being a PA.'

'I don't give a shit. You know how to answer a phone, stick stuff in a file, and keep an ear open for anyone trying to have one over on me. That's all I'm interested in,' Markie said.

It sounded fair enough to Leanne, but she was desperate to say something about Tony. As she made the tea she shouted to Markie, 'See Mum made the papers today? Can of lager and a fag on while she was pushing Kia on the swings.'

'You can't buy class,' Markie shouted back.

Leanne brought the coffee through and put the mugs on the desk. 'I bumped into Tony the other day,' she said, trying to sound casual.

'Yeah? What did that mong want?' Markie said, without looking up from his paperwork.

'Someone's battered him, but he didn't even mention it.'

'No? Well, why would he?'

'You don't know what happened to him, do you?' Leanne asked.

'Quit the cute routine, Leanne. You heard him say he knew what was going on behind my back.'

'So what? You had him done over?'

'Listen, Lee, there's stuff you tell your mates.'

'And there's things you don't do to your mates. Like beat them up.'

'Am I taking a lecture on life here before you've even clocked in?' Markie said, glancing at his watch.

'No,' Leanne said, trying to hide her anger. 'I was just saying.'

'Well, things with me and Tony are fine. As long as he doesn't darken my doors again he'll get to keep his head on his shoulders.'

'Right,' Leanne said, then ventured bravely, 'Tough talk.'

'Yeah? Well, you'd better get used to it.'

Leanne raised an eyebrow and cocked her head to

one side. 'I'm grateful you're giving me a job, Markie, but let's not get funny with each other before I start, eh?'

Markie picked up the papers and passed them to his sister. 'All right. Stick them in a file, then I'll tell you what else needs doing.'

Tony had been right, she thought. Markie didn't want anything to do with him. But she wasn't going to tread on eggshells with her brother for ever just because Tony wanted her to. For the time being, though, she'd keep her mouth shut and sort out the filing, like a good little PA.

*

It was Sunday morning and Jeanine hadn't shown up for work. Lisa, who had just about mastered the art of putting on a nappy, was joggling baby Blest up and down, singing 'Get The Party Started' by Pink. She wasn't sure why she was doing this but Blest seemed to like it.

Jay came into the kitchen, dishevelled, a towel wrapped round his taut torso.

'What time did you get in?' Lisa asked.

'Dunno,' Jay said, scrutinising the contents of the fridge. 'We got any orange?'

'Where were you last night?' she asked again.

'Panacea, Hilton. We didn't get bothered, though.'

'We?'

'Yeah, "we". D'you think I went out on my own?'

'Who's "we"?'

'Me, Joel Baldy and some of the other players. Team-building. We'll be in the papers this week. Got papped.'

'Did you do the look?' Lisa had decided that Jay looked far better in photographs if he made sure his left side was in profile, closed his mouth and put his tongue to the inside of his lips, affecting a slight pout.

'Yeah. Think I pulled it off.'

Lisa nodded, approving. 'Listen, Jay, there's something I need to tell you.'

'What?' Jay asked. He broke off from swigging at a milk carton.

'I met Leanne this week.'

Jay stared at her. 'What?'

'I went to that dump she's moved back to and offered her some money to keep her mouth shut.'

'And?' Jay asked, plainly wanting her to spit it out.

'She told me to shove it. Said she didn't need our money.'

'What else did you think she'd say?' Jay said, slamming down the milk carton.

'I thought she'd thank me and take the cheque.'

'There's no story in that, is there?' Jay cried, pulling at his hair. 'What if someone saw you? What if you were photographed?'

'We weren't. And why exactly are you having a go? In case you haven't noticed, it's me who sorts out the damage limitation in this marriage and you cause the damage. So don't get all uppity. It won't wash.' She thrust Blest at him. He took her, then held her as if he'd been passed a bag of snakes. 'Say hello to your daughter. She's not sure what you look like.' Lisa stormed out of the room.

The kitchen phone rang, stopping her in her tracks. The only person who called on a Sunday morning was Steve C their publicist. She stalked back in, past Jay, who seemed suddenly terrified.

'Hello,' Lisa snapped into the receiver.

'It's Steve. Bad news,' he said, cutting to the chase. Lisa had grown used to Steve's straightforward approach to delivering bad tidings.

'Go on,' she said, her eyes boring into Jay.

Jay mouthed '*What?*' at her.

'That nanny, Jeanine. Whatever credential checks you did weren't good enough. She's gone to the *News of the Screws*. "My Life with the Leightons" – some bullshit eight-pager.'

Lisa's jaw nearly hit the floor. 'Oh my God.' There was no way she'd thought Jeanine would go to the papers. She'd seemed like such a nice woman, such a *private* woman.

'What?' Jay demanded.

'The nanny, Jeanine. She's gone to the papers.'

'Shit! Shit! Shit!'

Lisa ignored him. 'Tell me everything,' she said to Steve.

'Right, page one in a nutshell, you don't know one end of a baby from the other and Jay's never there. You have two nannies – which, of course, is played out as pure decadence ...'

'We've got two *part-time* nannies because we couldn't get a full-timer ... fuck! What else?'

'You and Jay barely speak. He's got a roving eye, looked at her a few times –'

'Looked at her a few times? Even I know he didn't do her! She's old enough to be his fucking mother!'

'She said I was looking at her? Fuck me, don't flatter yourself, you old dog,' Jay said.

'What else?' Lisa needed to know it all. She wanted to get the embarrassment out of the way, then deal with the fall-out.

'You have a loveless marriage and everything you do is for show.'

'That is such bullshit!' Lisa said, without realising the irony of what she had said.

'And you tolerate Jay's indiscretions because you know that without him you're nothing. Sorry about all this, Lise, bearer of shit news and all that.'

Lisa was wounded. 'She only worked for us for two minutes. She didn't even know if I took milk in my tea! How the hell could she pretend to know all this?'

'She's also left a tidy little cliff-hanger ...'

Lisa felt every muscle in her body tighten. 'Go on.'

'She's said she knows something you did this week that'll blow the lid on your marriage. I've done some digging at the paper, but no one's giving an inch. What've you done?'

'I ain't done nothing!' Lisa squawked. She racked her brains. What *had* she done? She never did anything. It was Jay who dropped them in it all the time, not her.

'Well, you've nothing to worry about, then, have you? It'll just be some cobbled-together rubbish, no doubt.'

'Oh, shit!' Lisa moaned. 'I met fucking Leanne Crompton in a park in shit-tip Bradington.'

'Well, why don't you get a gun and shoot yourself?' Steve asked helpfully.

'Well, I don't know if that's what she means.'

'Right, sweetheart, let's run through this. Jay has a kid with a glamour model. The only people who know this to be a hundred-per-cent fact, as far as we're aware, are you, Jay, me and Ms Crompton. You've denied every rumour that's ever suggested they went near each other because you want everyone to believe your marriage is monogamous and that you and Jay are as besotted with one another as you were ten years ago. So, what do you do? You meet fucking Leanne Crompton. 'Scuse me if I don't give you a Mexican wave, darling, but I'm not that pleased to hear it. D'you wanna make my job any harder?'

'I just wanted to talk to her and ask what she was doing for money.'

'And I just want to talk to Nelson Mandela and ask him what makes him tick but it ain't going to happen.' Steve sighed heavily. 'Right. This is what you do. Before anything appears in any paper I'm going to set up a photocall for you and Jay tomorrow. I want you looking like the fucking Waltons. Piggybacks for that new kid of yours, the works. Then I'll arrange an exclusive with a rival newspaper next week, and you're going to bare your soul.'

'But I don't do tabloid interviews,' Lisa bleated.

'You do now,' Steve said harshly. 'I'll make some calls and be back in ten.'

'What we going to do?' Jay whinged. 'We've got to show it's bullshit.'

'Oh, shut up, Jay, for God's sake. You make me sick,' Lisa said, and marched out of the room.

*

Jodie was standing in Brian Spencer's dusty studio. She had finally plucked up courage to call the 'talent manager' who had given her his card in the Beacon a few weeks ago. He had asked her to come along at midday on Monday in something skimpy. He had met her at the door. Then, flattening down his comb-over and falling over himself, he ushered her upstairs. As Jodie looked around, she wondered if it would have been a good idea to ask Leanne what she could expect from a first photo shoot. But she didn't want her sister to know what she was up to. She wanted to succeed by herself without Leanne's help. It had never worked in the past, though. Now she was wishing she'd said something to her sister. If only so that someone knew where she was.

'Right, love. Go over there and take your top off,' Brian said, waving at a pile of furniture covered with a dust sheet.

'What? Just take it off?' Alarm bells rang. Jodie knew that when Leanne had done her first shoot she had been made to feel comfortable first, not ordered to whip off her top.

'That's right,' Brian said, producing a camera that looked like it had only ever been used to take holiday snaps.

'Can I see your portfolio before we start?' Jodie asked. She knew that if he was genuine he'd have photos of the girls he represented.

'My whatio?' Brian said blankly.

'Brian?' Jodie said, cocking her head to one side.

'Yes, love?' he said distractedly.

'Are you an old perv who gets young girls up here so you can see their tits?'

Brian's face went a funny colour. 'You cheeky little whore!' he shouted.

Jodie grabbed her bag and shot past him. 'Dirty fucker!' she yelled over her shoulder and barged through the fire door, running down the steps on to the street. There was no way she'd let him catch her. At the main road she saw someone coming out of a sandwich shop, dressed in a suit. It was Leanne.

'Bloody hell, look at you!' Jodie gasped, breathless.

'Look at me? Look at you more like! You on the run from the coppers?' Leanne was laughing.

'Worse. Fancy a drink?' Jodie asked. She could murder a G and T.

*

Leanne and Jodie were in a Bradington bar. Leanne had already received at least twenty nods of recognition, and a group of women behind Jodie were whispering about her. Jodie turned and gave them one of her best evil glares. They shut up.

'Doesn't it bug you? People talking about you everywhere you go? I'd go mad,' Jodie said, making sure the women could hear her.

'You get used to it.'

Jodie didn't think she could. She'd have a right go at anyone who sat in a bar whispering about her.

'So who were you legging it from?' Leanne asked.

Jodie began to tell her about Brian Spencer. When she'd finished, Leanne said, 'Why didn't you tell me? I could have helped you.'

Jodie shook her head. 'Remember last time? That witch manager of yours bawled me out of her office.'

'But you're so much more mature now.'

'You mean I don't look as much of a dog?'

'Bloody hell, Jode, you're your own worst enemy. First, you never pay someone for photos. If you're good, they'll take them for free. Second, managers don't take their own pictures, they have photographers for that, so you're right in assuming that Brian is a perv. Best thing to do is to have a couple of pictures done and I'll send them to an agency for you.'

'Would you?' Jodie asked eagerly. She really had changed in the last couple of years. She knew she was far more like the girls she saw in the lads' mags and the tabloids than she had been when she'd first set foot inside Figurz Management.

'Course I will. No problem.'

Leanne didn't see Jodie's face drop as she looked at the news report on the big-screen TV positioned behind her. The Witches of Eastwick were cackling again. 'Leanne,' Jodie said, nudging her and nodding at the screen. Leanne turned and stared. Jay and Lisa Leighton were in a public playground, pushing their poor child on a roundabout.

'Jesus,' Leanne said.

'The kid can't even hold its head up, it's that small, and they're doing that to it?' Jodie said, disgusted, waiting for her sister's reaction.

'Poor little thing,' Leanne said quietly.

'Leanne …' Jodie began. She had never had the courage to ask her sister if the rumours about her and Jay were true.

'I don't want to discuss it, Jodie.'

Jodie knew she meant it. She sipped her drink and tried not to look at the TV screen on which the banner headline read, 'Leightons Quash More Rumours About Their Private Life.'

chapter seventeen

'Bend forward and pull your top down,' Karina said. Jodie wobbled unsteadily on her high heels. 'Bloody hell, Jode! What's that?' Karina couldn't believe the face her sister was pulling. She looked like she'd been asked to do an impression of a sucker-fish and she was pushing her boobs together in a very unflattering pose.

'What's what?' Jodie asked, sounding put out.

'That! The whole thing! Big fish lips and the thing with your tits. No one asked you to push 'em together till your nipples touched.'

'Oh, and you know all about modelling, I suppose?'

'I know what a complete knob looks like.' Karina scowled at her sister, then took the silver ornament that hung round her neck, put it to her nose and sniffed. Gaz had bought her a coke pendant. It looked like a spherical locket but when it was tipped up and down it dispensed a snifter of cocaine, and allowed Karina to drop-feed herself her favourite drug without the nasty business of racking up lines and snorting off toilet lids.

'Is that what I think it is?' Jodie asked.

'It's my snowstorm,' Karina said proudly.

'Shit-storm, more like.'

'That doesn't make sense, does it?'

'Course it does,' Jodie protested. 'As in you'll cause a right shit-storm if you keep using so much coke.'

'Yeah, but I said, "It's my snowstorm," and you said, "Shit-storm, more like," and that doesn't mean anything. Now if you'd said, "Snowstorm? There's gonna be a shit-storm if you keep on using it," that would've made sense.'

'Jesus Christ, Karina, will you wind your neck in and take some fucking pictures?' Jodie said, throwing her hair over her shoulder.

Karina positioned herself professionally behind the disposable camera Jodie had bought that morning. 'Why's our Leanne not here, anyway? She's the expert.'

'Because she's working for our Markie and I didn't want to wait. I'll get them developed and then show her. That's if we ever get them bloody well done.'

'All right.' Karina decided to take matters into her own hands and give her sister some advice. 'You need to raise your eyebrow slightly and look straight at the camera, like it's just walked into the Beacon and is about to tip all night.'

Jodie gave the camera a smouldering, sultry look and Karina took the picture. 'Bingo,' she said, delighted. 'A couple more, and I think you're on to a winner.'

Karina had managed to get twenty-four shots, three or four crackers that Leanne could definitely send off to management companies. She was sitting on her settee smoking a cigarette as Jodie changed back into her jeans and T-shirt.

'I saw Leanne earlier, actually. Had a drink with her.'

'Really?' Karina said. She'd hardly seen Leanne since her return to Bradington.

'Yeah, she's all right, I think, despite everything.'

'Despite what?' Karina asked, with a sneer. 'Despite having had the life of Riley for the last seven years? Despite everyone thinking she's ace?'

'Fucking hell, what's she ever done to you? She always got us in free to places, took us abroad, looked after us when we went down to London, and all you do is bitch about her.'

'Oh, and you never have? You called her all the cunts under the sun when you came back from London that time and didn't get that modelling job.'

'That was ages ago. Bloody hell, Kar, life's hard enough as it is without us all back-biting. She's all right, Leanne. I've been jealous of her in the past but so what? I'm older now. Let bygones be bygones.'

'Very noble,' Karina said, stubbing out her cigarette. 'So, go on, "despite everything".'

'Well, we were sitting there and this thing came on the news with those two divs Lisa and Jay Leighton prancing around with that kid they've robbed from China. And I just wanted to crawl under the table.'

Karina threw back her head and sighed. 'Has Leanne ever told you that Jay Leighton's Kia's dad?'

'No, but –'

'No but nothing,' Karina yelled. 'I'm sick to the back teeth of this is-she-isn't-she bullshit. If I wasn't with Gaz I'd still say he was Izzy's dad. I wouldn't be going round all tight-lipped about it, not to family. What's the point?'

'Well, maybe,' Jodie suggested, 'she thinks someone'll go to the papers.'

'One of us?'

'God, I know,' Jodie said sarcastically. 'Imagine one of us selling a story on Leanne to the papers to earn a coin. That'd never happen.'

Karina huffed and flopped back in the chair. She'd sold a few stories, and they'd always been fairly mild. She hadn't caused Leanne much heat, but she'd earned a couple of grand without her sister knowing, and that, Karina thought, was fair enough. 'Well, so what if Jay is Kia's dad. I don't get what all the fuss is about,' Karina fibbed. Of course she knew what all the fuss was about.

'The most famous married man in the country and you don't know what the problem is?'

'Well, all right. But if he is, and Leanne says he is, it'll blow over soon enough,' Karina said, taking a bottle of midnight blue varnish and applying it to her chipped nails.

'Well, she got very upset when she saw those two idiots pretending to be mad about each other on telly so I don't think she'll be selling her story any time soon, do you?'

Karina shrugged. 'I would.'

'Course you would,' Jodie said. 'That's because you take after Mum.'

'Oh, and what's Leanne? Some throwback to a saint?'

'I'm not saying she's a saint, just that she's got more morals than you, and if you want to argue the toss with me when you've got a ball of coke swinging from your neck, go ahead.'

Karina looked down at her pendant. 'Why don't you piss off and get these developed? They'll give the Saturday lad in the chemist a stiffy.'

'Thanks,' said Jodie, getting up to leave. 'I might just do that.'

chapter eighteen

'These pictures are really good, Jode,' Leanne said, impressed.

'D'you think so?'

Leanne did. Jodie had a natural ability in front of the camera, she could tell. And she looked totally different from the podgy teenager she had sent to see Jenny a few years ago.

'What you two gawping at?' Markie asked, appearing from nowhere.

Leanne put the pictures back into the sleeve. 'Just some pictures Karina took of Jodie.'

'Give us a look, then,' Markie said, biting into his lunchtime pasty and thrusting out his hand.

'No!' Jodie squealed. 'They're glamour shots.'

'And I've not seen a picture before of a sister with her tits out?' Markie asked sarcastically. 'Give 'em here.'

'God, Markie, you're so mortifying!' Jodie complained.

Leanne passed the photos to her brother. He looked at the first, then the second and the third. 'You look knock-out, Jode,' he said, handing them back.

'Thanks,' Jodie said, sounding shocked.

'She does, doesn't she? I'm going to send them to a management firm I know. I think they'll snap her up,' Leanne told him.

'How much does a management firm take out of her wages?'

'Commission's anything from ten to twenty per cent,' Leanne said, trying to remember what Jenny had taken as her fee.

'Bollocks to that, Lee! Why don't *you* do it?' Markie said, as if he was suggesting the simplest thing in the world.

'Me?'

'Yeah. What's the procedure? You book a photographer, line up a page three, lads' mag, whatever, and Bob's your uncle?'

'It's not that simple,' Leanne said.

'No? Talk me through it. Which bit couldn't you do?'

'Well, I could do all of it – I know a lot of people. It's the money. I wouldn't know where to start.'

'With an accountant. I'd have thought that bitch manager of yours might have sorted one out for you until you rocked up here on your arse.'

'Thanks!' Leanne snapped.

'Oi! I'm not being funny, just saying. You should represent Jodie. Why not? You've got a high profile and you can make out this is your new business venture if anyone asks. Except you're not leaving me. Like I said, I need you to answer the phone and do the promotions. How's that thing for the Glass House coming on?'

Markie had asked Leanne to arrange an opening night for his new club. She had managed to secure a high-profile girl band – Party Hard – to play on the night, because she had helped out one of its members a few years ago and Markie was delighted. He didn't mind paying the five-thousand-pound fee they demanded for two songs. Having them there would ensure that the Glass House was *the* place to go for at least the next six months. 'It's coming along great. Now we've got Party Hard playing, the world and his wife want to be on the guest list,' she told him.

'I need you to get Mac to sign these papers. He's down at Poles.' Markie handed her an envelope.

'OK. What are they?' Leanne asked, so that she knew where to send them and where to file the copy.

Markie tapped his nose and nodded at Jodie.

Jodie clocked this immediately. 'All right. Bloody hell! I'm not arsed what your papers are for, Markie. Keep your hair on.'

Markie watched her go. 'They're about a house we've acquired,' he said.

'Right, I'll catch Twisted Knickers up. You know what, Markie?' He looked up from his computer. 'I might have a think about what you said about representing her. No one else could put up with her strops.'

*

Jodie had driven with Leanne to Poles Apart. 'I'm not coming in, the girls are knobs,' she said, less than charitably.

Leanne rolled her eyes. Jodie thought everyone she didn't like or didn't know was a knob until proven otherwise.

'It's only two o'clock and they don't start till eight. How long do you think it takes to put a thong on? There'll be no girls in there.'

'Even so, I'll stay outside, thanks,' Jodie said, leaning against the wall.

Leanne pulled at the main door but it didn't budge. She stood back and looked up at the pink unlit neon sign that read 'Poles Apart' and furrowed her brow. 'I'll go round the back. See you in a minute.'

She walked round the building, stepping over discarded bottle bags from the night before, and came to the door that led into the small kitchen – it produced such delicacies as chicken in a basket. It wasn't locked so she walked in. 'Hello?' she called. There was no response.

She went to the door that led into the main part of the club. The runway where the girls danced was lit, but the rest of the club was in darkness. There was no sign of anyone, but Leanne knew someone must be here or the back door wouldn't be open. She sat on the end of the runway. The place was eerily quiet. Then she heard a crack from one of the side rooms that were used for private dances and a strangled howl. She jumped to her feet and went to the door from which the noise had come.

'Please – just take the house. Have it!' There was another jaw-shattering whack and the man who had spoken began to sob. Leanne felt sick. The door opened and a breathless Mac came out. He shut it behind him so that she couldn't see what was going on.

'Leanne!' he said, walking over to hug her. 'You look bloody gorgeous as always.'

'Hi, Mac,' Leanne said shakily. 'Markie asked me to bring these down.'

'Good girl. I'll get them signed. You want a drink?'

'No,' Leanne said, feeling out of her depth. 'Got to get back to work.'

'Don't we all?' Mac said, smiling.

He vanished into the room, reappeared a moment later and handed the envelope back to Leanne. 'Markie was saying you're doing well with the Glass House opening.'

'It seems to be going fine, fingers crossed.' Leanne forced a smile on to her face, just as the man she had heard a few moments ago let out a whimper. She glanced at the door. Mac caught her eye. 'Toothache,' he said, smiling wickedly.

Leanne tried to smile back, but she couldn't make her eyes match her mouth. 'Anyway, Mac, nice seeing you,' she said.

'And you, darling. Come down soon. We'll get you comps and drinks all night.'

'Thanks, I will,' she said.

As she burst out into the daylight, she had a feeling she wouldn't take Mac up on his offer.

'Come on,' she said to Jodie, who was now sitting in the car, in the middle of texting someone.

'Hold your horses,' Jodie said. 'What's up with you?'

Leanne waited until she was safely back behind the wheel before she pulled out the document that had just been signed. Mac had scribbled his name as receiver of the property. Below that, the vendor's signature was accompanied by a streak of blood.

Leanne threw it into the back. 'What's our Markie up to?'

'What do you mean?' Jodie asked.

'I've just heard some bloke being beaten black and blue in there. And these papers are for his house.'

'Well, he might owe Markie and Mac money.'

Leanne looked at her sister. 'Is it only me who doesn't think that's normal? He was pleading with Mac to leave him alone.'

Jodie turned to face her sister. 'Look, Leanne, I don't one hundred per cent agree with everything our Markie does, but it's the business he's in. He lends money, he's involved with poker rings. You don't think all his cash comes out of a pole-dancing club and a few shops round town, do you? Mac's minted and our Markie will be too. He's just got to build up to it.'

'And by that you mean batter people and make everyone scared of him?'

'He doesn't need to make anyone scared of him. They already are.'

Leanne thought about her clandestine meeting with Tony and realised her sister was right. She drove along the road back to the office feeling deeply uneasy. If she was now working for Markie, wasn't she party to his activities whether she liked it or not? Well, she didn't like it one little bit.

chapter nineteen

Tracy and Paul were sitting in the lounge, drinking vodka and looking at holiday brochures. 'I'm not going to fucking Benidorm, that's for sure,' Tracy said snootily.

'What's up with Benidorm?' Paul asked.

'It's rough as fuck, that's what.' Tracy said, flicking through Thomson Worldwide. 'What about an all-inclusive in the Dominican Republic? Look at this, free booze *and* free fags. We can smoke ourselves daft.'

Paul nodded, impressed. 'How much?'

'Two grand a pop.'

Paul let out a low whistle.

'What's up with that, Money Bags?' Tracy asked. 'It was you who said I deserved a break.'

Paul touched her face. 'And you do. Right, let's have a look. When do you want to go?'

'Soon as,' Tracy said. 'Call 'em now. What time is it?'

'It's nearly midnight. They're not going to be open, are they? I'll go down in the morning.'

'Brilliant. It's about time I parked my arse on a nice

beach somewhere. It's been too long,' Tracy said. Something occurred to her. 'Stick the radio on and see if he's still banging on.'

Kent had been bombarding Tracy with texts and phone calls. On his radio show he had been talking about his broken heart and playing everything that had ever reminded him of her. 'Fuck me, he's running out of songs. It'll be "Una Paloma Blanca" next,' Paul had said the other day, which had made Tracy chuckle.

Paul tuned the radio into *The Late Night Love-in* as the last strains of a song died away. 'And that was Elaine Paige and Barbara Dickson with "I Know Him So Well". But did you, ladies? Did you know him?' Kent asked.

Tracy laughed and poured herself a vodka. 'He's so bloody dramatic, isn't he?'

'You think you know someone, and then they rip your heart out, trample it into the floor,' Kent went on. 'If anyone else has had a similar experience, call in this evening. We'd love to hear from you. OK, we're going to line one, Carrie-Anne ...'

'I'm just ringing in to tell you about my husband Pete ...' Carrie-Anne said, and droned on about how good he was to her, and how he'd held her hair back when she was sick on their first date and how there wasn't enough love in the world.

Tracy turned the volume down. 'When is he going to give it a rest?'

'Come on, love, he's upset. Let him have his moment,' Paul said.

Tracy sparked up a cigarette and dragged hard on it. 'He's flogging it, though. You'd think having the police called might sort him out, but no.' She didn't clock that she was talking to a man on whom she had called them countless times. The other day Kent had come round and spelt 'I love you' in daffodils down the middle of the road. By the time Tracy had opened the window it didn't read anything. It was just a mish-mash of flowers and the neighbours from whose garden he had dishonestly acquired them were kicking up a song and a dance with a policeman.

'Chuck us another vodka in there, will you?' She waved her empty glass at Paul.

Dutifully he got up and did as he was told, while she went back to her holiday brochure.

*

Tracy pushed open the door at the travel agent's and Paul followed her in. A very blonde, very made-up young woman looked her up and down and asked, 'Can I help you?' as if she knew she couldn't.

'We want to book an all-inclusive to the Dominican Republic,' Tracy said, giving her a piercing look in return.

'Anything at this time of year is quite expensive,' the woman said.

'Well, we'll worry about that. You park your arse in front of your computer and tell us how soon we can go,' Tracy told her with her best nasty smile.

It took the travel agent twenty minutes to confirm two weeks at the Esplendido resort travelling this coming Saturday. Paul handed over his credit card.

The woman swiped it and waited for the transaction to complete. 'Have you another means of payment?' she asked, not cracking a smile.

Tracy glared at Paul.

'That's not right. There's plenty of money in my bank account. Put it through again,' Paul said, panicky.

'I don't want to do that, sir, as the bank may ask me to destroy the card,' the woman said, giving Tracy *her* best nasty smile.

'Well, I'll tell you what, I'll go to the bank and sort this out, but we won't be coming back here to book with you, not wi' your attitude.'

'I'm sorry you feel that way, sir.' Her professional mask didn't slip.

'Course you are, you snotty cow,' Tracy said, and flounced out.

In the street she turned to Paul. 'What the fuck was that about? You out of money?'

'Course not. There's been a mistake. I'll go to the bank now.'

Tracy eyeballed him. 'Go on, then. I'm off to Yates's for a pint. You can come and find me when you're finished.'

Paul plodded off down the street. Tracy could smell a rat, but she wasn't about to go off at him. She needed to work out if something was going on, or if Paul was just being his usual slack self.

175

chapter twenty

Leanne was at her desk. She was holding the paper that had been signed the other day, the streak of blood still visible. No one else would be able to tell it was blood – it looked like a little brown smear – but Leanne knew what it was.

Markie walked in and Leanne hid it under the rest of the filing. 'Everything's gone off to the solicitor's,' she said. She wanted to test the water about what she had witnessed the other day. 'I've not sent off the thing Mac signed. I didn't know where it had to go.'

'Bloody hell, Lee! That's the important one. It needs to go to HJ Solicitors. Get a courier.'

'Sorry.'

'It takes them for ever to complete on house transfers as it is, without us sitting on paperwork.'

'When did you decide to go into property?' she asked.

'When I was staring at my ceiling in Strangeways on the four hundred and twenty-first night. Why? What's this? The Spanish Inquisition?'

'No, I'm just asking. You don't have to bite my head off.'

'Look, Mac said you might have overheard something the other day.' Markie paused, as if he was getting ready to make a confession. 'There are people we deal with, who borrow money from us when they can't get it from other places, and then they get into trouble. That guy the other day, he's run up a massive debt and was caught doing a runner to Spain. We've asked him nicely and it's not like he hasn't got money tied up – he's got the house. We tried to arrange for him to release some equity in it but the bank weren't having it, so we had to get him to sign the house over, all above board. We're even giving him a good whack out of it so he can set up again. But he got mouthy with Mac just as you walked in to get the paper signed. Sorry you had to hear that, Lee.'

Leanne wanted to believe him, and what he had said sounded plausible. 'Look, I'm not daft, Markie, and I know you aren't snow white, but I got a bit of a shock, that's all.'

Markie wrapped his arms round her. 'Next time you're worried, come and tell me, yeah?' He kissed the top of her head.

They were interrupted by the door buzzer. Leanne activated the lock and a bike courier came in. 'Delivery for Mr M. Crompton,' he said.

'That's me.' Markie took a box from him.

'Bit whiffy that, mate,' the courier said.

Markie sniffed it and recoiled, as Leanne signed for it. 'Don't suppose you can do a job for us while you're here? I just need this envelope dropping at Rawson

Street. I'd walk down myself but can't leave the phone,' she said.

'Give it here. What number?'

Leanne smiled gratefully and popped the blood-smeared document into an envelope. 'Four. HJ Solicitors.'

Markie was trying to open his package.

'You were the first poster I had on my wall when I went to college,' the courier told Leanne bashfully. 'I can't believe you're not still modelling. You're well fit,' he said, forgetting himself.

'Oi, that's my sister!' Markie said, as he opened the box. 'Fuck!' He threw it onto the desk and reeled backwards. Then the smell hit Leanne, who put a hand over her mouth. 'It's a fucking rat!' Markie shouted at the courier. 'Who sent it?'

The courier looked at his delivery sheet – he was gagging too. 'It just says Mandy.'

'That bitch!' Markie said. He put the lid onto the box and thrust it back at the courier. 'Well, you can take it to forty-nine Letchworth Street.'

'Come on, mate! It's a dead rat! I can't take that.'

'You brought it here. You can fucking take it back.'

'Markie …' Leanne said.

'Right! I'll take it my-fucking-self.'

'What will you do with it?' Leanne asked, as her brother marched to the door.

'Feed it to the cunt,' he said, without looking back.

*

Leanne had sprayed air-freshener round the room and opened the windows, but there was still a distinct smell of dead rat in the air. Mandy wasn't one for going quietly. Leanne knew that Mandy wanted Markie to go round to see her, even if it was to feed her her own gift. For Mandy any contact with Markie was better than none at all.

Leanne's desk was clear. She had done all of the morning's jobs and the phone wasn't ringing, so she took the photos of Jodie out of her bag, then scrolled through her mobile phone until she came to Victoria Haim's number.

Victoria had been a gossip columnist for one of the red tops when Leanne first knew her. Contrary to popular belief, the gossip columnists weren't parasites whom celebrities avoided at parties. They were almost celebrities in their own right. They had so much power that they were treated exceptionally well by the people they often lambasted.

Leanne had always got on well with Victoria, not because she had had anything to gain from it, but because they had hit it off. Victoria's rise had been meteoric and she was now editor of the *Globe*, a leading tabloid.

'Victoria, it's Leanne – Leanne Crompton.'

'Leanne! How are you? Did you get my text? I've been meaning to call but I've been up to my eyes ...'

Leanne had received a text from her the day after Jenny had sacked her, saying how sorry she was and offering help. Leanne hadn't taken her up on it because she knew Victoria was just being polite and that a couple of high-days-and-holidays snaps of her on page three wouldn't extend her career any further.

'I did, yeah, thanks. I've been keeping my head down.'

'What can I do for you?' Victoria asked warmly.

'Well …' Leanne began. She told Victoria about her sister, how Jodie was six years younger than her, had great energy and a look that would, in Leanne's opinion, shift papers.

'Who's managing her?' Victoria asked.

'I am,' Leanne said. 'I've moved back up north because so many good-looking girls are being taken advantage of by old pervs when they could have a good career if they had the right person to look after them.' She hadn't thought about this until she'd said it, but it made sense.

'Good for you,' Victoria said. 'Send her pictures to me now and I'll put you in touch with the person in charge of page three.'

'Great,' Leanne said. They chatted for a few more minutes, and Victoria assured her she wasn't missing much in London. Then Leanne put the phone down, beaming from ear to ear. She called Jodie. 'I've got some good news for you.'

'What?' Jodie asked blankly.

'I've spoken to the editor of the *Globe* and she's asked to see your pictures. I'm sending them to her now.' Leanne winced. Jodie's excited scream had threatened to burst her eardrum.

chapter twenty-one

Leanne stepped out of the taxi and looked at the tiny bistro, Barolo's, tucked away along a back-street not far from Little Venice. Tony had chosen it, and she had asked him if he was happy to go somewhere so close to where Markie was living. Until recently Tony had known Markie's every move and assured her that there was no chance her brother would come into a place like this. His week nights were spent in Poles Apart or at the new Glass House premises, Leanne knew, but she had wanted reassurance. Jodie was looking after Kia. She was so excited about her pictures being sent to the *Globe* that she had promised to baby-sit free for the rest of her life.

Leanne opened the door to the dimly lit bistro and saw Tony sitting in the corner. He stood up as she entered and walked over to kiss her cheek. Leanne blushed girlishly.

'You look beautiful,' he said.

She was wearing a short black dress she had been given by a young fashion designer for whom she had modelled about a year ago. 'Thank you,' she said. 'You're not so bad yourself.'

Tony laughed. 'Yeah, less like Quasimodo than last time you saw me, eh?'

The bruising had faded now, and the swelling around his eye had all but disappeared. Leanne smiled. 'But you looked like Quasimodo anyway,' she joked.

'All right, Esmeralda. What you having to drink?'

'G and T, please.' Leanne looked round the restaurant, then back at Tony. 'It's really nice to see you again,' she said.

Tony fiddled with the butter knife and, unable to meet her eye, said, 'You've no idea how much I've missed you. I've been such a dick, Lee. I should have come with you. What was I staying here for? So I could kiss Markie's arse? He's got enough hangers-on around him without me.'

'You're not a hanger-on,' Leanne said. He had always stood on his own two feet where Markie was concerned, unless Leanne was involved and then he had tried to play it safe.

'Well, I might not be a hanger-on but I'm a mug,' he said angrily, then caught himself. 'Sorry, Leanne, I wanted tonight to be really nice. Let's not talk about me and Markie.'

'Fine by me.' She picked up the menu. Then she remembered what she had wanted to ask Tony. 'Sorry, I promise this is the last time I'll mention my brother, but he's being a bit cagey about something and I was wondering if you could shed any light on it.'

'Go on.'

Leanne told him what she had heard and seen at Poles Apart, that Markie had explained it away, but it didn't sit right with her, people losing their homes for the sake of a gambling debt.

'Well, what Markie's told you isn't a million miles from the truth. The only thing is, he knows when he lends these mugs money that they're not going to be able to pay him back. And he only ever lends it to someone who's bought their own house. Usually they got it off the council for thirty grand and it's worth more than a hundred now. He gets them to sign over the house in case they can't pay back what they owe him, then lets them run up a bill for more than they paid for it. Simple. He takes the house but makes out he's doing them a favour because he's letting them off the difference between the debt and what they paid for the house. But in reality he's pocketing all the equity. He only deals with people too stupid, lazy or blinded by a gambling addiction to see what's going on. It's dodgy, but if him and Mac weren't doing it someone else would.'

Leanne knew her brother was into all sorts of illegal activities, but she had somehow convinced herself that since he'd come out of prison he'd been on the straight and narrow. She'd been reassured of this when he'd given her the job in his office. But now she knew she was being paid with money gained from other people's pain. 'I don't like it.'

'Shit happens, Lee, bigger shit than this. You've just got to accept it.'

Leanne didn't think she had to accept anything, but now – on her first date in years with Tony – wasn't the time to point it out. 'Yeah. Maybe.'

The waitress was hovering.

'I'm ready. Are you, Leanne?'

Leanne ordered soup and a medium rare steak.

'Medium rare?' Tony said, after he'd handed the menus to the waitress. 'I'm impressed. Time was, you'd have had it cremated.'

'True. I'm dead refined now, me.'

The waitress came back with the wine Tony had ordered. 'Just stick it in the glasses, I'm sure it'll be fine,' he said. Once it was poured he lifted his and said, 'To having you back in Bradington.'

Leanne raised hers. 'Cheers.'

Just then a bell chimed and the door burst open.

Tony's face paled. Thinking it must be Markie, Leanne turned. To her greater dismay, she saw her mum and dad.

'Eh, it's all right in here, innit?' she heard Tracy say.

'Told you I'd take you somewhere posh.'

'I'm not having no frog's legs.' Tracy was taking off her coat.

The place was too small for Leanne and Tony to pretend they hadn't seen them, and only three other couples were in the room. Leanne put her head into her hands.

'Eye-eye, Tony boy!' she heard her dad say. 'And who's the lovely lady? If it isn't our Leanne!'

Leanne arranged her face into a smile, then turned

round to greet them. 'What are you two doing here?' she asked.

'Might ask you the same. That poor kiddie of yours is going to think our Jodie's her mum.' Tracy cackled to indicate that she was joking, but Leanne knew a not-so-veiled dig when she heard one.

'She's looked after her three times since I've been back.' She bit her lip. Tracy could talk, her mum had buggered off to Rhyl for a week, leaving her kids home alone with Markie. He had been thirteen and Jodie five months.

'So, how d'you hear about this place, Paul?' Tony said, making idle chit-chat. Leanne knew what he really wanted to ask was, 'How the hell did you hear about this place, Paul, and why, tonight, of all nights, are you here?'

'Write-up in the paper said it was pricey, so I thought, that's where I'm taking Tracy for some slap-up nosh.'

'Yeah, finally got his finger out of his arse and decided to bring me somewhere that's not a Berni Inn,' Tracy added.

'Could I take you to your table?' the waitress asked. Evidently she was anxious to seat them down. Then they might lower their voices.

'We'll sit here,' Tracy said. Leanne felt the colour drain from her face. 'Only joking!' Tracy chortled. 'Look at the chops on you! Look like you've seen a fucking ghost. We'll go over there, leave you two lovebirds to it.'

Leanne smiled tightly, and Paul rubbed his daughter's hair. 'Look at you, all grown up,' he said, then winked at Tony before he allowed himself to be ushered to his table.

'What does that mean?' Leanne whispered, through gritted teeth. 'He's seen me I don't know how many times since I've been back and he says, "All grown up." He's weird.'

Tony started to laugh.

'What?' she demanded.

'When did those two get back together? I thought they hated each other.'

'After the wedding.'

'Bloody hell. Chances of 'em coming in here tonight!'

'Chances?'

'It's not just bumping into them,' Tony muttered. 'I mean, no disrespect intended – but when have your mum and dad ever been to a place like this?'

'*Never* is probably the answer. Mum'll be asking them for scampi in a minute.' Tony sniggered. 'What you laughing at? I'm serious.' Leanne could hear Tracy asking for a bottle of their most expensive red wine. She rolled her eyes. 'Not the best, but the most expensive. That's her all over.'

'Has she robbed someone's benefit book?'

'No, surprisingly, she hasn't. Believe it or not, Dad's come into money.'

Paul had phoned Leanne to tell her. It was part of his campaign to get back into her good books because he'd been so contrary before she had left London.

He'd offered to take the family out to Maxwell's, a nightclub that no one other than Paul, it seemed, ever went to. Everyone had politely declined and Leanne had pointed out to her dad that his son owned the best nightclubs in Bradington, and if they were to go anywhere maybe they should go to one of them. 'When was the last time one of our Markie's clubs played "My Coo Ca Choo"?' Paul had asked.

'What?' Tony nearly jumped out of his seat.

'Horses or something. Hard to believe, eh? He went to book a holiday the other day and his card got refused so he promised Mum he'd make it up to her. Suppose this is part of him making it up.'

'How much?'

'Fifty grand, apparently.'

'He'll piss that away in no time if he's booking holidays and buying two-hundred-quid bottles of wine.'

Leanne nodded. 'You're probably right but I think he might actually be happy at the moment. God knows why because she treats him like dirt half the time, but he loves being with Mum.'

Tony leant forward. 'Shall we get this down us as quick as we can, then go somewhere we can be on our own?'

'Great idea,' Leanne said, her eyes twinkling.

*

Two hours later, Leanne and Tony were sitting in a small car park on the outskirts of Bradington. Below them stretched the city lights. 'It looks like the view from Mulholland Drive from up here.'

'I can only agree because I've seen the film, even if I couldn't make head nor tail of it. But Los Angeles it isn't.' Tony paused. 'You been to LA, Lee?'

'A few times.'

'Bloody hell.' Tony sounded embarrassed. 'I keep asking you daft stuff like that but what do I think you've been doing for the last seven or so years? Not sitting on your backside in Bradington like me. And it's not like all the pictures of you on some beach are just fake backgrounds. You're probably somewhere exotic, aren't you?'

'Was, Tony. That's in the past and now I'm just trying to get myself sorted.'

Tony leant across and, without a word, he kissed her and she responded – she didn't want to break away from him and wished it could last for ever.

chapter twenty-two

Lisa was in Steve C's London office, with Jay beside her. The receptionist, Liliana, was walking around outside singing a Polish lullaby to baby Blest.

'Right,' Steve said. 'Before they get here, is there anything else I need to know?'

'It's all there, I swear,' Jay said. Lisa threw him a poisonous look.

Jay had been asked to list every indiscretion he had had, from the cloakroom attendant at the 101 Club in Hale to the A-list movie star who had been in Italy promoting her latest film.

'You're a fucking dick, Jay,' Lisa said, fighting tears. 'Why can't you keep your cock in your pants?'

'I'm sorry,' Jay said pathetically.

'So these *women* are all you need to tell me about?' Steve asked.

'What d'you say "women" like that for?' Jay snapped defensively.

Steve leant forward in his leather chair, propped his elbows on the desk and steepled his fingers. He was quite good-looking in a Daniel Craig sort of way, Lisa thought. If he'd only smile a bit more. Not that either she or Jay gave him a lot to smile about.

'Well …' Steve began slowly. 'The thing is, Jay, I've heard a few rumours on the grapevine, and, as it's my job to hear rumours on the grapevine about you two, I listened. A little bird tells me you might be having a little bat for the other side.'

Lisa threw up into her handbag. Steve grabbed some tissues from his desk and handed them to her. She spat into them, then screamed at the top of her lungs, 'Is that what you were up to on the plane?'

'This is disgusting! I can't believe you're listening to that rubbish!' Jay said indignantly.

'Well, were you? That trolley dolly on the flight from Thailand? The one who was smiling at you? What happened there, Jay?'

'Nothing! Nothing at all! I swear to God!'

'You always swear to God and then what happens? I find out you've been with someone else,' Lisa said. She thrust her handbag, full of sick, at her husband. 'I'm going.'

'Where you off?'

'To sort my face out. Where else?'

*

Lisa looked in the toilet mirror at her tear-stained face. She felt old. She opened her bottomless pit of a makeup bag, took out her Touche Eclat and her bronzer, then set about making herself look normal. But she couldn't remember what normal was.

When she had been at school she had been naturally pretty. She wasn't big, just a size ten, but over the years she had shrunk to size eight and, in times of stress, to a bony size six. She knew that clothes hung better on her when she was smaller but she would never admit this to the press. She often said she was so tiny because she had a high metabolism, but that was rubbish. She ate less than a thousand calories a day and *that* was why she was tiny. Nobody batted an eyelid about her size, though. So many celebrities were dieting themselves into non-existence. What Lisa would give to have a day in Greggs going through the cakes! But she couldn't. Her image was sacrosanct and she had to maintain it at all costs. At times like this she wondered if it was worth it.

She checked her reflection one last time and then made her way back to Steve's office.

'I'm not gay!' Jay said, as soon as she came through the door.

'I don't think you are, Jason.' She only ever called him Jason when he was really in trouble. 'But you can't stop thinking of new and more ridiculous places to stick your dick.' Steve winced. 'And seeing as you've not gone down the man route yet, as far as I'm aware, you've probably just thought, Fuck it, why not? Am I right?' She glared at him, demanding an answer.

'That's your problem, Lisa. You always think you're right, that you've got everything sewn up. Well, you're talking bollocks,' Jay declared.

'Listen to me, you shit. I've put up with your lies

and your cheating for years because I truly believe – believed,' she corrected herself, 'that we were meant to be together, but at this moment in time, I feel like throwing in the towel.'

'Woo! Lisa, come on,' Steve said. 'I'm sorry I asked that but I need to know all the facts. I'm sick of being hit from left-field by some stupid story about your extra-maritals, Jay. It makes us all look like dicks.'

'Well, I'm not gay, that's for sure,' Jay said, folding his arms, his eyes glassy with tears.

'Oh, don't start fucking booing as well, Jay. We can do without that,' said Lisa.

'You're the one who's just puked in a handbag and flounced off to the toilets. Jesus!'

'Right!' Steve shouted. 'Time out. Jay? There's no substance to these rumours?'

'None whatsoever.'

'Lisa, you're in the paper on Sunday talking about how solid your marriage is. Last thing you or anyone else needs is you storming out the door right now.'

Lisa nodded. He was right.

'So here's what we do. You need to sort your heads out. Go home, talk to each other. Sunday, you'll look lovely in the paper and that nanny of yours with her week-old news will be tomorrow's chip paper, yeah?'

'What if she says something really bad about us?' Jay asked.

'Lisa's tackled anything we think she might say. We've got editorial control on it, so we're fine. They can't print anything I've not signed off first.' Lisa had even answered questions on Leanne, saying only that she wished the girl well and she was sure that Leanne was as fed up as she and Jay were with the rumours that dogged her.

'Listen, Jay, when this goes in the paper tomorrow, people'll like us again, I'm fairly sure of it. Aren't you, Steve?'

Steve nodded. 'Lisa's done a great job.' He paused for a moment. 'But you, Jay, have got to sort yourself out. There's only so long the great British public will put up with your shit and your denials. And when they turn, you don't want to be on the receiving end.'

'What they going to do? Stone me in the street?' he asked petulantly.

'No. They'll just dislike you, and that means they'll want feeding stories about what a twat you are and the papers will be only too glad to dish them up. And you know as well as I do, Jay, that those stories are easier to find than the ones about you being a good little boy.'

Lisa stared at her husband. He couldn't meet her eye. 'Well, thanks as always, Steve. Hopefully, Jay, you might learn to keep it in your pants and we won't have to go through all this every three months.' She stood up and shook Steve's hand.

His grip was firm and strong and Lisa knew he was the only person in the world who understood what she was going through because her useless lump of a husband certainly didn't. He just thought the entire world was conspiring against him.

Jay shook Steve's hand limply and shuffled out of the room.

Once they were alone in the foyer, waiting for their driver to pick them up, Jay said, 'Lise.'

'What?'

'I think I might be a sex addict.'

Lisa looked him up and down contemptuously. '*I think you might be a dick.*' She didn't give Jay a chance to answer, just turned her back and called the driver to find out what was keeping him.

*

Wine glass in hand, Karina gazed at the six-page tabloid exclusive on Jay and Lisa Leighton's nanny while Izzy played on the floor in front of her. In the first picture the woman was mumsy-looking, the sort you'd entrust with your kids. She didn't seem the type to hot-foot it to the nearest rag. And what exactly was the story? Karina wondered. The six pages were filled with a lot of pictures of the Leightons, a few of the nanny, Jeanine, in the customary wronged-woman pose, and the rest was just bits of claims she was making.

She had alleged that Lisa had seen Leanne to try to silence her in case she had any bright ideas about going to the papers herself to put paid to the rumours about Jay's extra-marital affairs.

Karina couldn't believe her sister had met Lisa and not said anything. How could she keep something so juicy to herself? She'd always been like that, Karina thought, peeved. Always made out she was better than everyone else, not one to stoop to gossip. Karina couldn't believe her sister had never read *Heat* or followed a *Closer* diet. Too busy living the dream instead of reading about it.

The other rag in front of Karina contained the scoop of the year: Lisa Leighton speaking out about her marriage. There she was, arguably the most famous woman in Britain, talking about her life and mentioning Karina's sister. 'I wish Leanne Crompton all the best, I really do. I believe she's a very nice young woman, but any rumours surrounding her little girl are malicious and haven't come from myself, Jay or Leanne. It's just people wanting to make money out of our lives.'

Karina sat for a moment and wondered how much people actually made from these stories. She and Jodie had always known that their mum made a few pence out of 'exclusives' she dropped to the weekly gossip magazines. She never gave them anything truly revealing, just something about Leanne's latest trip to Bradington or her new haircut. Imagine if you had some real gossip, something more than this Jeanine had, with her six-page spread, or even Lisa Leighton herself. There was probably a small fortune to be had, Karina thought.

As she threw back her wine and helped herself to more, Gaz came in. He had been working till five that morning and had just got out of bed. 'You on the booze already?'

'It's Sunday,' Karina reminded him.

'"It's Sunday,"' Gaz mimicked. '"It's the weekend." "It's the Queen's birthday." Any bloody excuse.'

'All right, fucking hell! And what were you drinking last night? Mineral water? I don't think so.' Karina hated it when Gaz got snippy with her. She deserved a glass of wine when she wanted one – after all, she stayed at home and looked after their kid while he was out working in knocking shops and lap-dancing bars. Other girlfriends would have put their foot down, but not Karina. She saw herself as Girlfriend of the Year and thought Gaz should too.

'Who brings the money in round here – and the coke? Me,' Gaz said.

'Well, big fucking deal,' Karina retorted. 'For your information, I'm going to be earning something this month too, so stop whingeing.' She folded the papers and put them under the settee. She hated it when Gaz made out he was the sole breadwinner while she just sat in the flat enjoying the spoils.

'You been selling your dirty knickers on eBay again?'

Karina threw a cushion at him. 'You cheeky bastard,' she said indignantly. 'I haven't done that since Izzy was born.'

'So where's the money coming from?' Gaz asked.

Karina tapped her nose. 'Never you mind. Let's just say I have ways and means.'

chapter twenty-three

Jodie was standing behind the bar of the Beacon watching Brian Cooper, Bolingbroke's worst drunk (and he had his fair share of competition), lurch from side to side on 'his' bar stool. 'Down at the Old Bull and Bush, da da da da da ...' he sang tunelessly.

'Give me strength,' Jodie muttered.

'What's up wi' you?' Brian asked, switching to accusatory-psycho mode.

'Nothing's up with me, Brian. I just hope to God that one day, very soon, I won't have to hear "Down at the Old Bull and Bush" again.'

'You know what's up wi' young uns like you, these days?'

'We're not as pissed as you?'

'Oi, mouth! I could have you sacked,' Brian said, pushing his big red head across the bar in Jodie's direction.

Jodie took the empty pint glass from him. 'Yeah, you've got a lot of sway round these parts.'

'I bloody have!' Brian said, jumping up off his stool. 'Too right. Where's Val?'

Jodie looked at her watch. It was a quarter past two.

'She's not back till four, so you'll have to wait for her to sack me then.' By which time you'll be on your back under a table and will have forgotten this conversation, she thought.

'Val knows a good tune when she hears one, not like you, you bloody upstart. "We're on the one road, singing the one song, we're on the road to God knows where …"' He was off again.

'Hear, hear to that,' Jodie said wryly.

'See? You liked that one,' Brian said, breaking off briefly, then launching into another.

Jodie popped his glass into the dishwasher and looked round the bar. There was an old couple in the corner. He was hunched over a pint of mild and a Sudoku book and she was sipping a Gold Label and staring into space. If that's me in fifty years' time, Jodie thought, then someone please shoot me.

She wiped down the bar as Brian continued to sing. When the door opened, she glanced up to see which exciting daytime clientele were darkening her doors. It was Leanne. 'Save me!' Jodie shouted.

Brian stopped singing and Leanne laughed. 'Well, as you mention saving you …'

'What?' Jodie threw down the cloth. 'Tell me!'

'Victoria wants to meet you.'

Jodie's jaw hit the drip trays. 'Oh, my God! Get me out of here!' she squealed. She was so excited that she vaulted the bar and flung her arms round her sister.

'Bloody hell! Chill your boots!' Brian said, but Jodie continued to scream with excitement.

Leanne hugged her back. When Jodie pulled away from her, Brian was leering at them. 'Now, that's what I'm talking about!' he said, as if he was impersonating Sammy Davis Jr. 'Bit of hot girl-on-girl action.'

'Right!' Jodie said, in stand-in landlady mode. 'You, out.'

Brian was about to protest but then, seeing she meant business, thought better of it. He lurched off his stool and headed for the door. 'I'm going to tell Val,' he said.

'Oh, boo-hoo!' Jodie sneered as he huffed his way out. 'Come on, then – tell me what'll happen,' she squeaked to Leanne, as the door closed behind him.

'Well, we'll go to London and you can meet the page-three people and they'll get some professional shots of you done. If they like what they see they'll give you a page-three slot. Then they have to attract public interest so they might pit you against two other girls and do one of those daft high-street-honey things. I think that would work in your favour. You've got a great personality.'

'You mean I'm mouthy?' Jodie asked.

'Call it what you want. Anyway, I can't wait for them to see you. I think they'll snap you up.'

Jodie was thrilled to the marrow. She didn't usually have good luck – she didn't usually have any luck. She worked in the crappy Beacon, lived with her wayward mother and generally just got on with it. Things like this didn't happen to people like her.

'My only advice is to be polite to everyone, no matter what. No one likes a diva.'

'Oh, yeah, and I'm *such* a diva,' Jodie said sarcastically.

'I'll book the train tickets. Will you be able to get time off work?'

Jodie arched an eyebrow. 'No, probably not. I'll have to stay here and look after George and Mildred in the corner. Duh! I'll be there with bloody knobs on.'

'Great,' Leanne said. 'I'll call later when I've arranged times.' She gave Jodie a quick kiss and disappeared.

Jodie's world had changed totally, but the Sudoku man was still ignoring his staring-into-space wife – Jodie wanted to go over and push her to find out if she was stuffed. She peered out of the window. There weren't hordes of marauding punters battling their way up the hill to the Beacon. She could pop to the loo for five minutes.

The toilets at the Beacon were a real treat. Years ago Val had stopped bothering about the graffiti and, strangely, this had led to some interesting, thoughtful reflections rather than the usual 'Baz was 'ere, 04'. Jodie gazed into the mirror. Her nose always seemed out of proportion to the rest of her face. She turned sideways and ran a hand over her non-existent stomach, then ran into a cubicle and stuffed her fingers down her throat. She threw up her breakfast, which, as ever, had been an apple.

Jodie threw up every day. And she never ate more

than twelve hundred calories in twenty-four hours. But some days she found herself throwing up more than others and she knew that today would be one of them. When she did it, she felt elated. It was the one small thing in her life that she had firmly under her control.

She turned back to the mirror, stuck out her belly and stroked it. Once more, she thought, and went back into the toilet. She shoved her fingers down her throat, but this time nothing happened. Jodie was empty. She felt pleased with herself. She washed her hands and went back to the bar. She knew she wouldn't make herself sick for ever. One day she'd start eating healthily, she was sure, but she didn't have time for all that at the moment.

She often made herself little promises about not throwing up and becoming healthy one day. That way she didn't have to acknowledge the shame that crept in after the elation every time she did it.

*

Leanne had finished work and was sitting on a park bench as Kia fed the ducks. Suddenly she realised that Tony was walking towards her. She waved awkwardly. She knew he was nervous. He had seen Kia only briefly at Markie's wedding and had told Leanne he wanted to make a really good impression on her little girl.

'Kia, come here, darling,' Leanne said. 'I've got a friend I'd like you to meet.' The little girl left the ducks and climbed on the bench beside her.

'Hi,' Tony said, sitting down with them.

'This is Tony.'

'Hi, Tony,' Kia said.

'Hi, Kia. How are you?'

'I'm good. I'm feeding the ducks.'

'Want some help?' Tony asked.

'Have you brought any bread?' Kia asked.

Tony produced a plastic bag from his back pocket. 'Never go anywhere without it.'

'Good. Because birds really like it and people forget that sometimes,' Kia told him.

'Bird woman of Alcatraz.' Leanne laughed.

'What does that mean?' Kia asked.

'It means you know a lot about birds,' Tony said.

'Come on, Tony,' Kia said, 'and I'll show you what to do.'

Tony winked at Leanne and walked with Kia to the water's edge. He crouched so that he was at the same height as Kia, then began to rip pieces off a stale loaf and throw them into the water. When all of his bread and Kia's was gone, they came back to Leanne.

'He's good at feeding ducks, Mummy.'

'Is he?' Leanne ruffled her daughter's hair. 'Well, that's good. Shall we go and get an ice-cream?'

'Yeeees!'

Leanne and Tony stood up and the three set off for the ice-cream van, Kia running ahead.

'She's a sweet little girl,' Tony remarked.

'She is,' Leanne agreed. Since Lisa Leighton had reared her not-so-ugly head, Leanne had thought more about Jay and the role he didn't play in his daughter's life. It wasn't that she wanted him there. It was just that he was always in the papers or on the TV. There was no escape from him. Most women who were foolish enough to fall for a married man's chat and end up pregnant didn't have to face him on a weekly basis once they had decided never to see him again, but Jay was everywhere.

Over the past few weeks Leanne had wondered whether it was a good idea to introduce Kia to Tony. She knew how aware Kia was that other people had a daddy and she didn't, but she didn't want Tony to become a father figure to her only for him to disappear out of her life as quickly as he had entered it. But she and Tony had been getting on so well that she had run out of reasons not to let him meet her. And from the early signs she was glad now that she had. It would do Kia good to see her mum with a man. She was too used to having Leanne to herself.

Tony approached the ice-cream van and put out his hand for Kia to hold. She took it. Leanne was amazed – her daughter was usually standoffish with new people. All those don't-talk-to-strangers lectures had made an impact on her, but she was relaxed with Tony.

'What do you fancy, Kia?' he asked.

'Strawberry ice-cream, please.'

Tony ordered three then handed one to Kia, one to Leanne, keeping the last for himself. 'Want some raspberry syrup?'

'Yes, please!' Kia carolled.

Tony squirted on far too much, and Leanne raised an eyebrow.

'More! More!' Kia squealed.

'I think that's probably enough,' Tony said, and handed the bottle back to the ice-cream man.

'Your teeth will fall out,' Leanne said, with mock-reproach. 'And what do you say?'

'Thank you, Tony.'

'No problem.'

As Kia concentrated on her ice-cream, Tony said, 'I bought these because I'm celebrating.'

'What?' Leanne asked, eager to know.

'I've got a job.'

'Oh, that's great news.' She was genuinely pleased for him. After he and Markie had fallen out, Tony had found that no one in Bradington would employ him as a doorman because they knew Markie would have something to say about it.

'Yeah. I'm working for a construction firm in Manchester, heading up their security.'

'Congratulations!'

'Well, it's a lot of sitting around and dealing with jobsworths but I don't mind. It's money, and that's all I'm bothered about.'

Leanne threw her arms round his neck and kissed his cheek.

Kia screwed up her face, looking more than a little perplexed. 'What are you doing, Mummy? Is Tony your boyfriend?'

Leanne glanced at Tony, then back at her daughter.

'Yes, I think he is,' she said, smiling. Just then a flash went off beside her and she whirled round. A photographer with a long-range lens was snapping pictures of them as he straddled his moped.

Tony marched over to him, but Leanne shouted, 'Leave it, Tony. They're not worth it.'

'What's your problem, mate?' Tony growled.

'Only doing my job,' the photographer replied.

'Well, why don't you piss off and do it somewhere else?' Tony suggested menacingly. Leanne grabbed Kia and walked away.

The photographer bypassed Tony and drove in front of Leanne, still snapping.

Tony ran after him but this time it was Leanne who lost the plot. 'What the hell do you think you're doing?' she asked, pointing a finger at the man. 'I'm trying to have a walk in the park. Is that against the law?'

'No.' The paparazzo snapped away.

'Leave. Us. Alone!' Leanne yelled. He kept taking pictures. Kia dropped her ice-cream and burst into tears. 'Now look what you've done,' Leanne complained.

Tony ran towards the photographer, who slung his camera over his shoulder and twisted the throttle on his bike. 'If I see you again, I'll have you!' Tony shouted.

'I'm sorry,' Leanne said, as the photographer sped off. 'That hasn't happened for ages.'

'I can't believe it happens at all,' Tony said angrily.

Kia was still crying. 'I didn't like that man.'

'Neither did I, darling,' Leanne said, exchanging a glance with Tony, who, she could see, was trying to keep a lid on his anger for Kia's benefit.

*

Markie was sitting at his desk, boiling with rage. He had been there since seven that morning, but he wasn't going to call Leanne. He'd have it out with her face-to-face as soon as she came into the office.

The door opened and Leanne walked in. She didn't look at Markie's desk, as she was usually first in the office. Then she turned – and nearly jumped out of her skin. Her hand flew to her heart. 'Jesus Christ, Markie!'

Markie threw the tabloid paper at her. 'What the fuck is that?' he asked.

Leanne stared at the picture. She looked up at him, then back at the paper. 'Another Married Man For Leanne,' the headline screamed.

'I feel sick,' she said.

'Not as fucking sick as I do,' Markie said. The picture showed his sister embracing Tony O'Brien, with Kia, utterly bemused, beside them. 'Tony?' he said. 'What the fuck are you, of all people, doing with Tony?'

'We went for a walk. I like him.'

'So it's not enough that you two are talking behind my back at the wedding, you have to hook up with him afterwards. He's no one to you, just an ex-mate of mine who used to work for me. You can go out walking in the park with anyone you want – but, no, you have to make things difficult and go with Tony. I'm beginning to think you have fuck-all sense of loyalty.'

Leanne's eyes flashed. 'That's utter bollocks and you know it. I'm as loyal to you as the day is long. But I like Tony and I happen to think you've treated him like shit.'

'Really? Well, thanks for the lecture but you can get home and sort your head out.' Markie had had enough for one day.

'What?'

'You heard. Go home. Have the rest of the week off. Sort your head out about Tony and come back to work when you've kicked him into touch and you're not making a show of yourself.'

Leanne grabbed her bag. 'You're the one making a show of yourself, shouting the odds, telling people who they can and can't see. Who do you think you are, Markie? God?'

'I'm your brother and your new boss, so get home and don't come back until your head's screwed on right.'

Leanne fled and Markie remained seated, staring after her. What the bloody hell was she thinking? A soft arse like Tony? He rolled the newspaper into a ball and stuffed it into the bin. When he found Tony he'd let him know exactly what he thought.

*

Leanne was sitting in her car, parked outside a new housing development in Manchester, wearing shades and hoping to God that no more photographers were lurking about. She had driven there erratically from the office, feeling sick and angry that her not-very-interesting private life had been dragged once again through the papers.

Tony came out to her. When he saw she had been crying he marched around to check that no one was watching, then jumped into the passenger seat. 'I saw it this morning when I got in. The lads have been ripping into me ...'

'I'm sorry you've got involved,' Leanne said.

'Eh? Come here. I'm big enough and ugly enough to look after myself. I'm only bothered about you.'

'Everyone's going to think I'm some sort of marriage wrecker.'

'Listen, no one's going to think that. Monica's gone off her head,' he said, referring to his 'wife', 'but that's just tough shit. She was getting on my nerves anyway, cluttering up my flat.'

'I bet she wants to kill me.'

'Will you stop stressing about her? She was a very savvy girl. She'd saved up a pot of money and was always moaning that she hated England and couldn't wait to get back to Russia.'

Leanne didn't feel any better for Tony's reassurances.

'I don't like you having to read that crap about yourself,' Tony went on.

'All I'm bothered about is Markie.' She wondered if she should have said that, considering the bad blood between Tony and her brother.

'What's it got to do with him?'

'He's just told me to go home and sort my head out. He thinks we've started seeing each other to kick him when he's down.'

Tony exploded. 'Fuck him! What's he got to gripe about? His life's fucking hunky-dory. Me and you have never done anything but bend over for your Markie, so we don't upset him, so he doesn't get pissed off, and for what? So he can upset you and sack you? So that I'm not allowed in a three-mile radius of a Bradington club? Well, fuck him. I'm fed up with worrying about what Markie thinks, because he sure as shit doesn't care what I think.'

Leanne was worried – Tony was really angry. 'What are you going to do?'

'I'm going to tell Markie to stop taking the piss out of me.'

Leanne grabbed his arm. 'Please don't. Not today. Can we have a couple of days to cool off and think about it? If you do that and anything happens, some paper will make a story out of it and I'll end up as the home-wrecking psycho.'

Tony leant back against the head-rest. 'OK, Leanne, but only a couple of days. If I still feel like this at the end of the week I'll go to see Markie, have it out once and for all. I don't want him thinking he can run our lives for ever.'

Leanne kissed him. 'Neither do I,' she said.

As Tony walked away from the car, Leanne felt relieved. Even though she knew that a considerable percentage of the country was waking up to the story of her latest fling, she had never seen Tony like that. He had always been so careful to keep quiet where Markie was concerned. Not that Leanne wanted an all-out fight in the street, far from it, but she wanted to see Tony stand up for himself and for what he believed in. Because as much as Markie was her brother and she loved him, she knew he was a bully and always got away with it.

chapter twenty-four

Leanne had decided not to waste the week moping in front of the TV, wondering if Markie would call and tell her he'd made a mistake. She knew it wouldn't happen.

She had booked herself and Jodie onto a train to London the following morning after Kia had gone to school. She had asked for her mother to pick the little girl up afterwards. Tracy was acting as if she'd been asked to look after Kia's entire class for a month.

Leanne was in the spare room she and Kia were sharing, sorting out what to wear the next day, and Kia was downstairs watching TV. It was great that they could stay here for the time being but she knew it was time she and Kia moved on. Finding the deposit for somewhere half decent was the sticking-point. She didn't want to ask anyone for it and she didn't have anywhere near the thousand pounds she needed. Leanne berated herself yet again. That amount had come and gone many times when she'd lived in London. She'd never thought about money when she'd had it, which was why she didn't have any now. She'd spent it all.

The door flew open and Tracy stuck her head in. 'You've got a visitor,' she snapped.

'Hi,' Charly said.

'Hi,' Leanne replied.

Tracy stood in the doorway, waiting to hear what the woman who'd got her claws into her son wanted with her daughter.

Charly looked at Tracy. Tracy stared back. 'Don't give me that you're-dismissed look in my own house. You're lucky I let you in without our Scott with you.'

'Mum!' Leanne remonstrated.

'Bloody hell.' Tracy stomped off down the stairs.

'Sorry about that. How are you?' Leanne asked. She knew Charly must be there for a reason because they didn't catch up on a social level. She was Scott's girlfriend and that was that.

'I'm good,' Charly said. 'Listen, Leanne, tell me if I've got completely the wrong end of the stick but Scott was saying you're representing Jodie for page-three stuff.'

Leanne wasn't sure how Scott had heard about it but probably from Jodie. She nodded. 'That's right. Why?'

'Well ...' Charly began, then looked at the floor as if she was unsure what to say next. 'I was wondering if you'd think about taking me on.' She flushed.

Leanne was surprised. Charly was usually so self-assured, and she'd never thought for a moment that she would be interested in modelling – Charly liked lording it around Bradington. Suddenly, though, it made sense. And, looking at her now, Leanne thought she'd be perfect. Charly had an innate confidence in herself – so much so that she wasn't scared of Tracy, even though Tracy had made it known to everyone that she couldn't stand the girl. She was pretty and cocky, a good combination.

Leanne had never mastered cocky. Her look was more wide-eyed or smiley, but the girls who pulled off cocky got the sexier bookings.

'I'd be delighted to,' Leanne said.

'Really?' Charly asked, sounding genuinely shocked. 'I thought I might need a boob job first.'

'Don't do that. Natural's big at the moment. Anyway, that's way off. I'd have to take a couple of pictures of you.'

'Well, er, Scott took some. I don't know if they're good enough though.' Charly produced them from her bag.

'Bloody hell – you've come prepared!' Leanne exclaimed. Charly smiled, and Leanne was willing to bet that she'd run Scott ragged trying to get the perfect picture.

'He got a new camera specially,' Charly added proudly.

The pictures were a bit readers'-wives, and Leanne felt a little embarrassed to look at them, but once she'd got past that, she saw that Charly knew how to work the camera. She sorted through the pictures and handed back the ones in which Scott had been concentrating on her breasts. 'I'm going to London tomorrow with Jodie so I'll take these with me and see what they think.'

'Really?'

'I can't guarantee anything, but you look good, so we'll see.' One thing she had learnt from years of having Jenny as a manager was not to promise too much. It only came back to bite you. Let people be pleasantly surprised by the outcome rather than banking on it.

Charly kissed her. 'You're a star! I owe you big-time for this, Leanne.'

'Just buy me a drink, yeah?' Leanne was glad to be of service.

*

The next morning, Leanne and Jodie were running through Manchester Piccadilly to make the eight forty-five train. They jumped on at eight forty-four. Leanne had completely misjudged the rush-hour traffic.

'Jesus!' Jodie plonked herself down next to a businessman, who obviously wasn't in the mood for being interrupted. He rustled his newspaper and threw her a look of disdain. 'I'm sorry, are we bothering you?' she asked.

'No, not at all.'

'Good,' Jodie said, and made herself comfortable.

Leanne giggled. Jodie was a law unto herself, especially when she was out of Bradington. It was as if she'd been given a new lease on life.

The businessman got up. 'Would you two like to sit next to each other?'

'Too right. Thanks,' Jodie said, smiling at him. He ran off down the train like a startled rabbit as they pulled out of the station.

'Get in here, then,' Jodie said.

As Leanne was sitting down a voice behind them said, 'That's that slag.'

Leanne's blood ran cold.

'That Leanne thingy.'

Leanne wanted to be sick, she wanted to run off the train, but most of all she wanted Jodie not to have heard.

Too late. Jodie was out of her seat and staring at the woman and her friend. 'What did you just say?'

'I didn't say anything to you.'

'That's not what I asked. What did you just say?' Jodie repeated.

From where Leanne was sitting she could only see Jodie's legs and stomach, but she guessed her sister's head was waggling from side to side and her finger jabbing in the air.

'I was just saying that the woman sitting next to you is a slag.' The words hung in the air. Then Jodie grabbed the woman by the scruff of the neck.

'Get off me!' she screamed. Her friend pressed the emergency button and the train ground to a halt as Jodie whacked the offender.

Leanne was on her feet now, trying to drag her sister off, as the train manager piled towards them.

'Look, I'm sorry, there's been a misunderstanding,' Leanne said. They were drawing disapproving stares from the entire carriage. The train manager gave her the double-look to which she was accustomed. The first look is the look anyone would receive in such circumstances, the second is the look of recognition.

'She attacked me!' the woman screamed.

'You were being a bitch about my sister,' Jodie said.

'She was goading her,' a weary passenger said from behind.

'Could you come with me, please?' the train manager said to Leanne and Jodie.

Brilliant, Leanne thought. I've just been called a slag, everyone's staring at me and, to top it all, we're about to be slung off the train.

'That's right. Chuck 'em off,' the woman shouted.

'I'll be back to ask you and your friend some questions once the train is moving again.'

As Leanne and Jodie walked quickly along the carriage, Leanne's head bowed, Jodie's held aloft – so that if anyone else wanted to chip in she could put them back in their box – Leanne knew they would be unceremoniously ejected at the next station. They would miss their meeting and she'd have to strangle Jodie for sabotaging their chances. They walked through two more carriages to first class.

'Here you are, ladies. You shouldn't have any more bother,' the train manager said, pointing at an empty table.

'We can sit in here?' Leanne was dumbfounded.

216

'Course you can. Someone will be along in a while to get you some breakfast and a drink.'

'Yeees! Check it out,' Jodie said gleefully.

'Thank you,' Leanne said.

He smiled. 'No problem, Ms Crompton. Might be along in a bit for your autograph, though, if you don't mind. My son thinks you're great.'

'No problem.' Leanne beamed. He smiled back shyly, then walked away.

'Son? Get lost! It's for him,' Jodie said.

Once the man was out of earshot Leanne said, 'Right. Rule number one.' Jodie looked at her to see if she was joking. Leanne was never usually stern with her. 'You need to keep that –' She pointed at Jodie's mouth '– buttoned. Another train manager would have slung us off.'

'But she was calling you a slag! I was sticking up for you!'

'Well, let me fight my own battles. You need to keep a low profile for the time being. Rule number two, be polite to everyone.'

'I know, I know. You've already said.'

'Well, do it, then.'

'OK,' Jodie said. 'Is there a number three?'

'Yes. If you start to get some decent work, and I'm not promising anything, you've got to save some money.'

'Boring!' Jodie said, leafing through the free paper in front of her.

The train jerked into life.

'Well, it might be, but the alternative is that you end up working for Markie and living at Mum's when you could have your own place and a nice little nest egg.'

'Right. I'll do whatever you tell me.'

Leanne assessed her sister, sure she had only agreed for the sake of an easy life. 'I know you will, because I'm your manager,' she said, and pulled the breakfast menu towards her.

*

The train drew into Euston station at ten past eleven, which gave them plenty of time to get to Canary Wharf for half past twelve.

'I need the loo,' Jodie said.

'You've been about seven times on the train,' Leanne said, gazing around to check that the woman who had caused the altercation wasn't nearby. It felt weird to be back in London, but she had a purpose, which made her less anxious than she might otherwise have been.

'Weak bladder.' Jodie marched off to find the toilet. Leanne put her twenty-pence piece in the slot and then went through the barrier.

'Twenty pence for a pee. Cheek,' Jodie said.

Leanne walked to the mirror and checked her reflection. She prodded the non-existent bags under her eyes and applied some bronzer to her cheeks. She was pulling a brush through her ponytail when she heard retching from Jodie's cubicle. The flush went on a number of toilets at the same time, drowning the noise. 'Jode, you all right?'

'Fine,' Jodie said chirpily. 'Why?' She opened the door and came out, smiling.

'Thought I heard someone being sick,' Leanne whispered.

'Well, it wasn't me.'

As Leanne was zipping up her makeup case, Jodie grabbed an eyeliner and a lip gloss. 'What?' Jodie said, in response to Leanne's mock-annoyance face. 'I need to look my best, don't I?' She applied the eyeliner, replaced the lid and turned to the side. 'Thank God smock tops are in. I look preggers.'

Leanne dragged her away from the mirror. 'You look like a stick with boobs. Now, come on.'

*

Karina couldn't believe that those two had gone to London for a big glamorous day out and left her in Bradington. They hadn't even invited her. It was their loss, the silly cows, she thought. She'd have treated them if they had. She'd just come into a bit of cash and was up for a spending spree. She'd parcelled Izzy off to Gaz's mum's and was on the bus to Manchester, ready to hit the shops.

It was ages since Karina had had any money of her own. Gaz usually gave her house-keeping every week and she had what she claimed on the social, but a good whack of money, five grand to be precise – she'd never had so much that she'd acquired herself.

First stop was the Arndale Centre, where she'd buy herself some new clothes. Then she was going to Pizza Hut for a slap-up all-you-can-eat lunch, and then to Harvey Nicks for a couple of glasses of champagne to celebrate her windfall. Then, Karina thought, she might have a look at a few tops for Gaz and some bits for Izzy.

She loved coming into Manchester. It made her feel important. She wasn't sure why, probably the coke she'd had this morning, but the city gave her a swagger she didn't have in Bradington. Manchester was as cool as Karina, or so, at least, she thought.

She wandered into Topshop and looked around, not knowing where to start. The cash was burning a hole in her pocket and she wanted to spend, spend, spend.

*

Leanne was sitting at the side of the studio watching Jodie take instruction from the photographer. Leanne hadn't liked Canary Wharf when she had started modelling. It had always seemed a soulless outpost with lots of people walking around at speed with brief-cases, too busy to stop and talk to one another. But over the last five years buildings had sprung up thick and fast and it had taken on a life of its own. The sun was shining and as it reflected off the water and the surrounding buildings the area looked extremely impressive.

'She's good,' Victoria Haim whispered to Leanne. The editor of a newspaper wouldn't usually hang round a photo shoot for a potential page-three girl, but she had come to see Leanne. 'Fancy a quick coffee?' As good as Jodie was, there was only so much time that they could spend watching her pout and preen.

There was a coffee shop at the foot of the building. Leanne and Victoria sat outside in the sunshine. 'So, how's life treating you?' Victoria asked.

'OK,' Leanne said. She really liked Victoria but she wasn't about to show a load of ankle and say, 'I've been living in my mum's box room wishing I'd not frittered away every penny I've ever earned'. 'Good, actually. I'm really enjoying helping Jodie do this, and it's nice to get back to my roots – at the risk of sounding like a div.' She laughed.

Victoria ran her fingers through her mane of curly black hair. 'You don't sound like a div. I sometimes wish I could run for the hills.'

'How's work for you?'

'Oh, you know, meetings with the Prime Minister one day, Heather Mills the next.'

'Really?' Leanne was surprised.

'Yeah. This job involves a lot of high-level schmoozing.'

They used to have a real laugh together when Victoria was a gossip columnist, Leanne remembered, pulling apart the wannabes that clamoured for Victoria's attention. Yet now she had one of the most powerful jobs in the country and Leanne couldn't even hack it doing the filing for her brother.

'Victoria,' Leanne said, 'can I be honest with you?'

'Course you can.'

'Well, I think there's a lot of girls, like our Jodie, who end up doing promotions in seedy nightclubs because they'd never think to get a manager to guide them through their career. Now, I'm not saying I know anything about contracts and that stuff, but I know what the pitfalls are, and I have all of the contacts …' Leanne trailed off. 'God, I suppose what I'm trying to say is that I think I'd be good at looking after models, bringing them through the ranks, reining them in when they're acting up, advising them when they're blowing their money, pointing them in the right direction. All of the things that no one did for me. Not that I'm slagging off Jenny …' she added hastily.

'You'd be well within your rights to do exactly that. From what I've heard she treats people like cattle.'

It was true. 'Well, I just wanted to know if you think I'm barking up the wrong tree.'

Victoria put her hand on Leanne's knee. 'If you can get someone to do the contracts for you, you'll fly. You've got a natural humility that goes a long way in this business as there's so little of it about.'

'You really think so?'

'Of course! Let me have a think who I can put you in touch with for the contracts. As for the modelling, we need girls like Jodie. Give the white-van man something to look at in the morning.'

'I've been trying to read up on contracts, but I don't think it's really me.'

'Leanne, people train for years in contract law. You just worry about supplying good models.'

Leanne rummaged in her bag. 'Talking of which, I was going to see Gavin about this.' Gavin was head of new model talent for the *Globe*. 'But what do you think of her?'

'She's good too. Very pretty.'

'She's my brother's girlfriend.' Leanne thought she might need to cast her net a bit further than her immediate family in her hunt for clients.

'Must be something in the water up there in Bradington.'

'Yeah. Lead,' Leanne said.

Victoria laughed. 'We get a lot of girls who haven't got a manager. Usually we send them a polite thanks-but-no-thanks letter. It's easier to deal with the ones who are represented. But I could get Gavin to send you details of girls we get through on the proviso that we'd always be your first port of call.'

'Of course you would.' Leanne was excited.

'So,' Victoria said, 'Lisa Leighton. Any truth in the rumour that she came to visit you?'

Once a hack always a hack, Leanne thought. She couldn't blame Victoria for trying. After all, she was the editor of a tabloid. Not that Leanne was going to tell her anything, even off the record.

'None.' She shook her head.

'And do you think, purely from the perspective of someone who's met him a few times …'

'I've seen him out and about, I haven't met him,' Leanne said, her tabloid radar on high alert.

'As someone who's seen him out a few times, do you think there's any truth in the rumour that Jay Leighton is gay?' Victoria let the words hang in the air, studying Leanne's face.

Leanne was flummoxed. 'Jay Leighton? I wouldn't have thought so. But,' she added, not wanting this to come back and haunt her as in the form of a 'Mother of Gay Jay's Child Defends His Straight Honour' article, 'you never can tell.'

'No,' Victoria said. 'That's what I thought.' She sipped her latte and stared out over the river.

Leanne wondered what on earth Jay had been up to now.

*

On the way back the train was packed but Leanne and Jodie didn't have the pleasure of a free up-grade. Jodie didn't mind. 'Have I told you how much they loved me?' she said, for what must have been the hundredth time.

'Yes,' Leanne said wearily, trying to read her magazine.

'Next Monday, watch out, world, Jodie Crompton's coming your way.'

'Will you keep your voice down, Jode? It's like sitting with Foghorn Leghorn.'

'Whatever. Anyway, I don't care, 'cause I'm going to be in the paper. Get your autographs here!'

Leanne shook her head and laughed.

There was no shutting Jodie up this afternoon. When Leanne and Victoria had returned to the studio, the photographer had raved about her, and Gavin had already booked her to be one of their promotional girls. That meant on days when the temperature went over twenty-five degrees Celsius, Jodie would be sent to a beach to pose in a *Globe* bikini, or if they were launching the paper in a new territory she and a gaggle of other models would be sent there as braless ambassadors.

Leanne knew that there was a lot more to managing a team of girls like Jodie than sending a few pictures to London and claiming her ten per cent. But she was ready to start looking for clients. It was something she could do in the evenings when she had finished work – if Markie wouldn't have her back she'd have to find something else to pay the bills.

She got out her diary and made a note to call the contracts adviser – Maurice – whose number Victoria had given her. Then she thought about the brief conversation she and Victoria had had about Jay. She was glad now that he wasn't in her and Kia's lives. He had far too many issues of his own to know what to do with a daughter.

chapter twenty-five

Tracy helped herself to a tumbler of Courvoisier. She'd developed a taste for brandy recently – it went particularly well with the new coke Karina had delivered the previous evening. It was really good stuff, Tracy thought, not like the usual brick dust Gaz sourced. She counted out the cash she had received in benefits this week, rolled it up and put it into the shoebox she kept under the floorboard nearest to the window in the lounge. She didn't want Paul seeing it. He'd only want to spend it.

Tracy kept meaning to ask Paul what had happened to their glamorous foreign holiday. He kept saying he was going to book it, then always had a reason why he hadn't got round to it. He also kept coming home with little trinkets for her. If she saw another Lladro figurine she'd swing for him. And she knew that little gifts were a sure-fire giveaway clue that he was up to something.

The door opened and he bustled in. 'Morning, Princess,' he said, as Tracy hoovered up her third line of the day.

'You booked that holiday yet?'

'Well, it's funny you should say that because I was just in town and I was about to book it and then I thought I'd come home and check where we're meant to be going because it'd slipped my mind. Has there been any post today?'

'How can the fucking Dominican Republic slip your mind? It's not like we'd been tossing up between Filey and Cleethorpes, is it?'

There was a thud at the letterbox and Paul jumped.

'You expecting a present?'

'Just some bills,' he said, as he went into the hall.

'Right. Let's get dressed, go into town and book this bleeding holiday before it slips your mind again and we end up in Morecambe.'

'What you doing on the Courvoisier?' Paul asked, picking up the bottle.

'Sun's past the yard arm, I can do what I want,' Tracy said indignantly.

'I'm not on about the time, I'm on about the price. It's fucking expensive stuff, that.'

'Oh, all right,' Tracy snapped. 'Get your foot in the door and then deny me. That's lovely, isn't it?'

'I'm not denying you anything, just wondering why you can't drink the cheap stuff. It's not like you know the difference.'

'I'll pour it down the sink and drink strychnine,' Tracy said.

'Don't be so bloody stupid. Call a taxi and we'll go into town.'

Tracy threw the brandy down her neck. That's more like it, she thought.

*

As Paul handed over his credit card to the travel agent, Tracy took a good look at it. It was different from the one that had been declined last time. It was even different from the one he'd used to pay for the meal in the restaurant where they'd bumped into Leanne. It was different, too, from the one he'd used at Booze Busters the previous evening. It was even different from the one Tracy had chopped up her lines of charlie with that morning.

'I'm sorry, sir, it's been declined,' the woman said, embarrassed.

Tracy didn't want to have to sit there and be shown up again. She glared at Paul.

'It can't be,' he bleated.

'Bleeding Groundhog Day,' Tracy said.

'There's money on that card,' Paul protested.

Tracy stood up. 'Come on.' Paul followed her sheepishly out of the shop. Outside she prodded his chest. 'You haven't got any money, have you?'

'What d'you think I've been spending for the past few weeks? Scotch mist?'

'All right, I'll put it another way, shall I? You haven't won any money, or got any money of your own.'

'I have!' Paul shouted angrily.

'Prove it!'

'How?'

'Take me to a bank and get some money out without using a credit card.'

'I can't. It's all on one card.'

'Don't talk bollocks to me about money, Paul. I know when someone's on the fiddle. So, I'll ask you one more time. You haven't got any money, have you?'

Paul's face screwed up. 'I just wanted you back.'

'So you haven't?' Tracy asked. 'Bang goes our fucking holiday to the Dominican Republic. Is that it?'

Paul crumbled. 'I applied for credit cards and they gave 'em to me. God knows why but they did.'

'And how much have you spent?'

'About twenty grand.'

'Twenty grand?' Tracy shrieked. She'd not seen anything like twenty grand. 'And you're moaning about me buying brandy that's not fucking blue stripe. You cheeky sod.' She wanted to kill him. 'And what happens now you've got no money left?'

'I'll apply for some more.'

Was she really hearing this? Tracy wondered. She was all for free money, but even she knew that credit-card companies might want theirs back at some stage. 'You'll be black-listed, you knob. Anyway, fuck that – I'm not interested. How you dig yourself out of the shit is your lookout. What I want to know is what I'm meant to do now.'

Paul wiped the tears from his eyes. 'What do you mean? We'll get out of this together.'

'"We?" Sod that for a game of soldiers. There is

no *we*. You lied to me and I'm meant to stomach it, am I? Sit back like a good little girl and pretend I don't mind?' Tracy asked, blind to the fact that she had never sat anywhere and pretended to be a good little girl.

'Course there's a we. How much have we been through, Trace, me and you?'

Tracy walked off. She wasn't listening to him. Paul chased after her and grabbed her arm. 'Get off me!' Tracy shouted, drawing stares from passers-by. 'What you lot looking at?' she screamed. No one bothered to respond.

'Don't go, Trace. I love you!' Paul pleaded, but she ignored him.

Stomping up the street, Tracy was outraged. What had she done, kicking Kent out and replacing him with that lying, two-faced Paul? She forgot that the only reason Paul had done any of it was so he could be with her.

*

Jodie was inspecting her cheekbones in the mirror. She had to be at work by three but she had half an hour to kill. The door to the bathroom flew open and Tracy fell through it, looking the worse for wear.

'Nothing like knocking,' Jodie said indignantly.

'It's my bathroom. I'll come in when I like,' Tracy bellowed.

'Yes, Mum, I got on dead well in London, thanks

for asking, and, yeah, it looks like I'm going to be in the papers next week.'

'Like I give a shit,' Tracy said nastily.

'Course, I forgot for a moment. Thought this was *Neighbours* and I'd been adopted by a nice family.' She added, under her breath, 'Twat.'

Tracy spun round and grabbed her daughter's hair. 'What did you call me?' She slammed Jodie against the bathroom wall.

Jodie panicked. Her mum hadn't flown at her like this in ages, and the last thing she needed was a black eye in case she got called to anything by the *Globe*. She shielded her face and tried to duck away from her mum, but Tracy kicked out and caught Jodie across the shins, sending her flying on to the floor.

Jodie scrabbled to her feet. 'Come on, then, Mum, have a go, if you think you're so hard,' she spat, finding her feet. She'd tackled bigger than Tracy at the Beacon.

'You ungrateful little bitch!' Tracy yelled.

Jodie didn't know what any of this was about but she wasn't planning to ask. Her mum didn't need a reason to kick off.

'Oh, yeah, dead ungrateful. You've sweated blood for us over the years, haven't you?' Jodie ran past her and down the stairs.

'I fucking have!' Tracy howled.

Jodie grabbed her bag and ran out of the door. She didn't stop until she was at the Beacon. Inside, she flew to the back of the bar.

'You all right, love?' Val asked, as Jodie sped past her.

'I'm fine.' But once she was upstairs in the staff changing room she realised she wasn't fine at all. She threw back her head, wishing the tears away. She needed to leave this place. She needed something that meant she could choose when to see her mum, so she wasn't forced to face her every day. Because even when Tracy was happy and smiley everyone knew it was only a matter of time before she'd blow again.

*

Tracy was necking brandy and listening to Burt Bacharach, feeling sorry for herself. What had she done to deserve her mob? she thought. Ungrateful, grasping lot. And that Paul, pretending to have money.

Tracy crawled across the lounge on her hands and knees to the phone. Then she crawled to the table where she dumped any bumph that came through the door. She had just filled up on more coke so her movements weren't those of a drunk but of a wired madwoman. She searched through the letters until she got to the one she was looking for. One from some shady bank promising her that she had qualified for a credit card. She punched the number into the phone.

'Hello, I'd like to apply for a credit card, please,' she said, thinking, If you can't beat them, join them. One of the reasons she was angry with Paul, although she didn't want to admit this, was that she'd never thought to do this herself. What did she care if she ended up bankrupt? At least she'd have a royal knees-up between now and then.

The woman at the other end of the line went through the application form with Tracy – who was dabbing the remains of her last line of coke and rubbing it on her gums – then put her on hold.

Eventually the woman was back. Tracy couldn't believe her ears. 'What do you mean I've already got a card and it's at its limit? What limit?' Tracy tried to piece together what this meant in her addled mind. 'Four grand! Fuck off! … I don't care if you shouldn't have to listen to language like that, I've not got no frigging credit card. Someone's got one out in my name and gone on a spending spree, haven't they, you silly cow?'

The line went dead. Tracy sat staring at the receiver then took out her frustrations on it. She smashed it against the table. It broke. 'For fuck's sake!'

She jumped up and poured herself another brandy. That fucker Paul, she thought. He's gone and got credit cards in my name as well as his own. Well, I'll show him. She wasn't sure how she'd show him, she just knew she would. What she *was* sure of was that she'd developed a liking for money and wasn't about to be left in the poorhouse again.

Since she'd destroyed the landline, she located her mobile. She scrolled to K in her address book and pressed dial.

Kent answered almost immediately.

'Kenty, baby, it's me,' Tracy said, and burst into

tears – of self-pity, but he wasn't to know that. They could double up as tears of regret for now. 'I'm so sorry, I want you back,' she sobbed.

Kent was all ears. He said he'd known she'd change her mind because they were meant to be together. He promised to be round as soon as he could. Tracy smiled through her crocodile tears. At least someone was bothered about her.

chapter twenty-six

It was Saturday and still Leanne hadn't contacted
Markie. The more she thought about it, the more she
didn't want to. She loved her brother but she hated the
way he had to be in control of everything. She knew
she'd have to call him today, but for the moment she
was avoiding her phone.

She had spent the morning with Tony. They had
been looking at two-bedroom flats in town. Leanne
couldn't afford anything but she was desperate to get
out of Tracy's house – if not for herself, for Kia. Tony
had said he'd lend her the deposit and Leanne still had
one overdraft that wasn't at its limit, so she could use
that for the first month's rent if she needed to. It
wasn't much of a way to live, she thought. She needed
security for Kia.

She had seen a place she liked not far from where
Markie was living. It was seven hundred pounds a
month, which, compared to Greenwich, was a
pittance. Tony had persuaded her to call the estate
agent and sign up for it. The place would be free for
her to move in next month, and if she couldn't afford

to do it by then, she could pull out and lose the deposit. Tony said he didn't need it back, but Leanne told him she wouldn't take money off him if she didn't think she could repay it. She had arranged to go to the letting agency at lunchtime on Monday to sign up for the flat.

Today the house was eerily quiet. Tracy wasn't about – in fact, Leanne hadn't seen her for days – and Jodie had been staying at a friend's because she and their mother had quarrelled earlier in the week.

Kia came into the room with a drawing she'd been doing in the kitchen. It was of three stick people, one of whom looked like the Incredible Hulk. He was even painted green, but that, Leanne thought, was because green was Kia's favourite colour. The stick people were holding hands.

'That's lovely, sweetheart,' Leanne told her.

'That's me, that's you and that's Tony,' Kia said, pointing at the Hulk.

'Is Tony green?' Leanne asked.

'Don't be silly,' Kia said, as if she was dealing with an imbecile. 'I ran out of pink paint.'

'Shall we put it on the wall in the kitchen?' Leanne asked.

As she tacked it up, she remembered it wouldn't be too long before she had a kitchen wall of her own to pin things to.

Her phone rang. She picked it up from the worktop. Victoria Haim was calling. Why's she ringing on a Saturday? Leanne wondered.

'Hello.'

'Hi, Leanne.'

'Everything all right?' Leanne had sensed that everything *wasn't* all right.

'One of the other tabloids is printing an exposé on you from a family member.'

Leanne felt every muscle in her body tighten. 'Oh, my God.' She put a hand to her mouth. She felt as if she was about to be sick.

'They claim to know for a fact that Kia is Jay Leighton's child. They're going big with this one. It'll be a front-page splash. Unfortunately the informant's been promised anonymity and I can't find out who it is.'

'Oh, my God,' Leanne said again, fighting back angry tears.

'I'm sorry to be the bearer of bad news, but I didn't want you to wake up tomorrow morning and see it. I wanted you to be prepared.'

'Thanks for letting me know.'

'Do you think you might know who it is?'

'I haven't a clue who'd do this to me,' she said. But there was only one person she had told about Jay Leighton and he was proving time and again not to care how ruthless he was when it came to earning money.

*

Leanne had asked Tony to take Kia to the park for an hour but hadn't said where she was going. She had wanted to tell him about the conversation she'd had with Victoria but she knew he'd talk her out of what she was about to do.

She waited outside Markie's flats until someone went in and followed them into the lift. She got out at Markie's floor and walked to his door. She had never felt so angry. It was one thing making money out of a picture of her having her hair done, as she knew Tracy had done a couple of times, but this? It was diabolical.

Leanne tried the door, which was open. She burst into the apartment. Markie sat bolt upright in bed, as did the woman next to him. 'You.' Leanne pointed at the woman. 'Piss off home. Now!'

'What the fuck is this about?' Markie grabbed the sheet and pulled it round himself. His companion grabbed her stuff, jumped into her clothes and made for the door. 'You mental bitch!' she shrieked, as Leanne glared at her brother.

'This better be fucking good,' Markie said.

'Oh, it's that all right,' Leanne said. 'It's blinding, Markie.' She stepped closer to him. 'I know I'm from a scummy family, I'm not under any illusions about that, but selling something to a tabloid that I told you in complete confidence? It doesn't get any lower.'

'What are you on about?'

'That's right. Play dumb. There's only you in the whole world knows that Jay is Kia's father, only you, and just because I've pissed you off by going out with your mate, you sell me to the highest bidder.'

Markie got up, grabbed her and threw her onto the bed. 'Sit down and shut up,' he hissed. 'You think I've gone to one of the papers? You seriously think I'd do that?'

'You're the only person who knows.'

'But I'm not the only person who *thinks* they know, am I? There's a queue a mile long of people who'd make some money off you, but I'm not one of them, you stupid little girl.'

'Don't call me stupid! You think you can sweet-talk your way out of everything. I saw what goes on with you and Mac. You beat people up and take their houses from them. You had Tony beaten up. You're a nasty piece of work, Markie, and I'm not falling for it any more.'

Markie ran his fingers through his hair, then spun round and punched the wall. He pulled his fist back, shaking his hand. His knuckles were bleeding and there was a dent in the plasterwork. 'Fuck you, Leanne. You come back up here on your arse and I sort you out a job, one I didn't need anyone to do but so you had some money coming in. And what do you do? Bang on about how hard-done-by you are and accuse me of stitching you up. Well, bollocks to you. All I've ever done is look out for you – and this is how you repay me. Get out of my sight.'

Leanne's resolve was wavering. No matter what she thought of Markie's shady business practices, he really didn't seem to know what she was talking about. 'Well, even if you didn't do it, what do you expect me to think?'

'What do I expect you to think?' Markie echoed. 'I expect you to think that I'm the only one who's stuck by you through thick and thin.' He pulled her up and marched her to the door, then manhandled her out of the flat. 'And don't come back in a hurry.'

He slammed the door. Leanne heard the lock being turned. She stumbled to the lift, mind racing. If Markie hadn't done it, she had irreparably damaged their relationship for nothing. She was shaking and on the verge of tears as she fell out of the lift into the downstairs foyer.

She got into her car and was about to call Markie to say that if he hadn't done it she was sorry, but she knew he was in no mood to listen to her. Instead she headed off to Tony.

She found him and Kia at the swings in the park. She had to tell him about the news that would break the next day. 'Tony, I don't want you to think bad of me. I knew he was married and I was young and stupid, but I can't regret it because I have Kia ...' she said. If Tony was going to be part of Kia's life he, above anyone else, deserved an explanation.

'You don't need to explain yourself to me,' he said, drawing her close to him. 'Just talk me through what you're panicking about.'

Leanne told him exactly what Victoria had told her on the phone. By the time she had finished she was crying.

Kia got down from the swing and came over to them. 'What's wrong, Mum?' she asked.

'Nothing, darling. I banged my knee this morning and it keeps hurting.'

'Want me to rub it better?' Kia asked.

'Yes, please,' Leanne said.

Tony squeezed her hand. 'Who would do this to you?'

'It's not just me, though, is it?' Leanne said, nodding at Kia.

'Just because someone says they're a family member doesn't mean they are. If they're not identifying themselves, it could be anyone.'

Leanne shrugged. 'I really don't know.'

Suddenly Tony looked as if he'd seen a ghost.

'What's wrong?' she asked.

'It could have been Monica,' he said.

'But why would your pretend-wife go to the papers about me?' Leanne looked at Tony warily. 'And how would she know anything about it for that matter?'

Tony looked startled that Leanne might think that he had told Monica anything.

'I'm not saying she knows anything, certainly not from me. But she's read the papers and the gossip mags enough to cobble together a story.' Tony sighed.

'She thinks we've destroyed her life. She needs to pull something good out of the bag to convince the authorities she should be allowed to stay.'

'Do you think she would have gone that far?'

'Only one way to find out,' Tony said, and called her. He walked away so that Kia didn't hear the conversation. A few minutes later he was back.

'What did she say?'

'She wasn't very polite about my mother, put it like

241

that. I didn't mention specifics, just asked her if she'd called the papers about us. She didn't seem to know what I was talking about, just told me I was an ego-maniac.'

'Do you think she could have done it?'

'She doesn't know anything, other than what she's read herself. Anyway, she doesn't get English newspapers. Everything she ever looks at is Russian – Russian food, Russian papers. It's a wonder she ever wanted to stay here. My gut instinct is to say no, but you never know …' Tony sat down next to Leanne.

Leanne thought about her mum, Scott, Karina and Jodie. None of them would have wanted to make money out of Kia. They just wouldn't. She had cousins strewn around Bradington, but she couldn't think any of them would sell her out, but whoever it was would have received a pretty penny for the story, so maybe … Leanne decided she couldn't wind herself up about it any more. She would just have to weather the next few weeks. She knew from previous experience that it would be rough, and if she ever found out who was behind it, she'd never speak to them again.

chapter twenty-seven

When Jodie had arrived back from work the previous evening, Leanne had treated her to a little chat about what they could expect the next day. She had had a few gin and tonics after work and even though she'd heard what Leanne had said, she'd taken it with a pinch of salt.

So, when Leanne shook her and Tracy awake the next morning and ordered them not to open the curtains, Jodie was, to say the least, a bit surprised. She couldn't help but do the opposite of what she was told, though, and opened the curtain a notch. More than thirty photographers were standing outside the front wall and began frantically taking pictures.

Jodie tugged the curtain shut. 'Shit!' she said. She galloped downstairs to the lounge where Kent and Tracy were smoking nervously. She couldn't be bothered to ask what Kent was doing back – she'd said barely two words to her mother since their fight.

Leanne soon followed her into the room. 'I've left Kia in bed. No point waking her. I've got to ask this, and it breaks my heart, but does anyone know how this got into the papers?'

'How what got into the papers?' Tracy asked blankly.

'A family member has gone to the tabloids and told them that Jay Leighton is Kia's dad.'

'Well, that's charming, that is,' Tracy said. 'You think we'd shop our own to the papers? Sometimes I don't know where your head is. Up your arse, I suspect.' She stabbed her fag out exaggeratedly.

'I'm not accusing anyone, just telling you what I've been told. And someone's done something, haven't they, because Brad Pitt doesn't get this much press!' She nodded at the drawn curtains.

'I wouldn't know. We've not been allowed to look out.'

'Well, it's not me, Leanne, I promise,' Jodie said.

'And I'm not going to sit here saying it's not me because I shouldn't have to,' Tracy put in loftily.

Leanne sighed.

'And it's not me.' Kent jumped on the band-wagon.

'Well, it wouldn't be you, Kent, would it, because you're not family?' Jodie said, having a dig at her mother through Kent.

'Oi! He is!' Tracy claimed.

'This week,' Jodie retorted.

There was a knock at the door. 'Jode, will you get that?' Leanne asked. 'It's Tony. He's bringing the paper so we can see what's been said.'

Jodie ran to the door and the noise from the crowd outside spilt into the house.

'Can we have a comment from Leanne on today's revelations?'

'Is Leanne in there?'

'Does she expect to have any contact with the Leightons on this matter?'

'Piss off!' Jodie shouted, as Tony rushed in.

'I wanted to knock out each and every one of them.' Tony threw the paper on the floor. 'But I didn't say anything. On my best behaviour, like I promised.'

They stared at the headline, which read, 'The Leightons, Leanne and the Love Child'. Underneath it said, 'By the person who knows her best'.

'Who knows me best?' Leanne asked angrily.

Jodie could see that her sister didn't want to read the article, but she had to know what was in it.

Tracy began to read: '"The sordid love triangle between Jay Leighton, Lisa Leighton and Leanne Crompton has finally been exposed today as true. A close family member who has asked to remain nameless told us, 'Kia is Jay's. There's no two ways about it. Leanne often talks about Jay in glowing terms and she even has a picture of Jay that she points to and calls Daddy.'"

'That is such bollocks! Who would say this shit?' Leanne shouted angrily.

The door edged open and Kia came in. 'What's going on?' the little girl asked sleepily.

Jodie went to her. 'Nothing, darling. Just reading the paper,' Jodie said. 'Want some breakfast?'

Kia nodded and followed her into the kitchen.

Tracy continued to read the article aloud, but Leanne swiped it from her. 'Mum!' she said sternly, nodding after Kia.

Tracy tutted and rocked back in her chair.

Jodie had an idea who might have sold this eight-page story. And when she'd got dressed and battled her way through the paparazzi, she was going to wring her scrawny neck.

*

Lisa was staring at the paper in horror. This was such a non-story, but it condemned her and Jay. The paper had spun the article in such a way that it read as if everything it said was the truth when in fact it was some lily-livered family member, who wasn't even brave enough to put their name to the article, trying to make a quick buck out of someone else's life.

A few paparazzi were gathered at the gates, but Lisa knew that most them would be at Leanne's house, making her life a misery.

Jay wandered through from his games room. He had read the article and had needed an hour on his Wii to get his head together. 'What are we going to do?' he asked, slumping on to the bed.

'"We" are going to do nothing,' Lisa said. 'You can do what you like. It's a farce anyway. That kid's yours. You don't look after the one we've adopted, so you're hardly going to look after one you fathered seven years ago and clapped eyes on once.'

'Why does life have to be so difficult?' Jay whined.

Lisa gazed at their magnificent bedroom. Neither she nor Jay would ever have to go out to work again if they didn't want to. Something inside her snapped. 'Life is easy, Jay. So easy that we – or should I say *you*? – concoct little bullshit exercises to make it difficult. If you didn't we'd have the easiest life of anyone in the country.'

'You want all this as much as I do.'

'All what?' Lisa asked. 'I want the house, I want the car, I want the nice clothes. But I don't want the loveless marriage and the shitty, snivelling husband who goes with it. You used to be a man. What happened to you?'

'I *am* a man!'

'Then why are you wailing like a little girl?'

The phone rang. 'Who's that?' Lisa asked. 'Steve C with more good news? I do look forward to his weekend calls.' She picked it up. 'Yes?'

'Lisa, it's Steve.' She glared at Jay. 'I've got a helicopter picking you, Jay and Blest up this afternoon at two. I've booked you a week away on a private island. There'll be a cook, a nanny and a butler, all vetted by Madonna's people so you've nothing to worry about. You two need a break. Time to reconnect. What do you think?'

Lisa sighed. The idea of getting away from the madness was heaven, and even the knowledge that she'd have to come back to it at the end of the week didn't cloud it. Jay was off before pre-season training started. There was nothing stopping them. The only problem was that she'd have to spend the week with Jay.

'Send it. We'd love to go.'

She clicked the phone off. 'Pack your bags,' she told Jay. 'We're going on holiday.'

'Where?' Jay asked.

'Somewhere even you can't manage to get your end away.'

*

'All right, all right, I'm coming. Jesus! Don't put the door through,' Karina moaned. Whoever was banging on her door meant business.

She opened the door to find a fire-breathing Jodie in the hall.

'So, all your new clothes you've been bragging about, your week in Marbella, all bought and paid for by you, you said. Not Gaz this time, you've got your own money. Isn't that what you told me?'

Karina stepped out of the flat and pulled the door to behind her. Izzy was playing in the hall and she didn't need to hear this. She pushed Jodie towards the main entrance to the block. She could do without the neighbours hearing it too. They moaned enough about her and Gaz playing music. She didn't want them griping about her noisy sister as well.

'So, what's your problem? You jealous 'cause I've got a decent wedge and you have to graft your tits off in that shithole pub for a fiver an hour?' Karina wasn't having Jodie coming round shouting the odds like this.

'Me? Jealous? And you're not? You think that me and Leanne are off living the high life while you have to sit here with no chance of modelling?'

That hit Karina hard. It was one thing for her to think she wasn't as good-looking as her sisters, but to have one of *them* say it was quite another. She grabbed Jodie's hair and marched her to the door. 'Is that what you've come to say to me, Jodie? That you think you're fitter than me? Because if it is you can fuck off.' She launched Jodie into the car park, still clutching a clump of her hair.

Jodie flew at Karina and grappled her to the floor. Once she was straddling her, she tried to pin her down, but Karina kicked and flailed. There was no way she was lying still so that Jodie could take a free shot at her.

'No. I've come to say I know it's you that's gone to the papers about our Leanne. It's you, you spiteful bitch. Selling your own sister out, dragging our Kia through the mud. You're nothing but a piece of shit.' Jodie swiped at Karina's face.

Karina screamed. 'I don't know what you're talking about, you demented bitch!' she shouted.

'You do! Where's all the money come from then, if you didn't shop Leanne?'

'I've done a coke deal, you cunt! Now, get off me!' Karina pushed with all her might and sent Jodie flying backwards. Now it was her turn to leap on her sister.

She was so intent on slapping the face off Jodie that she didn't see the two photographers standing in clear view, taking pictures.

It was only when Gaz pulled in on his way home from a late Saturday night at work, jumped out, rugby-tackled one and sent the other fleeing down the street that the two women noticed they weren't alone.

'What the fuck are you doing, you pair of tits? Your Leanne's all over the papers so you two brawling in the street is just want they want. Get inside,' Gaz said angrily.

Karina and Jodie stood up, pulling bits out of their hair, then went in sheepishly. Gaz showed Karina the paper.

'You thought I'd done this?' Karina gawped at it, then at her sister.

'Well, you've done it before.'

'Get lost! I once told a newspaper our Leanne would be in town at a certain time with Jenna James and made up a story – but I couldn't do this to our Kia! You must think I'm a complete bitch.'

'So where's the money come from?' Gaz asked.

'Not you an' all.'

Karina couldn't believe that Gaz was ganging up on her. Izzy was wandering about between them, mainly wondering what all the shouting was about. Karina calmed down and admitted meekly, 'I got a stash from that guy you know – the heavy-metal roadie bloke.'

'My supplier, you mean?'

'I wanted to earn some cash for myself, do some real

dealing instead of getting it for people and not charging them anything. I just bought a load and flogged it.'

'And sniffed half of it,' Jodie swiped.

'So what if I did? Why's it your business? Come round here accusing me of all sorts! You going to apologise?' Karina demanded.

'Well, I still think it's sus,' Jodie said.

Karina knew her sister would rather poke her eyes out with a sharp stick than say sorry.

'Well, are you?' Gaz asked.

Jodie had grass stains up her back and scratches on her face. She picked the remaining twig off her shirt and raised her head. It pained her to look Karina in the eye. 'Sorry,' she said.

'Fuck off and don't talk to me for a bit,' Karina said, 'because you've well and truly done my head in.'

As Jodie sloped off, Karina grabbed the paper and began to read. She had a fair idea who might have done this, but it was only a hunch and she knew that Leanne would work it out before she could prove it.

'See this picture of our Leanne here? She looks good, doesn't she?' Karina said to Gaz.

'Yeah – better than you two dicks are going to look in that picture of you scrapping in the car park.'

*

'Thank fuck for that,' Tracy said, relieved, after Tony and Leanne had left to a flurry of questions from the reporters outside. Leanne had decided it was best to go to Tony's as he lived in a flat and they could leave any reporters who followed them at ground level.

Monica had been to collect the last of her stuff a few days before. She had moved out telling Tony that he had ruined everything for her. Her parting shot had been to scream at her husband that she had put a curse on his car.

Kent was feeding Elvis and Presley, singing 'His Latest Flame'. Tracy shook her head. 'Anyone'd think you were always having to fight the national press off your doorstep.'

'Well, back in the seventies when I was roadying with Showaddywaddy it was like this every day,' Kent said.

Tracy bit her tongue. If she heard another rock-and-roll-telly-through-the-windows-in-the-seventies story she was going to lamp Kent. It was his default mode when he wanted to impress her, and because he felt he was back on probation, the stories were flowing thick and fast.

'Did anyone ever give a shit about Showaddywaddy? I can't remember girls flinging their knickers at them.'

'Oh, you'd be surprised,' Kent said, still feeding his birds.

'I'd get more attention, if I tarred and feathered myself and got on that perch,' Tracy said sulkily.

Kent spun round and took her in his arms. '"Are you lonesome tonight?"' he sang.

'Give up!' Tracy wrestled free.

'I can't win with you.' Kent said, apparently resigned to the fact.

'Well, that's where you're wrong,' Tracy said cockily.

'What's that supposed to mean?' Kent asked, curious.

'It means I need to get away from here and from the snotty Londoners hanging round the house asking questions about our Leanne.'

'So? What's that got to do with me?'

'Me and you are going on holiday. My treat.'

'Really?' Kent was so gobsmacked he dropped his bird seed.

The next day Tracy and Kent fell through the door of the travel agent's as it opened.

It was the snotty girl she and Paul had got the first time. 'Hello,' she said sniffily, looking Tracy up and down, then taking in Kent.

Tracy knew what she was thinking. This was a different fella. But Tracy couldn't give a monkey's what some bleached-blonde upstart thought of her. She dumped the carrier-bag she was holding on to the desk. 'Two weeks all-inclusive in the Dominican Republic, going as soon as. And I don't think your computer's going to decline that little lot, is it?'

The young woman looked at the bag, overflowing with twenty-pound notes, and logged on straight away.

chapter twenty-eight

Markie was at his desk. It was Monday. He hadn't looked at yesterday's papers. He couldn't be bothered to find out what rubbish had been printed about Leanne, especially since he'd been accused of having sold it to them. But he knew that there was a lot of interest in the story that wasn't a story. Today he had glanced at the front pages on his way in and seen pictures of Karina and Jodie fighting outside Karina's block. No change there then, he had thought. He had received three calls this morning from journalists asking him if Leanne had said anything about her affair with Jay, or about Kia. He was about to leave the office to meet Mac for lunch when the phone rang again. He picked it up. Another journalist looking for a scoop.

'Yes, Leanne told me something …' Markie paused for effect. 'She told me that if any journalists rang up I should tell them to kiss my hairy ring-piece.' He slammed the phone down. 'Wankers.'

As he grabbed his wallet from the desk, he heard a noise outside the office. The door opened and there stood Tony. Markie hid his surprise. 'Wouldn't have thought you'd dare show your face.'

'The same face you were too chicken shit to come and smash in yourself? Had to get your arse-crack lickers to come and do it for you?' Tony walked in, uninvited.

Markie stared at him, deciding how to play it. Tony was a hard bastard, but had always been loyal to him – until the Mandy fiasco. Now Markie knew he had to face him down. 'Fuck you,' he said.

Tony grabbed his arm. 'Sit down and fucking listen to me for once.'

'Take your hand off me before I snap it in fucking two.' Markie matched Tony's menace. Tony held his gaze for a moment, then released him. 'Sit down,' Markie said. Tony sat. Markie had won the first battle.

'Give me one good reason why I should give you air space?' Markie said, perching on the edge of his desk.

'Because me and you go way back. Because I've always bent over backwards for you. And because I'm going out with your sister.'

'That what you call it? You've been together for all of ten minutes.'

Tony sighed. 'Me and Leanne go way back, if you must know. And I don't care if you kick off, Markie. You can do what you fucking please. I've spent enough years pussy-footing round you and I'm not doing it any more. I love Leanne and we hid it for long enough.'

'Hid it when?' Markie said.

'Before she moved to London.'

'When she was a fucking kid? Are you some kind of nonce?' Markie stepped towards him, but Tony stood up. He didn't look like he was in the mood for an argument.

'She wasn't a kid. And it wasn't like that. Think what you want – you fucking will anyway.'

'You lay a finger on her ...' Markie began, blood boiling.

'Lay a finger on her? What are you on about? I fucking love her. I'm not some jumped-up cunt footballer who's going to fuck off when the first bit of shit comes along. I'm in it for the long haul. And that's what I've come here to tell you. You can badmouth me, you can make sure I don't work in Bradington, but you're not sticking your oar in with me and Leanne because I love her and, worst of all for you, she loves me. Geddit?'

'She's my sister!'

'And you want what's best for her, don't you? Who d'you think is sorting her out while all this shit's hitting the fan? It sure isn't your mum.'

Markie was about to fly at him and tell him not to bring his mum into it, but what purpose would it serve? And anyway, wasn't it better to have Tony on side than as an enemy, especially if what he was saying about Leanne was true? He couldn't appear to be the one to back down, though. He walked over to the filing cabinet and opened it. He produced a bottle of Hennessy XO and two glasses. He slammed them down on the desk, poured hefty measures and passed one to Tony. Tony accepted it, surprised. 'You'd better look after her,' he said, raising his glass.

Tony raised his glass with a sigh of relief, and Markie relaxed. He'd known he had to keep his head in this stand-off and that he'd come out, as always, on top. Tony was back where he wanted and, more importantly, needed him.

*

Leanne was astonished that Tony had been to see Markie and even more so that it hadn't ended in tears. 'Did he mention me?' she said, knowing it would take Markie a while to stop being angry about her accusations.

'He said to look after you, which I do anyway.' He twirled her round.

He was right, Leanne thought. He did. Only that morning he had taken Kia to school, then gone to the letting agency and signed for the flat because Leanne couldn't face any more press intrusion. Yesterday had been bad enough.

Leanne could have sat and cried all day but where would that have got her? Instead she had explained to Kia that a long time ago, before she had been born, Mummy had been friends with a man who was now very famous. The reason the cameramen were following them was because they wanted to ask her about it.

She would tell Kia when she was older about Jay, Leanne thought. Now was not the time.

Last night she had worked out a plan for what to do next. She was sick to death of people making money out of her and of being the object of press fascination even when she wasn't doing anything. She and Tony had ordered in a pizza, and she had decided to take the apartment they had seen and borrow the deposit from Tony. Leanne had made a lot of decisions over the past few days. It was amazing how national press intrusion could focus the mind. She would start up her management business in earnest this week. Now she would kick-start it with a call to Victoria Haim.

Tony had taken the day off and was about to head to the shops to stockpile provisions in case there was an influx of press. He kissed her goodbye and Leanne picked up the phone. She had one call to make before she rang Victoria. The contracts man, Maurice, had been surprised that she didn't have possession of her own contracts now that Jenny no longer managed her.

Leanne punched in Jenny's number and pressed call.

'Yeah.' The woman's familiar snappy tone rang in Leanne's ears.

'It's Leanne.' She was nervous, but she wasn't about to let it show. She'd have to talk to people like Jenny every day when she was managing new talent, so she might as well get used to it, not curl up in a ball and die at the first hurdle.

'Leanne?' Jenny said, as if she didn't know.

Leanne rose above it. 'Crompton. Your biggest earner for the last five years.'

'Oh, yeah. What can I do you for?'

Leanne wanted to say, 'You've done me for enough over the years,' but held her tongue. 'I'd like you to send me all my documentation. Any contracts I've signed, anything from when I first started with you.'

'And why would you need it? You haven't got any work at the moment and everything you've had in the past is paid up. What's the problem?'

Leanne paused. Since Maurice had pointed out that she should be in possession of her own contracts, she had been reading up on people who had been stung by their agents. The resounding piece of advice for anyone who had been treated in this way was to take back control from the person who had been responsible for their affairs. Leanne didn't think anything was due to her, but she wanted to have her contracts rather than leaving them with Jenny. And if it meant making a bit of work for the woman, good. She'd hung Leanne out to dry without a second thought.

'There isn't a problem, Jenny. I'd just like all of my contracts, please.'

'I'll have them sent today.'

'Good.' Leanne should have put the phone down now that she was playing the hot-shot, but her natural inclination to be polite got the better of her. 'So, how's everything?'

'Everything's fine. Bye,' Jenny said, and hung up.

Next Leanne scrolled to Victoria's name. 'Hi, it's Leanne.'

'How are you?' Victoria asked. Leanne could hear that she didn't expect her to be too good.

'You know something? I'm actually all right. I've decided to make a statement, once and for all.'

'Really?' Victoria's voice rose an octave.

She could smell an exclusive, Leanne thought. 'And I'd like you to have it.' She paused, trying to hide her nerves. This was a big step, one that she wasn't sure she wanted to take.

'Well, that's great news.'

'And I want to make sure I'm well paid for it, because it's the one and only time I'll be speaking about it,' she said. She hated being so forthright but she had to be.

'Well, it depends what you're going to say …'

'No, it doesn't. You put me on the front of a paper saying I'm going to talk about Kia's paternity and the papers will fly off the shelves.'

Victoria laughed. Leanne knew she was right.

'OK. What's your price?'

Leanne didn't want to be greedy. She knew she could make a fortune out of this, but she wanted to lay it to rest so it wasn't hanging over Kia's head. The money was for Kia when she was older.

'Well, there's two things. I'd like to build a working relationship with the *Globe* and I'd like first refusal as manager for any new talent you're sent.'

'That's a tall order. We can't demand that girls go with a particular agent.'

'No, but you can recommend me to them. Also, and I know this from experience, when you're new you're delighted if *anyone* wants to represent you.'

'Fine by me. And money?'

'Twenty grand.' Leanne held her breath. She was pretty sure that wasn't much for this sort of thing.

'That should be fine,' Victoria said. 'I'll get the contracts department on to it. Can we send a reporter up on Thursday?'

'As long as you tell your photographer to back off. They've practically been posting themselves through the letterbox.'

'Well, you'll let him in now, won't you? We'll need a few shots of you for the front page.' Leanne sighed. 'They're only doing their jobs, same as us, Leanne.'

'I suppose,' she said reluctantly.

'Someone will be with you tomorrow before lunchtime.'

Leanne gave Victoria Tony's address. 'You still don't know which "family member" it was who went to the other paper, do you?'

'Not yet. But it'll come out sooner or later.'

'Sooner, I hope.'

'By the way, you might want to invoice us tomorrow and buy a copy of the paper. There's someone you'll recognise on page three.'

Jodie would be delighted. 'Thanks,' she said.

chapter twenty-nine

Jodie had made the paper for the second time in two days, but this time instead of fighting Karina she was beaming on page three. She had already been on the phone to Leanne for half an hour but now she was running to the Beacon to show Val. She would have woken her mum up to show her but nothing ever impressed Tracy so there was no point in trying.

When she got to the pub there was a copy in the window and a makeshift sign above it saying, 'Our very own Jodie'. She burst through the door. Val was cleaning behind the bar and a couple of the regulars were perched on their stools. When they saw Jodie they cheered.

'I'm famous!' she squealed.

'Again,' Val said, smiling.

'Yesterday I was just showing that people shouldn't mess with me. Today my showbiz career starts,' Jodie said. 'Give us a G and T, Val.'

'G and T? Bollocks! I'm opening the oldest bottle of champagne in the country,' she said, bending down to the fridge. Val and Jodie often joked about the one and only bottle of champagne at the Beacon. Val couldn't remember ordering it from the brewery and was convinced she'd inherited it from the previous landlord. They often placed bets on someone buying it, but no one ever had.

'Not the champagne?' Jodie said, clutching her heart in mock-shock.

Val popped the cork. 'Get your laughing gear round that, Perky Tits.'

Jodie took the glass Val offered her. 'I could get used to this,' she said.

'Well, don't get too used to it because you're on the rota for at least the next two weeks.'

Jodie drank some champagne. She'd give Val plenty of notice, but one thing was for sure. She was leaving. Things were looking up for Jodie.

*

Leanne ignored the buzzer. Over the last few days the reporters had trickled away, but she wasn't taking any chances. After the third buzz her mobile rang. It was Markie.

'Hello,' she said tentatively. If he wanted to tell her not to come back to work, fine. She was too tired after the week's events to argue with him.

'I'm outside, Leanne. Let me in.'

She walked to the door and pressed the buzzer. A few moments later he was in the hallway.

'Hi,' she said awkwardly.

'Hi,' he replied.

'Listen, Markie, I'm really sorry for accusing you of being behind the story about Kia. It's just that you were the only person who knew and I flew off the handle.'

'That's for sure.'

'It's hard to know what to think sometimes.'

'Yes, it is, but I would never sell you out. Common sense might have told you that.'

Leanne dropped her eyes. 'Well, it didn't, did it?'

'Come here.' Markie took her in his arms, and Leanne hugged him back. 'You're my sister and I'd protect you all day long, you should know that.'

Tears plopped down her cheeks on to Markie's shoulder. 'I do, Markie ... I do,' she breathed.

'You know what you need, Lee? A good night out. Chill out a bit, enjoy yourself.'

'I can't with all this going on. I'll be papped in a taxi with a nipple hanging out when I'm not even drunk.'

Markie laughed. 'No, you won't. Let's have a knees-up. And what better knees-up than the opening of the Glass House?'

Since they'd parted company so acrimoniously, Leanne had felt guilty about the Glass House. It had been her project, and although she'd arranged most of it she felt she'd let Markie down by not being around to see it through to opening night. 'Are you sure?' she asked.

'Course I am. It'll be blinding. Anyway, if you come it's more publicity.' He winked.

Leanne laughed, but her mind was whirring. She had been thinking about how to get Charly and Jodie some exposure, this would be ideal, even if it was only a club in Bradington. For the first time she was thinking with a commercial mind, rather than waiting for an opportunity to come to her. If she was going to represent them and other girls she'd have to push them forward.

'You're on. But only if I can bring Jodie and Charly.'

'Charly?' Markie was startled.

'She's all right. Anyway, I'm going to represent her so I want to see what she's like when she's out. Iron out any Canterbury Avenue traits that might still be lurking.'

Markie smiled. 'Nice one.'

*

For Bradington the Glass House was a daring enterprise. It felt like a London nightclub, and had an air of professionalism that Leanne had never seen in a Bradington nightspot. There was usually a scrum for the bar and it was a major achievement if a night ended without a fight. Even the toilet attendant was officious, which didn't wash with Jodie.

'She needs to straighten her face,' Jodie had said, as the woman handing out towels in the ladies' toilet looked her up and down. 'She cleans bogs for a living. Less of the attitude.'

Leanne grabbed her sister by the arm and hauled her out. 'Remember what happened to Cheryl Cole? No kicking off with the staff,' she warned.

'It's Markie's club,' Jodie reminded her.

'And Markie'll throw you out, so button it,' Leanne said.

Party Hard had just finished singing two of their number one hits and had been greeted as heroes by the Bradington throng, who usually had to count themselves lucky if Roy 'Chubby' Brown agreed to make a tour stop there.

They found Charly chatting to Markie, who had ensured they had their own booth and would be well looked after. He had said he'd leave the girls to it once they had their drinks, but that he'd be around if they needed him.

'Are there no photographers tonight?' Charly asked.

Leanne knew she was trying to sound casual, but she was desperate to know. 'Photographers aren't allowed in,' she said. 'In fact, if anyone so much as holds their phone up, they're out on their ear. It's a marketing ploy. Makes everyone think that people worth photographing will be here.'

'Really?' Charly's face fell.

'Look, you've been brought out for a nice night and you're whingeing because your mug's not going to end up on page twenty of the *Star*. Chill out and have a drink,' Jodie said, raising her glass.

'It's all right, Charly. We're in the right place to be noticed and there will probably be photographers outside when we leave, so we mustn't get too legless,' Leanne reassured her. She was nervous. She was almost certain there would be photographers when they left the club. It would be good for the girls, but she wasn't too keen on the idea.

'Probably? Get lost. Definitely, more like,' Jodie said tactlessly. 'You can't go anywhere this week, Lee, without being followed. Someone'll tell them you're here. Everyone's rubbernecking as it is.' Leanne knew this was true. She'd felt eyes boring into her as she walked back from the toilet.

'Scott not want to come out tonight?' Markie asked Charly, in a bid to change the subject.

'He wasn't given the choice. This is work for me. I don't go to the factory with him and get in the way of his pallets, now, do I?' Charly said.

Markie raised an eyebrow. 'Work? You wouldn't know work if it bit you on the arse, Charlotte.'

'No one calls me that. It's Charly,' she said tightly, then turned back to Leanne. 'By the way, do you think when I'm in the papers I could be known as Charly M? It sounds more mysterious than Charly Metcalfe.'

'Shall we wait to see what the *Globe* says about your shots before we give you a stage name?'

'Fine.' Charly picked up her glass.

'I'll leave you lot to it,' Markie told them. 'I'm going for a little mooch.'

Leanne watched him move through the club, stopping to talk to people as he went. 'He knows everyone, doesn't he?' she said to Jodie.

'Yep. Look at that limp imp shaking his hand and pretending he's his best mate.'

Leanne saw a good-looking young guy dancing round Markie.

'Markie hates him. He's unbearable, always up Markie's arse when he goes anywhere, pretending he knows everyone and saying he's some sort of hot-shot businessman when in fact he just rents out two houses his dad bought him. Embarrassing. He'll be over here in a minute when he clocks you. Any Z-list celebrity and he's over them like a rash.'

'Thanks,' Leanne said, smiling wryly at her tactless sister.

'Oh, shit, here he comes.'

'Leanne!' he said, dragging out her name as if he was doing an impression of Dev in *Coronation Street*.

Leanne smiled vaguely.

'Dean Hirst. Good friend of Markie's. Might I say that you girls look amazing tonight?' He smiled cheesily.

Jodie grabbed the ice-bucket and pretended to vomit into it.

'You OK?' he asked her.

'Fine.'

'Leanne. You're a really beautiful human being. I know that from your brother and the papers. I think you need to centre yourself and search within your heart to do the right thing for you at the moment.'

Leanne's skin crawled. Jodie spluttered into her drink, and Charly looked at him as if he had a screw loose. Dean stood up, took Leanne's hand, kissed the back and said, 'Peace.' Then he wandered off to pretend he knew someone else.

Leanne shuddered. 'I feel dirty.'

'Well, he's the cock-end to end all cock-ends, isn't he?' Jodie said, and fell about laughing.

'What a total twat,' Charly agreed. Suddenly she spotted someone in the corner and sat up straight. 'Oh, my God, is that ...' She didn't finish her sentence.

Leanne did it for her. 'Joel Baldy,' she said. Her stomach knotted. If he was here, Jay might be lurking around. They were always in the papers together. Joel was with a gaggle of admiring girls. He glanced round and caught Leanne's eye. 'Listen, girls,' she said, 'if Jay Leighton's here we have to go. I don't want to see him and I don't want anyone thinking we're here because he is.'

'No one's going to think that,' Jodie said. 'This is your brother's club, for God's sake. Of course you're going to be here on its opening night.'

Joel excused himself from the group and came over to their table. 'Hi, Leanne.' He stuck his hand out for her to shake. 'Joel Baldy.'

'Hi, Joel ...'

'Rough week, eh?'

'Fairly.' Leanne nodded. She felt exposed. People were staring at her.

'Jay's gone away for the week – can't say I blame him.'

Relief washed over her – not that she'd thought even Jay Leighton would be stupid enough to come to a club that was part-owned by her brother in this week of all weeks, but still …

'Any idea who shopped you to the papers?'

'It's not something I want to discuss.'

'Fair enough.' He shrugged. He turned to Jodie and Charly. 'I don't believe I've had the privilege?' Jodie smiled.

Leanne wasn't sure Joel was her sister's type, but she'd enjoy the attention.

'Jodie, Leanne's sister.'

'Of course,' Joel said. The resemblance between the two was marked.

Jodie wiggled out of her seat. 'I'm off to dance. Anyone coming?' she asked, eyes on the famous footballer. He shook his head.

'I'll stay here,' Charly chirped.

Jodie's eyes narrowed. 'Fine.'

Leanne looked at her poor sister, who obviously didn't want to be left standing on her own. She got up and pulled Jodie towards the dance floor.

By one o'clock the girls were flagging and Markie had arranged for one of his lads to drive them home. Leanne went to check on Charly, who was still with Joel. They had holed up in a dark corner. As Leanne approached, Charly sat bolt upright and pulled her skirt down. 'Are you coming, Charly?' she asked.

'I was thinking of staying for maybe one more drink,' Charly said, testing the water.

'Well, I think it's better if you come home now. Scott will be worried about you,' she said.

'OK.' Charly was clearly trying not to sound disappointed, but there was no way Leanne would let her make a mug of Scott under her nose. Charly said goodbye to Joel and followed Jodie and Leanne. Outside five or six photographers snapped away. Leanne had told the girls that if anyone was waiting they should smile and put their best side forward. No point in getting the paper the next day to see your face all scrunched up. Leanne beamed at the cameras, and Jodie and Charly followed suit. Then they dived into the car Markie had provided and headed home.

'Well, we might have got you some exposure there. What do you think?' Leanne asked.

'I think Charly was trying to get off with Joel Baldy,' Jodie said glaring at her.

'No, I wasn't. He was just a nice guy.'

'A nice guy with pots of cash and a big sign saying, "This way out of Bolingbroke".'

'Get fucked, Jodie. You're just jealous.'

'Of you?'

'Yeah, me. Sitting there bitter because Joel liked me. Looking down your nose, judging me by your standards.'

'At least I've got some. You're the one who sits on your arse and sticks it in the air every now and again for our Scott to wipe.'

'Fuck off, you bitch!'

'Ladies! Ladies!' Leanne shouted. 'Time out! Jesus.'

Both girls crossed their arms and stared sulkily out of the window. 'You two work together now and if I see anyone arguing I'll be having words.' Neither girl spoke. 'Understand?' Leanne said sternly.

'Yes,' Charly and Jodie said, in sulky unison.

'Good. Now shake hands.'

Charly and Jodie turned to one another as if they'd rather amputate than shake them, but they did as they were told.

'That's better.' Leanne felt firmly in control of the pair – and if she could control Jodie and Charly, anyone else would be a piece of cake.

chapter thirty

'Where's Kia? What time is it?' Tracy said, running her fingers through her matted hair.

'You look like the Wreck of the *Hesperus*,' Leanne said, taking in her mum's stained nightie and cigarette-stained fingers.

Tracy began to cough, and then to retch, and before Leanne knew it her mother was over the sink, hacking up whatever her gut hadn't wanted to hang on to. 'Nice,' she said.

'Don't give me your sarcasm,' Tracy said, wiping her mouth on her sleeve. 'Ever thought it could be cancer what makes me like this?'

'Ever thought it might be too much booze and too many fags?' Leanne asked.

Tracy ignored her, grabbed her cigarettes and lit one. 'So, where's Kia?'

'She's at school,' Leanne said, confused.

'Why did I think it was Saturday?' Tracy said, almost to herself.

'Listen, we're going to stay at Tony's for a while until I get this new flat. It'll give you a bit more room.'

'What's up with here?'

'Nothing. But if we move out you'll have the house back. That's all.'

'Well, I was trying to be helpful, but if you want to throw it back in my face …' Tracy said, leaning over the kettle and gazing out of the kitchen window.

'Oh, God, Mum! I don't want to throw anything in anyone's face.' Leanne hated it when Tracy was like this. She was fine one day and unreasonable the next, utterly impossible to gauge.

'Fine. You want a brew?'

'Yes, please. Tea,' Leanne said, and sat down at the kitchen table. She looked at the piles of paper that were a permanent dust-gathering fixture, and noticed some airline tickets sticking out from the usual array of catalogues and Lidl special-offer leaflets. She pulled them out. Tracy was making a racket finding cups in her jumble-sale of a cupboard. 'You off on holiday?' she asked.

Tracy didn't turn round, just slowed in her rummaging. 'Yeah. Kent decided to treat me. Thought I deserved a break.'

Where had Kent got the money to pay for a holiday? Something dawned on Leanne that made her feel sick.

'Yeah,' Leanne said carefully, trying to disguise what she was thinking. 'You do need a break.'

'I bloody *deserve* one. I've had a hard time of it with your dad. He's still coming round, you know, shouting the odds.'

'You used him, though, didn't you, Mum? You thought he had some money and then when you found out he didn't you kicked him out. Isn't that right?' Leanne was angry now.

'Why you getting all uppity?' Tracy said. When she faced Leanne her eyes had narrowed to slits. 'Oh, I get it. You've put two and two together and got five, haven't you? Our Jodie was fishing the other night about the mysterious family member who's shopped you to the papers. And you think it was me, don't you?' Tracy was walking towards her menacingly. 'Well, if you think I'd do that to my own flesh and blood, then you don't know me at all.'

'I never said I thought it was you.'

'You didn't have to. It's written all over your face. You think I'd stoop so low as to tell some snotty-nosed twat from a rag about you? About my beautiful grand-daughter?'

Leanne felt terrible. Her mother was so adamant that she was now certain it hadn't been her. It had to have been someone pretending to be family, just to make some money, and now she'd all but accused her mum, had come straight out and accused Markie, and hadn't even had to bother accusing Karina – Jodie had done it for her. Leanne's mind was racing. It definitely hadn't been Scott – he didn't have a bad bone in his body – but Charly might have seen the pound signs. Even that didn't make sense, though. If Charly had made a packet in the last few weeks she'd have been out spending it. She wouldn't have been able to stop herself.

'I'm sorry, Mum,' Leanne said, 'I really am. I'm just paranoid.'

'Well, you can stick your paranoia. We're family. We stick together.' Tracy was shouting now, right in Leanne's face.

'You've made money out of me before,' Leanne said.

Tracy slapped her daughter across the face. Leanne jumped to her feet, clutching her cheek.

'Get out of my house!' Tracy shrilled.

Leanne fled. Outside, as she got into the car with tears rolling down her cheeks, a lone photographer was snapping away.

'Have you nothing better to do?' she shrieked out of the window.

'Live by the sword, die by the sword, love,' he said cheerfully, as he changed his film.

*

Even three thousand miles away on a desert island Lisa and Jay were not alone. The last couple of days had been heaven, as far as Lisa was concerned. She and Jay had sunbathed, played with Blest and had even had a few frank conversations. For the first time in years he hadn't been out of Lisa's sight for more than two minutes.

The butler approached her in his sombre I-used-to-work-for-the-Royal-Family manner. 'There's a call for you, Mrs Leighton.'

'I'm not accepting any this week.'

'It's from your publicist. He says he must speak to you.'

Lisa looked at Jay. 'I haven't done anything this time, scout's honour,' he said. He was usually hopping all over the place like Rumpelstiltskin when Steve called, panicking about his latest indiscretion. This time he was so calm that Lisa was inclined to believe him.

She walked from the white sandy beach to the grand hand-carved entrance. The butler pointed her towards a beautiful airy room with a sea view. She picked up the ornate phone.

'Steve?'

'Lisa. I wouldn't call you on holiday if it wasn't serious,' he said.

Lisa's heart sank. 'Look, Steve, just tell me …'

'Some rent-boy has come forward with a video-recording of him and Jay. It's damning stuff.'

Lisa's knees buckled. 'What sort of damning stuff?' she asked weakly.

'Whatever you think two men might get up to in the sack. I don't want to go into details, darling.'

'Oh, my God.' Lisa collapsed into a nearby chair and put her free hand to her forehead.

'This is fucked-up, Lisa. When it gets out there's not much we can say to make it look better.'

'Oh, my God,' Lisa said again.

'Did you hear what I said, Lisa? Do you understand what I mean?'

'Yes,' she whimpered. For the first time in her life, she felt she had lost the fight.

'There's only one thing we can do,' Steve said.

'Go on,' Lisa said. God knows what he's going to pull out of the bag now, she thought.

'We go to Leanne Crompton, sign a massive deal for her to go public and you tell everyone you were going through a rocky patch at the time but now your marriage is as strong as ever. If we get a story like that we can whitewash some skanky little rent-boy and his money-grabbing antics, and you'll come out on top.'

Steve's words washed over Lisa. She was aghast at what her life had become. She was living a lie. 'You know what, Steve?' She sighed. 'I can't do it any more.'

'Can't do what?'

'This … this … bullshit.'

'But "this bullshit" is what you're good at.'

Lisa digested his words. It was true. And *this* was what her life had become – a long-running farce. 'That, Steve, is not a compliment.'

'Sorry, Lisa, but you know what I mean.'

'I think I'm going to put Jay on. This is his shit. He can deal with it. I'll speak to you when I get home.'

Lisa put the receiver on the side and walked back to the beach, where she had left Jay sunning himself. 'Phone for you,' she said quietly.

'But I'm on my holidays!' Jay whined. When he saw

Lisa's face he knew she was in no mood for his baby voice. 'What's up?'

'You've done some barrel-scraping in your time, Jay, but this takes the biscuit.'

'What?' he asked, panicking.

'Some *rent-boy* –' She spat the word '– has a very clear video of you and him shagging that he's touting round to the highest bidder.'

Jay leapt up as if someone had fired him out of a rocket. Disdainfully, Lisa watched him run inside. The butler came over to her. 'Can I get you another drink, madam?' he asked.

'No. But you could get me and the baby on the first available flight to the UK.'

'Will your husband be travelling with you?'

'No,' Lisa said, looking the man in the eye. 'He can swim back for all I care.'

*

Leanne was dreading the interview with the *Globe*. What had seemed like a good idea at the time was now looking like something that might spell the death of her private life. She had ordered a Chinese takeaway, and she and Tony were going to talk to Kia about the three of them. Then Leanne and Tony were going to discuss the article and how she should best play it in order to be left with some dignity.

'Kia,' Leanne said to her daughter, 'me and Tony want to tell you something.'

She let Tony take over. 'You know how you were saying that other people have a daddy and you haven't and that you'd really like one?'

'Yes,' Kia said, nodding.

'Well, I'll be your daddy, if you like.' Leanne could see how terrified Tony was as he waited for the little girl's response.

'Will you?'

'I'd love to be. I can train you up to play rugby league and everything.'

'Girls can't play rugby, silly!' Kia said, giggling.

'My girl can.' Tony winked at her.

'So do I call you Tony or Daddy?' Kia asked.

Leanne laughed. Her daughter liked to have things straight in her head.

'You can call me Dad if you want.'

Had it been any other man, Leanne might have thought she was rushing things, but now she knew that things between her and Tony were meant to be.

'OK, Tony – I mean Dad.' Kia giggled, and Tony kissed her forehead.

Leanne looked at him with her daughter. She was so glad he was back in her life.

chapter thirty-one

Leanne had spent the morning in Markie's office. She had promised to man the phones and train an agency temp. As it turned out the young woman who arrived could have done the job standing on her head so Leanne was left to get on with organising some things of her own.

She had received the contracts from Jenny and was surprised by how soon they had appeared. Now she was leafing through them and trying to work out which one related to which job. There were few surprises, she thought. From what she could see, Jenny had represented her fairly and well.

'My brother's got that poster of you on his wall,' Jacinta, the temp, said.

Leanne rolled her eyes. 'Oh, God, which one?'

'The carwash one. I used to go off my head about it. "Do you think anyone seriously washes their car with their knickers up their arse like that?" I used to say, but it was only because I was pissed off that he was allowed to have a picture of a girl he fancied and I couldn't have lads on my wall.'

'Sorry I caused some hassle.' Leanne grinned.

'Don't worry about it. He's a div, anyway, my brother. If you met him you'd be like "Er, I don't think so in a million years, thanks, love."'

As Leanne was putting her contracts into files she remembered that she hadn't seen one for the carwash picture. She riffled through the paperwork again and when it became obvious that it wasn't there she picked up the phone and called Jenny.

'Oh, it was so long ago, darling. I'm not even sure I kept it. Don't worry, though. You got what was due about six years ago, didn't you? One-off payment, wasn't it?'

'Yeah …' Leanne said, suddenly doubtful. 'That's right.'

'Well, there you go. I see that bucktoothed sister of yours finally got down the gym – she looked all right.'

'Thanks. Bye now.' Leanne put down the phone and silently congratulated herself on not being a walkover where Jenny was concerned. Then she called Maurice.

'I've got all my files back from Jenny except one, and when I questioned her about it I thought she was fobbing me off.'

'Which assignment was it?' Maurice asked.

'The big one. I got a flat fee for it but it's been syndicated.'

'Right,' Maurice said. 'Give me the details of the publisher, how much you were paid and when, and I'll do a bit of digging. I thought it sounded a bit odd that you got so little at the time.'

'I was just starting out.'

'Even so, knowing that a picture is going to be syndicated means you've a fair idea it'll sell. Why would she agree to a one-off fee?' he asked.

Leanne didn't know the answer to that. Maurice promised he'd get back to her as soon as he knew anything. Leanne didn't hold out much hope. She was just glad to be regaining control of her life.

*

Jodie looked in the mirror. She had lost more than half a stone since her photo had appeared in the paper and she wanted to get down further if she could. She had told her mum that she was going out but she had sneaked back into the house for a last up-chuck – as she liked to call it – before she went to meet Leanne.

Jodie had throwing up down to a fine art. She only had to put her finger into her mouth and her brain thought it was going down her throat and handily did the job of telling her stomach it was time to evacuate itself. She felt terrible, but she thought she looked great. She loved it every time someone said to her, 'Have you lost weight?'

Since the picture had been in the paper and she, Leanne and Charly had ended up in the gossip column of the *Mirror*, pictured coming out of the Glass House, Jodie had had a lot of attention. Which all served to enforce her own skewed idea that the thinner she got the better she looked. And a wealth of magazines supported it – a celebrity put on a few pounds and their picture was plastered over the pages of the very publications that had purported to be 'concerned' when the same celebrity had got too skinny. Why else would they use wafer-thin models and constantly print articles about the new size zero? The celebrity world was shrinking and Jodie was happy to shrink with it.

She spat the remaining bile into the toilet, grabbed the mouthwash she kept close to hand and swilled out her mouth. She checked her reflection in the mirror again, in case it had changed in the last five seconds, and, almost happy with what she saw, set off to meet Leanne again.

She was coming out of the bathroom when she heard Tracy complain, 'I've paid for the holiday. You can get some spending money from somewhere.'

'But it's all-inclusive,' Kent replied.

'Just because it's all-inclusive doesn't mean you turn up frigging penniless. What if I want to buy some table mats or have my hair braided or something? Use your head. Anyway, we're stocking up on fags when we get there, so don't pack too many clothes. Box of two hundred is three quid there. Flog 'em at the Beacon when we get back and it'll pay for the holiday.'

Jodie tiptoed down the stairs. She couldn't wait until her mum buggered off on holiday.

*

Jodie walked into Markie's office. '*Bonjour*, all,' she said to Markie, Leanne and some new girl who was sitting in the corner.

'You disappearing?' Markie asked.

'What d'you mean?'

'Well, you're nearly skin and bone.'

'I've got a high metabolism,' Jodie replied defensively.

'Like fuck you have.' He got up to answer a call on his mobile.

'What's that meant to mean?' Jodie squealed at Leanne. 'Cheeky bastard.'

'Shall we go for some lunch?' Leanne asked.

'Fine.' Jodie flounced out.

In the nearby pub, she ordered soup and a sandwich. She wasn't stupid. She was going to eat in front of Leanne because she didn't want her nagging. There were probably about six hundred calories in what she'd ordered but she'd soon get rid of them with a visit to the toilet.

'I wanted to talk to you because I'm getting a lot of girls from the *Globe*.' Leanne hadn't signed a deal with the paper but the page-three team had been putting people in touch with her. 'I want you to know that whatever happens you're my number-one priority.'

'Thanks, boss,' Jodie said, tucking into her sandwich.

'I'm playing it by ear, really, trying to build your profile. I've lined up a shoot for two men's magazines. They're really keen. I think you'll do well on some sort of nostalgia level. They liked me when I was younger, but now I'm old and knackered there's a new version.' Leanne laughed.

'You're not knackered!' Jodie assured her, and spooned up some soup.

Leanne's phone rang. 'Hello?' She frowned as she listened to what the person at the other end was saying. After a few moments she asked, 'What exactly does that mean?'

Whatever the person said to Leanne, it made the colour drain from her face and her jaw drop. 'No way,' she said.

She cancelled the call and stared at her sandwich.

'What?' Jodie asked.

'Nothing. It can't be right. I need to get it checked out.'

'Get what checked out?' Bloody hell, Jodie thought, it was like pulling teeth.

Leanne looked at her. 'You know that picture of me? The carwash one?'

'Duh!' Jodie said. Of course she did. It had somehow become one of the most widely recognised images of the decade.

'Well, according to the guy who was just on – he deals with contracts all the time – Jenny's been claiming royalties on my behalf and keeping them.'

'Does that mean you'll get some money?'

'If what he says is right I'm due more than fifty grand.'

'Get lost!' Jodie said.

'Seriously.' Leanne was in shock. 'That would sort me out, Jode – fifty grand.'

'I should bloody hope so. Do you know how many hours that is at the Beacon?' She looked at the ceiling, which she always did when she was working out the price of a round. 'Ten thousand! Fuck me! All you had to do was wash a car in your knickers. Not a bad day's work.'

Leanne laughed. 'Since you put it like that ...'

Jodie had noticed that Leanne hadn't touched her sandwich. Now her sister took the top slice off it, looked at the contents, then picked it up and bit into it. This was a good time to go to the toilet, Jodie thought. Leanne wasn't about to follow her while she was preoccupied with eating. She threw her napkin over her own half-eaten lunch and excused herself.

A moment later she was in the toilet, hunched over the bowl, the usual mixture of elation and disgust flooding over her.

She flushed the toilet and opened the door. Leanne was standing outside with her arms folded. 'What you doing?' Jodie asked defensively.

'Listening to you throw up by the sound of it.'

'The soup went down the wrong way.'

'How many times a day, Jodie?'

'What do you mean?'

Leanne's eyes bored sternly into her. 'You know what I mean.'

'I don't do it often.'

'Then how come I hardly ever see you eat, and how come you're now unnaturally thin?'

'Get off my case, Leanne. It has nothing to do with you,' Jodie said, and went to the basin to scrub her hands.

'I'm your sister and I care about you, so it does have something to do with me.'

Jodie gave her a withering look. She didn't need this right now.

'I'm also representing you. And I'm not going to put you forward for things if you're skin and bone.'

'I'm not skin and bone, I'm fat.' Jodie grabbed at her stomach.

'There's nothing there!' Leanne said angrily.

'There is!' Jodie said, and a single tear rolled down her cheek.

'Jodie.' Leanne's voice softened. 'How long have you been doing this?'

Jodie looked at her and began to cry, lurching, heavy sobs. 'Years. I don't know what else to do to look good,' she said, knowing it sounded stupid.

Leanne took her in her arms. 'We'll get you help.'

'But I don't want to be fat.'

'It's not about being fat, it's about being well.'

But Jodie knew it wasn't. It was about looking good, and she was a long way from thinking that being well was a decent trade-off.

chapter thirty-two

'I feel like I need a PA,' Leanne joked, looking at her to-do list. She was meeting a string of girls who had been recommended to her by the *Globe*. Later she and Jodie were going to the doctor to find out if the NHS offered help to people suffering from bulimia, but first Maurice was coming to run through her options with regard to Jenny and what seemed to be a case of misappropriated funds, and she had to call Victoria Haim.

When Maurice arrived, he shook Leanne's hand and got straight down to business. 'Jenny has two options. She settles out of court and sends you a cheque for, by my reckoning, sixty thousand four hundred and eighty-two pounds and fifty-six pence, then pays all future royalties to you. They won't be as substantial as the first amount because the popularity of something like this is rarely sustained for more than a few years. Or she refuses and you sue her. She'll be dragged through the courts and no doubt the papers will make sure her name is mud. Either way, you can't lose.'

'I don't want it in the papers,' Leanne said, full of dread.

'Believe me,' Maurice said, 'neither will she. Would you like me to call her now?'

'You'd do that?' Leanne asked.

'Trust me. With this snaky witch the pleasure would be all mine. I know plenty of people who've had a run-in with her and I'll feel I'm getting one back for more than you.' He dialled the number and waited.

'Hello, this is Maurice Grey. I represent Leanne Crompton.' He paused for effect. 'I know you have been accruing royalties for the carwash picture and I estimate conservatively, that it will have earned in the region of sixty thousand pounds. Will you let her have a cheque for the exact amount straight away? Then you can revert payment to her. Yes?'

There was a squeal at the other end. Leanne thought it sounded like the high-pitched gabble you heard when a cartoon character took a phone call. 'Well, no amount of abuse is going to change anything, is it? What's it to be, then? Court and a few months' exposure and humiliation at the hands of the media?'

Maurice hung up. 'She'll have an answer for me by tomorrow.' He beamed.

*

Tracy was itching to leave the country. Since she'd dumped him, Paul had been nagging her about his mounting debts. Her parting shot had been, 'Well, top yourself, then.' The last thing she needed was to open the door and find Scott in floods of tears, but that was what she was dealing with now.

'She's left me!' Scott said, blowing his nose and dissolving into tears again.

'Charly?'

'She's run off with Joel Baldy. How can I compete with him? He can buy her new boobs without having to save up. It's not fair!'

'Come in,' Tracy said, pulling him into the house. 'Who the fuck's Joel Baldy?'

'He plays for Manchester Rovers.'

'What is it with girls and footballers? They can't keep their knickers on when they're around,' Tracy said, without realising that her words cut through her son. 'I've always known she was a little slag. When I get my hands on her I'm going to knock fuck out of her.'

'No!' Scott sobbed. 'You can't! I still love her. Sting sang, "If you love someone, set them free." What am I going to do, Mum?'

Tracy looked at him. He was a pathetic mess. She wished sometimes she could take a bit of Markie and give it to Scott. He needed toughening up. 'You're going to get out there and shag anything you can get your mitts on. That's what you're going to do.' Honestly, Tracy thought, sometimes I have to be both mother *and* father to these kids.

'I can't do it, Mum. I can't! I just want *her*.'

'Bloody hell.' Tracy wanted to take her son by the scruff of the neck and shake sense into him. 'Right, well, you'd better go and sort him out, then.'

Scott gawped at her as if she'd gone mad. 'Joel Baldy? It'd be like trying to get at the Prime Minister.'

'Jesus, Scott! I know you're not the brightest star in the sky but even you must know that if you want to do something badly enough, there's always ways and means.'

Scott looked at his mum, but she couldn't be bothered with his swollen features any more. He'd soon forget about this and move on, she thought.

*

Outside the rain was beating down. It was six in the evening and Leanne was waiting for Tony to come home. The buzzer sounded.

'I'll go,' Kia said. She loved answering the door.

'Don't forget to check who it is.'

'It's Uncle Markie,' Kia called from the hall, 'I think.'

Leanne headed to the door to greet her brother – and froze when she saw who was standing, sopping wet, in the hallway.

Jay Leighton was unshaven and wearing a hoodie top. He held out his hands in a placatory way. 'Don't freak, Leanne, I don't want any trouble.'

'Get out of this flat.'

'Who's this, Mummy?' Kia asked.

'No one,' Leanne said pointedly, for Jay's benefit. 'I'll be with you in a minute, darling. Go and play.'

Kia eyed the adults, then headed into the spare room, her adopted bedroom.

'Come through,' Leanne said, walking into the lounge. Jay followed her. 'How did you find me here?'

'Photographer friend.'

'Does he know you're here?' Leanne asked, alarmed.

'Course not.'

Something else occurred to Leanne. 'Does Lisa know you're here?'

'I don't know where she is. She left me on holiday.'

Leanne wondered what he wanted. A bit of her couldn't help savouring the moment. Jay Leighton was a sorry sight. He'd promised her so much and not meant any of it. Now she wanted him to come good. She had no feelings for him but if he'd come because he wanted to see Kia, to build a relationship with her, Leanne would allow it to happen. His timing was perfect, she thought. If he'd arrived a day later, she'd have been in the papers saying he wasn't Kia's dad.

That was what she and Tony had decided to do. In time Leanne would tell Kia who her real dad was, but for now she was going to quash all speculation and tell the journalist from the *Globe* that Tony was Kia's father. They had been an item years ago and were again. Tony was more than happy with this, and it would free Leanne and Kia from tabloid scrutiny.

Leanne's nerves about the interview were getting the better of her, and Jay's presence in Tony's lounge was doing nothing to ease them.

'So, what brings you here?' she asked.

Jay stepped towards her and took her hands. 'Leanne, I'm really screwed and I need your help,' he gabbled. 'I've done a lot of bad things but in particular I've been seeing this guy. Now I've got no one else to turn to.'

Leanne was waiting for him to mention Kia, to talk about something other than himself.

'So, I was wondering ... would you come out and tell everyone that Kia's mine? No one'll think I've been anywhere near a man then. It'll kill two birds with one stone. You get to tell the kid someone's her dad, and I get to keep this quiet, because if it gets out I'll be finished.'

Leanne's eyes narrowed. 'After all these years the only reason you come round is to ask me to cover for you because you're gay?'

'Don't get me wrong, I'm not gay. It's just been a phase, something I thought I'd try. I'm definitely straight.'

'I don't care if you're into shagging horses. That's not the point. You only ever do anything that benefits you. You don't care about Kia, you just want to save your arse. Although, by the sound of it, you haven't been saving it, have you? You've been handing it round.'

'No! It's not like that! I'll give you money for the kid!' Jay scrabbled for the right words.

'Get out,' Leanne said, boiling with rage.

'No, Leanne, listen – this can work for both of us –'

'I said get out!'

'You heard the lady,' said a voice from behind Jay.

Leanne hadn't heard Tony come in but now he was blocking the doorway, looking as if he'd like to snap Jay in two.

'Please, Leanne,' Jay begged.

Tony grabbed him by his hoodie and dragged him into the hall. Leanne burst into tears.

Kia came out of the bedroom. 'Why's that man made you cry, Mummy?'

Leanne held out her arms and her little girl ran into them. She waited until Tony came back before she spoke. She could see that he was furious.

'That's the man I told you about, darling, who I was friends with before you were born.'

'What did he want?'

Whatever she said now could have a serious impact on her daughter's life, Leanne knew.

Tony knelt down beside Kia. 'He didn't want anything, darling. He might do in a few years' time, but at the moment there's nothing he wants that we've got, and nothing we want that he's got.'

'Is he a bad man?' Kia asked. Leanne could tell she was shaken.

'No. Just a bit of a silly billy.'

Kia giggled. 'Silly billy,' she said in a sing-song voice, then headed back to her room and her dolls.

Tony took Leanne in his arms.

'He just turned up,' she said, on the verge of tears again.

'Ssh. It's all right.' Tony said, stroking her hair. 'He's

gone now. And, trust me, he won't come back in a hurry. He's an arsehole, Leanne. Just forget him.'

'I wish I'd never met him. I wish you were Kia's dad, I really do.'

'I am. I'll do anything for her, and for you.'

Leanne pushed back the new surge of tears that was welling inside her. There was one thing in the world she was sure of. It was that Tony meant what he'd said.

*

Jodie was sitting in a room with a kindly woman opposite her. She didn't know much about therapy, only that celebrities were always in and out of it and it sounded a bit like going for a spa day.

'So, Jodie, these sessions are fairly informal. They're to help you to talk about why you make yourself sick.'

'I just do it.'

'And was there a time when you didn't?'

'Course.'

'Why don't you start by talking about when that was?'

'Well, it was when I was fat, wasn't it? I used to sit at the bar shoving crisps down my neck ...' She paused. 'Is that the right answer?'

The woman smiled. 'There are no right or wrong answers here. We just want to explore your relationship with food.'

'I haven't got one,' she said honestly.

'What do you mean by that?'

'If I could take a tablet instead of eating, that's what I'd do. I hate food.'

'Is there nothing you really like the taste of?'

'Yeah, course there is. Chocolate cake, curry, pizza. But I can't have them because I'll end up a fat arse again and I'm not having that.'

'So it's fair to say you have a love-hate relationship with food?'

Jodie thought for a moment. 'Yeah, I'd say that was fair enough.'

The woman got Jodie to talk about when she had first noticed herself becoming obsessed with what she ate, how it had made her feel, and what she felt now when she ate something she thought she shouldn't.

At the end of the hour-long session Jodie said, 'So, is there a way I can stay this weight without throwing up? Because, like I said, I'm not getting fat again. No way.'

The therapist gave her a sympathetic smile that Jodie thought suggested she might have a bit to learn.

*

Leanne's mobile rang, and she pulled it out of her bag.

'Leanne, it's Maurice. Are you sitting down?' he asked.

'Do I need to be?' Leanne asked excitedly.

'Jenny's agreed to settle. You'll receive a cheque within the month. Her only stipulation is that you sign a non-disclosure agreement about what she's referring to as her "oversight". Do you know what that is?'

'Oh, yeah. I know what one of those is all right.' She hadn't forgotten Lisa Leighton whipping papers out of her bag and presuming that Leanne would just sign them. This time, however, Leanne had no problem with signing. She wanted her money – but she wasn't interested in badmouthing Jenny. She felt like doing cartwheels down the street.

She said goodbye to Maurice and immediately called Tony. 'Are you at work yet?' she asked.

'Yes, why?'

'I'm coming over.'

'What's happened?'

'I've got some great news.'

Leanne jumped into her beloved Mini and grinned. She could keep it, after all. Her and Kia's secret was safe now too.

*

A few hours later Leanne was leafing through the pictures of the young women she had been sent by the *Globe*. Jodie had told her she would help with contacting potential clients, but Leanne had decided she wanted to do it herself. She had always felt intimated by receptionists and secretaries when she was modelling. Also her experience in the business would ease the girls' nerves and give them confidence in her as their representative.

She had already invited five to meet her and Markie had lent her a room at the Glass House for the interviews. After today, she was hoping to see ten girls every day for a week, then make her choice.

Leanne had a plan. She was going to promote her new team of girls as just that – a team. Over the last few years the glamour industry had become increasingly cut-throat and many of the girls who wanted to go into it felt they needed to act accordingly, they bitched about each other and sold stories about their sex lives. Leanne's girls would be different. They would get on with each other and if anyone didn't like it they were out. Leanne felt that if they pulled together they'd be calling the shots.

She would go big with the launch, she decided. She was going to re-enact the famous *Charlie's Angels* silhouette pose, but with as many girls as she took on. She had twenty in mind. Then she wanted a countdown in the *Globe*, a big filmic build-up: 'A new breed of woman has emerged, the like of which we have never seen before …' to get everyone talking. She wanted to start a whispering campaign through the *Globe*'s website – people could download the silhouette and when the girls were launched it would become the emblem of Leanne's Angels.

If all went to plan, and Leanne kept the girls in line, they could become successful very quickly. She had already gone over the idea with Victoria, who had said she loved it. Leanne knew she had to be careful. Victoria had become the editor of a tabloid newspaper by making sure she got a story. Leanne had agreed to sell hers but was going back on the deal, which might well damage their friendship. She had decided to continue working towards the launch as she envisaged, and if Victoria pulled out, she would just deal with the consequences.

She had Maurice on board, ready to draw up the contracts and make sure each girl understood everything that was expected of her and what she could expect in return. An old photographer friend would do the shoots. And should this year's venture be successful, Leanne would repeat it next year, but throw open to the public the opportunity to join her agency. Every year there would be another group of Angels. She was quietly confident about the project. The editors of three best-selling men's magazines had agreed to see her next week.

The door buzzer sounded in the apartment. Leanne looked at her watch. It was nearly midday and she wasn't expecting anyone. She got to her feet and pressed the intercom. 'Hello.'

'Leanne, it's Charly.' Angel number two, Leanne thought.

Charly fell through the door, eyes puffy. She didn't pause for breath. 'I'm sorry, Lee, and I completely get it if you don't want to represent me, but I can't do it any more, and I've tried loads of different things to make it better but it's just shit, and I know he's your brother and you love him, but I was looking at a lifetime of watching *Police, Camera, Action* and I was tearing my hair out...' She collapsed into a sobbing heap.

Leanne picked her up and hugged her. She'd got the gist of Charly's garbled explanation. Scott's girlfriend had dumped him. 'Come on, calm down.'

Just then the door burst open and Jodie marched in. 'Oi, Slag Features, fuck off and cry to someone who gives a shit.'

'How did you get in?' Leanne asked, shocked.

'She's dumped our Scott for Joel fucking Baldy and all you can say is, "How did you get in?"'

Leanne let go of Charly. 'Is this true?'

'We had a connection,' Charly said sorrowfully.

'Well, whoop-di-fucking-do. I've got a connection with most of the men who come in the Beacon,' Jodie snarled. 'Doesn't mean I drop my drawers as soon as they look at me.'

'I don't love Scott,' Charly pleaded.

'So you went out with him for security. Like I always said, you were only with him for the knock-off gear and the roof over your head. Well, now you're with someone who'll buy you proper Spy bags and let you live in a mock-Tudor mansion. You must be so proud!' Jodie sneered.

'And what are you? Mother fucking Teresa? You've got your tits out in a paper and you pull pints for a living. Get off your fucking high horse, will you?'

'Sit down and shut up, the pair of you!' Leanne ordered. Both girls were so startled by the force of her voice that they did exactly as they were told.

'Right, you first,' she said to Charly. 'You've just dropped your first bollock. You've got one more chance and if you blow it I'll make sure your modelling career begins and ends with the snaps our Scott took of you. And don't think I'm joking. No one wants to work with a troublemaker. There's so many girls out there clamouring to get into this business that I don't have to deal with people who aren't to be trusted. And I don't trust you, Charly, but I'll take a punt on you because I think you've got something. And that's it. So dry your eyes and don't you dare go near my brother again. The least he deserves is to be left alone.'

Charly nodded. 'Thank you, Leanne.'

'Go on then! What are you waiting for?'

Charly got to her feet and, head bowed, left the apartment.

'The look on her face! Silly cow,' Jodie scoffed.

'Who said you could start again?'

'Bloody hell, Lee! What's up with you?' Jodie said, narked.

'I don't need you shouting the odds for me, thanks very much.'

'I wasn't. It was for Scott.'

'Well, whatever. Where Charly's concerned, you let me do the talking when I'm around. Yes?'

'For God's sake!' Jodie was sulking now.

'Yes?'

'Yes,' she agreed reluctantly.

'Good.'

'Right,' Leanne said, 'I've got quite a bit to do this

afternoon, but I'd like to go over to Mum's and sort things out. I know she's a pain in the arse …'

'You can say that again.'

'… but she's been good to me since I've been back, letting me and Kia stay there, and I all but accused her of going to the papers.'

'Yeah, 'cause she's not the sort of person to do that, is she?' Jodie said sarcastically.

'I was wondering if you wanted to come with me. Play happy families for a bit before she goes away?'

'How's she affording this holiday?'

'She's not. Kent is.'

'Really?'

'Yes.' Leanne didn't want to believe Tracy had found money any other way. 'So, are you coming?'

Jodie shrugged. 'Yeah, why not? As long as you get me more work I'll go wherever you want.'

*

Leanne picked up the phone. This wasn't a call she was looking forward to making but she and Tony had discussed it and she knew what she had to say. Victoria Haim had done a lot for her recently and Leanne was about to pull her biggest exclusive.

It hadn't been a hard decision to make. Now that she was about to get some money from the carwash picture she couldn't justify selling a story to the newspapers – even if it was the one that would have meant she could lay everything to rest.

If she and Tony told the nation that he was Kia's dad it would throw up more questions in the public's mind. Where had he been for so many years and why was she willing to take him back now? Why was Jay Leighton so often linked with her, and why hadn't she come forward sooner to put the rumours to bed? She knew it was naïve to assume that if she said Jay had had nothing to do with Kia the whole thing would go away. But she hoped it might make a nice neat end to things and that the money would come in useful for Kia when she was older.

Tony had been the one to suggest it was the wrong thing to do. He thought it was blood money, however way they looked at it, and that Kia wouldn't be forgiving in years to come if they lied now.

So, Leanne picked the phone up and dialled Victoria. She explained that she couldn't go through with the interview because it would lead to even more press intrusion.

Victoria sighed. 'I'm pissed off, Leanne,' she said.

Leanne took a deep breath. 'I know you are, but it was either disappoint you or be dragged through the papers again but this time through my own doing. I can't. For me, for Tony but, most importantly, for Kia, I just can't do it.'

'Right,' Victoria said, giving nothing away.

'I hope this won't affect the page-three project, but if it does then I'm sorry.' Leanne thought she should get this out into the open now.

'Of course it won't. But next time you promise me a scoop, deliver on it, will you?'

'Of course.'

Leanne felt bad that she had let Victoria down, but pleased that she had had the conversation. She was quite impressed with herself. Tough conversations would be part and parcel of her new job and she was getting the hang of them. Suddenly a thought occurred to her. She picked up the phone and pressed redial.

'Victoria, it's Leanne again. Strictly off the record, a story will break this week that has nothing to do with me but would wipe me off any front page.'

'Really?' Victoria said. Leanne could tell her antennae were up. 'Go on.'

Leanne felt little loyalty to Jay, but she couldn't hand the story to Victoria on a plate for fear she might be implicated. 'Get your source at the other papers to sniff round about Jay and a rent-boy. That's all I'm saying because that's all I know,' she said.

'Are you *sure* that's all you know?'

'Yes,' Leanne said adamantly.

*

Tracy had packed her bags. Her airport outfit was hanging up in the front room – a pink velour tracksuit and some boots Karina had ordered from the catalogue. She had been sent two pairs by accident and Tracy loved it when that happened. Her case was full of sarongs from previous holidays and her lucky towel. It featured a line of cats pulling their pants down and looking cutely over their shoulders. 'Do cats have shoulders?' Scott had asked, when she'd brought it back from Magaluf.

'Do cats pull moonies?' Tracy had replied. 'It's a fucking joke towel, Scott. It's not a representation of a day in the life of cats.'

Kent was ready too. He had his two pairs of shorts, his pink neon trunks and his Elvis shades, which he saved for special occasions.

Tracy was watching an old episode of *Fifteen to One* on Challenge TV when she heard a rustle behind her. She took a gulp of her pre-holiday *piña colada* (her own concoction: one part orange juice, one part coconut juice, forty-two parts rum) and began to moan about the TV without turning to check that she was talking to Kent.

'Remember this? Rock-hard questions, went on for months and then at the end all the poor bastard won was a Grecian urn.'

'Yeah, we used to watch it together, didn't we?'

Tracy spun round. Paul was standing over her, with a manic glint in his eye. 'Get out!' she shouted.

'No use screaming at me – lover-boy's at the shops. I've just seen him go.'

'I'll call the police,' Tracy said. Paul wasn't a violent man, but everyone had their limit and she had the feeling she might have pushed him to his.

'I don't think they're going to run round here, are they? Not after all the wolf-crying you've done. I've come round so's me and you can have a nice little chat. You never give anyone the chance to have their say when you've decided you've had enough of them – and you've dicked me over one too many times.'

'Piss off! I'm not talking to you,' she said, and pushed him. Usually he would have backed away, but now he grabbed her wrists and shoved her into a chair. She sat down with a thump.

For the first time since she'd met him, Paul looked really dangerous. 'Come on,' she said, trying to sweet-talk him. 'Whatever's wrong we can sort it out.'

'We can't, though, can we, Trace? I know you too well. You're only interested if there's something in it for you. That's why I got the credit cards, because I was mug enough to think you'd be bothered about me when the money ran out. I'd be able to remind you of the good times we'd had together. But no. You just wanted the cash. Fuck me, fuck everyone else.' Paul took a step towards her. Tracy flinched. 'And what's this?' he demanded, flinging his hand back. Tracy ducked. 'Going away?' he asked. And she realised he was pointing at her going-away outfit.

'No! I'm just airing it.' She was panicking.

'Don't talk shit!' Paul shouted, lurching forward. 'Scott told me. The Dominican Republic, no less! And how've you paid for *that*?'

Tracy gazed at him.

'You've robbed me fucking blind! That's how.'

Tracy was genuinely shocked. 'What you on about?'

'Stock-piling money from my cards when I wasn't looking, weren't you? Drawing out whatever you felt like. You were on to my credit-card scam and you were milking me –'

'No!' Tracy shouted. 'Honest, Paul, I wasn't.'

'You knew my card would bounce because you had the money in your account so you could piss off with Elvis.'

'I didn't, Paul, I *swear*.'

'Stop lying to me!' Paul bellowed.

Usually, Tracy could talk her way out anything, but now, if Kent didn't make a swift appearance, Paul would do something stupid …

*

Leanne and Jodie were in the hallway, listening, petrified. Leanne was going to call the police, when Jodie reminded her that a domestic at the Cromptons' would be way down their list. They'd rescue a cat stuck up a tree first.

As they dithered Paul yelled, 'Stop lying to me!' and the sisters froze.

Then Tracy began shouting as if her life depended on it: 'I sold that story to the papers about our Leanne. That's where the money came from – the one about the footballer and our Kia. I got a decent wedge for it. I was going to tell you about it, Paul, honest.'

Leanne paled visibly as Jodie stared at her.

'I'd never rob you.'

'But you'd sell your own daughter out?' Paul raved. 'You're a cunt of the highest fucking order, aren't you?'

Rage filled Leanne and she flew into the room. 'You bitch!' she shouted. 'Drag me through the papers, bring the press to my door, fair enough, but your granddaughter?'

Tracy looked wildly at her daughter. 'Leanne – you've got to understand.' She glanced at Paul, stood up and sprinted to the other side of the kitchen. 'You bastard!' she spat at him. 'This is all your fault!'

'*He's* a bastard?' Jodie put in. 'Am I hearing right? You shopped your own daughter! You're a disgrace.'

'I didn't. I had to say that to yer dad to leave me alone.'

'And you couldn't have said you robbed the money from somewhere else? Your "lie" had to involve selling a story to the paper about your daughter?'

'Yeah,' Tracy lied again. 'No one else has owned up to it, so it was the first thing that came into my head.'

'You can't even admit it now, can you?' Leanne snapped. 'Not even now you're cornered and everyone knows you did it.'

'I didn't,' Tracy said weakly.

'Let's go to the bank, then. You can get a statement and show me where the money you paid for the holiday came from.' Leanne knew that any money paid by a newspaper would have been credited in its name to the account.

'After everything I've done for you, this is how you repay me,' Tracy whined.

'I'm not standing here listening to this. I'm going,' Leanne told her father and Jodie.

'That's it – leave!' Tracy shrieked defiantly.

Paul stepped towards his ex-wife, who shrank away from him. 'I don't know where we got these girls from, but the tips of their little fingers have more good in them than you've got in your whole rotten body, you bitch,' he said quietly. Then he put his hands on Jodie and Leanne's shoulders and guided them out of the house.

'Oh, and you lot are all so fucking perfect!' Tracy howled impotently after them.

They got outside just in time to see Kent coming back from the shop. He seemed shocked to find the three united outside the house.

'You're welcome to her, mate. She's a nasty bitch,' Paul told him.

'Enjoy your holiday,' Jodie said. 'Never thought to wonder where the money to pay for it came from, did you?'

Leanne glared at him. Any man who would take Tracy back after the way she'd treated Kent must be pathetic, she thought.

'Where's Tracy? What've you done to her?' he asked, waving a jar of pickles.

'We've done nothing,' Leanne said. 'She's done it all herself.'

chapter thirty-three

The papers showed Jay Leighton no mercy. The story of the football star and the rent-boy had been a massive splash and was showing no sign of abating. For the past few days, Lisa had been besieged in her home, but she didn't care any more. She was well past trying to hold together her sham of a marriage. She was packing her things, making sure she did it herself. She wasn't employing someone to come in and then sell the story of how she couldn't even put her own belongings into a suitcase.

Jay came into the room, his head twice its normal size. He'd been crying non-stop for almost a week. Lisa ignored him and went to feed Blest. She was getting the hang of having a baby, and enjoyed being a mum.

'Please,' he begged, for what must have been the eightieth time that day. 'Don't do this to us.'

'There is no "us". There's only ever been you, and I've been too much of a mug to see it. Prancing around you, covering up for you when all you do is shag around. Well, let someone else clean up your mess. Give that rent-boy a call. I'm sure he'd be happy to oblige.'

'What about the house?'

'Have it. What do I care? I've got enough money for the time being.' Jay looked puzzled. 'Oh, don't worry, I'm not losing my touch. I'll be making sure I get what's due in the divorce settlement.'

'You can't divorce me!' Jay moaned.

'Can and will,' Lisa said, wiping Blest's chin.

'Where are you going to live?'

'None of your business.'

'I'll find out. I'll ask Steve,' Jay said, like a sulky child.

'No, you won't. Steve's not going to represent you any more.'

'What are you on about?' Jay asked, stricken.

'He can't represent both of us and I'm the safer bet. He's staying with me.'

'You can't do this to me! I made you!'

'Well,' Lisa said, 'if you think that you're more deluded than I thought you were. I'll be out of here by tonight. If you want any contact with me you can call my solicitor.' She slid a business card to him. 'And if you want to see Blest that's fine, but I doubt you will, seeing as your track record with kids isn't great.'

Lisa knew he didn't believe any of what she was saying, but for the first time in her life she genuinely didn't care.

*

Leanne admired her reflection in the mirror. The simple black floor-length gown she was wearing looked perfect. As she twirled to see a glimpse of the back, Tony kissed her neck. 'You're beautiful,' he said.

Leanne smiled. 'You don't look bad yourself.' He was wearing a tuxedo, and his usually stubbled face was clean-shaven.

'You all set, then?' Tony asked.

'Ready as I'll ever be.' She squeezed his hand.

Tonight was the launch of Leanne's Angels. She had been trying to come up with a better, more original name for her girls but this one had stuck and the papers seemed to like it, so she had kept it. She had planned to launch them in Bradington – stick to her guns on representing girls from outside London and make the launch distinctly northern – but Tony had persuaded her differently, to Victoria's delight. He had said that the party needed to be in London so that the city would know what had hit it. So, Leanne had hired a banqueting suite in the middle of Mayfair and invited the tabloid press. She was sure she'd see a few familiar paparazzi but she didn't hold a grudge. As the man had said to her, live by the sword, die by the sword, and she would make sure she was on the other side of the lenses.

She, Tony and Kia were staying in a central London hotel. Kia was very excited to be back in London, but she wasn't begging to return to her old life. Leanne had promised she could come to the party for a bit, as long as she stayed with Tony. She herself had to be interviewed and, of course, keep an eye on the girls.

Markie, Scott and Karina were waiting in the foyer of the hotel as Leanne, Tony and Kia walked down the sweeping staircase.

'You scrub up well,' Markie said, kissing his sister's cheek. Then he shook hands with Tony. Leanne checked for any undercurrent of animosity, but if it was there, she couldn't detect it.

'Our Jode's shitting herself,' Karina said helpfully.

'I don't know why. She's the one everyone wants to interview from what I can gather,' Leanne said. She'd been fielding interest about her prospective clients all week and everyone wanted to know if her sister was one of the Angels.

'Good luck, Lee,' Scott said, smiling. Leanne squeezed his arm. She was so glad he'd come. She knew it was hard for him. He missed Charly desperately and it didn't help that she'd been in the gossip columns hanging on Joel Baldy's arm. Seeing her here tonight in the flesh was going to rub salt into the wound, but Leanne knew that he was putting his own feelings aside for her tonight. Leanne just hoped that Scott could get himself another girlfriend and forget about Charly. But she knew that was easier said than done.

Paul came round the corner. He was in a tuxedo too.

'Dad, you look really smart,' Leanne told him.

'No need to sound so bloody surprised,' Paul said, dusting himself down.

'Before we go, I'd just like to say I'm really glad you've all come this evening,' Leanne told them. 'It means a lot to me to have all my family here. And it'll mean a lot to Jodie too.'

'Well, I was at a bit of a loose end tonight anyway …' Markie joked.

Karina punched his arm.

'And I just want you to know that although Mum's not here I can't be bothered having a massive feud with her because I know she enjoys that sort of thing. I'm just going to keep out of her way.'

The others shuffled and glanced at one another as if they knew something Leanne didn't.

'What?' she asked. 'What's she done?'

'Nothing,' Markie said. 'Don't worry about it.'

'You can't say that half an hour before I've got to front this launch. Come on – what?' she demanded.

'She's been in an air-rage incident on the way back from the Dominican Republic. She kicked off with the steward, demanding to go in first class, pissed out of her head apparently. They grounded the plane and she was arrested in Jamaica. It was in the papers but she called me, looking for bail money,' Markie said, with a wry smile.

Before she knew it Leanne was laughing hysterically. 'Get lost! She's banged up? What did you say?'

'I said I'd get back to her.' Markie winked.

Leanne was still laughing. 'Good. Make sure you leave it long enough for her to be crawling up the walls.'

'Oh, don't worry. She's going to sweat, the silly cow.'

They had been appalled but not surprised that Tracy and Kent had gone ahead with their holiday, even when it was obvious where the funds had come from.

'What's Nana Tracy done now, Mummy?' Kia asked innocently.

'Nothing, darling,' Leanne said, feeling guilty that her daughter was now aware that Tracy was always doing something nobody approved of.

Tony took Leanne's hand. 'Come on. Don't be worrying about your mum. It's your big night.'

*

There were banners with the *Globe*'s name emblazoned across them all over the room. Leanne was grateful that they had continued to sponsor the event, even though she hadn't kept her end of the bargain. She had concluded that Victoria thought it best to keep her sweet so that one day, if she decided to tell her story, the *Globe* would be the only place she'd go.

A stage had been built at one end of the room and the silhouette of Leanne's twenty girls, in the *Charlie's Angels* pose, hung on the back. The hall was dimly lit as the guests took their places. It was filling fast. More than two hundred people had been invited and Leanne had been happy to receive a positive response from at least ninety per cent.

She was backstage now with her new clients, who were chatting nervously among themselves. Leanne remembered how she had wanted to do well, make a name for herself, but these girls understood they were a team.

Victoria popped her head round the curtain. 'Everyone ready?' she asked, with a smile.

'Just about,' Leanne told her.

'You'll be great. The buzz this has caused is phenomenal. Just go out there and knock 'em dead,' she said. 'Good luck, girls.' Then she shouted, 'Five minutes to call.'

Leanne straightened her dress and went over once more what she was about to say. She had been rehearsing it all week.

Jodie came up to her. 'Stop stressing.'

'If I was ever going to stress, tonight would be the night.'

'At least you don't have to get your baps out.' Jodie grinned.

'What a comfort.'

Jodie hugged her. 'Leanne, thanks for everything. You're amazing – you do know that, don't you?'

'Don't be daft,' Leanne said, hugging her sister back. She hoped Jodie would be all right, that thrusting her into the limelight would help her, not make her illness worse. She seemed to be benefiting from the sessions with the psychologist, but that was all Leanne could hope for. She had to take it a step at a time.

'One minute, Leanne,' Victoria said. 'Then you're on.'

*

The hall was in darkness as Leanne waited in the wings for Victoria to introduce her. Her friend's words of praise went over her head as, nervously, she recited for the last time her opening speech. As she stepped onto the stage a roar went up, and she beamed at her audience.

'All right. At least let me say something good before you start cheering me ...' she began, with a twinkle in her eye. That wasn't scripted. And suddenly she knew she was going to play it by ear, as she did most things. Why not? she thought. As a way to get through life, it had served her well so far ...